C000304113

COSMO COSMOLINO

1399

£5.99

By the same author

MONKEY GRIP
HONOUR & OTHER PEOPLE'S CHILDREN
POSTCARDS FROM SURFERS
THE CHILDREN'S BACH
THE LAST DAYS OF CHEZ NOUS

COSMO COSMOLINO

Helen Garner

BLOOMSBURY

First published in Great Britain 1993
Copyright © 1992 by Helen Garner

The moral right of the author has been asserted

Bloomsbury Publishing Ltd, 2 Soho Square, London W1V 5DE

A CIP catalogue record for this book
is available from the British Library

ISBN 0 7475 13449

Printed and bound in Great Britain by
Mackays of Chatham PLC, Chatham, Kent

'Every angel is terrible.'

Rainer Maria Rilke

ACKNOWLEDGEMENTS

I am grateful for the two-year fellowship from the Literature Board of the Australia Council which gave me the time and freedom to write this book.

'A Vigil' has appeared in the anthology *Soho Square* (Bloomsbury, London); and two excerpts from earlier drafts of 'Cosmo Cosmolino' were published in *Scripsi*. My thanks to these publications.

CONTENTS

RECORDING ANGEL

*S*OON AFTER the collapse of my last attempt at marriage, when it did not appear to matter much which city I was in, I passed through Sydney and called as always on my old friend Patrick, to tell him, among other things, that my Auntie Dot had died.

'Ah yes,' he said. 'The bottle blonde.'

'I thought you'd like to know,' I said, 'seeing you danced with her at my wedding.'

'And you were fond of her,' stated Patrick.

'Her hairdos,' I said, 'were Wagnerian.'

'Oh, come off it.'

'They were! She had all that hair piled up, and a big smiling mouth, and a great big beautiful bosom.'

'All the things you lack,' said Patrick, pulling out a chair for me. 'What did she die of?'

'The usual,' I said. 'Cancer.'

We sat down at the table.

'Actually,' said Patrick, 'we've got some news too. Remember those headaches I was always getting, that wouldn't go away? I had tests. There's something badly wrong. Inside my head.'

Now the contents of Patrick's head were of more than normal concern for me, for Patrick recited my life like a poem he had learnt by heart; and over the years of our friendship I had come to endure his version without open rebellion, since if in conversation I disputed even the most trivial detail of his discourse – a date, a setting, a dream – he exhibited signs of an existential alarm that verged on panic: his eyes widened, his nostrils went stiff, he breathed in sharply and shoved his palms against the table edge; and it was not only my life's patterns, its events and landmarks and the proper ordering and interpretation of them that he needed to hold a monopoly on, but also its aesthetic, the aesthetic of me.

In their back yard one day only a year before, under the wire on which their children's clothes, stained with vehement activity, were drying in the breeze, Patrick, his wife and I had regretted the passing of our youth.

'I can't drink any more,' said Patrick. 'It makes me dizzy and sick. I get headaches, real boomers that last a week. Night and day. And I'm starting to forget things. I'm losing my memory.'

'That,' I said, 'would be a blessing. There are so many things I'd like to forget that I hardly know what would be left standing, if I ever got started.'

Patrick was appalled. 'But the past is what we *are*,' he said. 'It's our *duty* to remember it.'

'Speak for yourself,' I said. 'I'll wipe it out as I go.'

'Over my dead body,' said Patrick.

'Getting old is worse for women,' said Natalie,

emptying the tea dregs on to a pot plant, 'because it's our boring fate to be looked at.'

'But imagine if we were beautiful,' I said.

'Natalie *is* beautiful,' said Patrick quickly.

'She means *Beautiful*,' said Natalie. 'She means how terrible, if you'd built your whole idea of yourself round the fact of being considered beautiful, to watch your beauty desert you.'

'I've never even been pretty,' I said, 'so for me it's probably less painful than it was for Ursula, for example.'

'Tell me who Ursula was again?' said Natalie, but Patrick was already firing up.

'You *were* pretty,' he said. 'You *were*! You never had that feminine quality, mind you, that Nat's got – you were never *composed* – but your face used to be *vivid*. Till it got hawk-like. We were saying the other night, weren't we, Nat, that you'd become hawk-like. And you used to have such pretty little breasts! Of course, they're sad now. Dignified, but sad.'

'Sad?' I said. 'They're not so sad.'

'Oho!' said Patrick. 'Now she wants to hear lies about herself!'

Natalie laughed and made an exclamation of reproach, but since I had recently been led to believe that my life as a lovable creature was over, I said nothing. Solitude, I thought. Forgiveness. On Melbourne summer mornings the green trams go rolling in stately progress down tunnels thick with leaves: the bright air carries along the avenues their patient chime, the chattering of their wheels; but although I did not speak, Patrick knew the words I would have used and so even the thought of home at that moment was not a refuge.

There must have been thousands of facts unknown to Patrick, ones I thought of as mine, but sweepingly he would correct me. He had mapped out the story of my life, and of the lives of everyone we knew, into a grid-like framework and nailed it down; and everything done, witnessed, dreamed, heard of or read he had lined up under cast-iron headings, those terrifyingly simple categories of his. Only *Dissatisfied Women* become feminists. Lesbians are *Heavy Drinkers*. Derelicts suffer from *Human Degradation*. Some women *Lack the Quality* to make a man *A Good Wife*. Ursula, for example, *Became an Alcoholic and a Prostitute*.

Hostile, I objected: 'She was drinking, for God's sake. She got a job in a massage parlour.'

'I think you'd be hard put,' said Patrick, squaring himself and whitening his nostrils, 'to draw a distinction between "drinking and getting a job in a massage parlour" and what *I* just said.'

When I stood next to you, Ursula, at your daughter's funeral, you were still wearing the gold ankle chain, the Indian ring on the forefinger. You said to me brightly, from behind your sunglasses, 'What a lot of people have turned up! You don't often see so many people at a . . . gathering.'

'*You* told me about her,' said Patrick. 'You were laughing and pulling faces. You told me that summer, remember? When you brought your new bike up here on the train and rode around in those silk shorts. It was an Italian bike with an unnecessary number of gears. You said you'd seen her at the swimming pool. Her face was red and coarse from the grog, you said, and she told you that the blokes she, uhm, serviced, that they all reckoned it was their wives' fault, that they couldn't get what they needed from their wives.'

Did I say those things, did I grimace? Forgive me, Ursula, as you stumble into the traffic on St Kilda Road.

I thought of you yesterday when I stood too close to the tracks and a tram, keeling fast, clipped the tip of my shoulder. Unlike you, I stepped back in time but I was shaking, because now I knew what you had already found out: the colossal weight of the thing, its dense rigidity, its utter lack of give.

Patrick was by nature not a guest but a host, the kind of person who had his own chair and always sat in it. My houses and my life upset him because they were not fixed, as the past is: I was always crashing, picking up the pieces and moving on, and he could not afford to be curious, because curiosity and its results might cause a shift in his taxonomy. He came into my room on one of his rare visits, stepping gingerly to where I was reading at the table with my back to the door, and peered over my shoulder at some lines on a card that was pinned to the window frame: '*What are you waiting for? What are you saving for? Now is all there is.*' He turned away with a tongue click, relieved and vindicated.

'Oh, how shallow,' he said. 'I'm disappointed in you.'

I hung my head. I did! I was choking with indignation, but I hung my head and fiddled with my fingers. The words on the card, no matter who said them first, were what Balanchine used to shout to his dancers – a dare, a challenge, not a philosophical position to be argued; and yet Patrick went home again happy, furnished no doubt with a fresh subheading: hippy? grasshopper? clapped-out party girl? What do they say about me, when they lie alongside each other in their upstairs room, talking after midnight in their quiet, civilised voices? He is my *oldest*, my *most loyal friend*, who loves me and seems to want the best for me; but loyalty is not as simple as it looks, and the truth is that for the comfort of the contrast he needs to go on believing that my life is lonely, chaotic, wrecked, loose, without meaning: 'a blasted heath'.

On that same last visit to Melbourne I took him to a coffee shop and we sat up at the bar. Patrick looked round him with cheerful pleasure.

'It's years,' he said, 'since I've sat on a high stool like this. It must be, oh, eighteen years ago, when Natalie and I lived over in Darlinghurst.'

'I never knew you lived in Darlinghurst,' I said.

'Yes you did!' said Patrick. 'Because you saw me there once, way back in the early seventies. You told me about it years afterwards.'

'I don't think that can be right.'

'It is!' he said. 'How can you forget these things? You'd come to Sydney with some bloke or other, in a band, remember? I suppose you'd been taking drugs with him and so on – anyway you saw me walking along the other side of Victoria Street with my shopping basket. You were about to yell out to me, but something made you change your mind. You didn't call out, and I walked on round the corner without knowing you were watching me.'

'Funny,' I said. 'I don't remember that at all.'

'It's rather like a Poe story, isn't it,' said Patrick luxuriously, unfocusing his eyes. 'A person sees the chance of a better life passing by, and he makes as if to call out' – he flung forth one arm in the imploring gesture of a soul in torment – 'but something in his nature makes him hesitate. He pauses . . . he closes his lips . . . he steps back . . . and then he slides down, and down, and down.'

I stared at Patrick, breathless.

'*Who* did?' I whispered. '*Who* slid down, and down, and down?'

He turned his full front to me and sang out, laughing, with both arms spread wide, '*You* did, my dear! You!'

There was a lunch for those who rallied round, the day Patrick was to go into hospital. Rain was falling, birds flew low, air was damp and hair turned wavy. Another university relic of Patrick's spotted me in the kitchen, nodded coldly, then said to Natalie with a sentimental smile, 'Patrick's still looking after people, I see!' The phone kept ringing, people were drinking and laughing and taking terrible liberties with the unspeakable.

'I've got a really good brain tumour story,' said Max from where Patrick worked, 'an absolutely true and recent one. A woman I know, our age, lovely girl but never had much success with blokes – well, she gets a tumour, a bad-looking scan. Goes to a top surgeon, he operates. Every kind of treatment available, she gets it. He does a brilliant job on her. Off she goes. A year passes, they do another scan. She comes in to get the results, the surgeon sits her down and gives her the news: perfect. Clean as a whistle. They're both excited, laughing and congratulating each other. Then the surgeon says, "Would you mind waiting here for a moment?" He gets up and goes out of the room, closing the door behind him. Then he opens it again and comes straight back in, without his white coat. "I'm no longer your doctor," he says. "Will you come out to dinner with me?" And they've been together ever since.'

Later in the afternoon, when the other guests had wished Patrick well and departed, Natalie unplugged the phone and Patrick put to me a formal request.

'I want you,' he said, 'to take two photos. One of me, Natalie, and our children, and the other of me and Natalie.'

Cheerful from the afternoon's society I replied, 'Okay. Of course – with pleasure. And then Natalie can take one of you and me.'

I sprang up from the table to reach for my camera, but with a slow movement of the kind permitted to those behind whom death already stands, Patrick put out his hand and restrained me, saying, 'No. With a camera I've got upstairs. I borrowed one with a flash.'

'You don't need a flash,' I said. 'There's still plenty of natural light left.'

'No,' said Patrick more firmly. 'Natalie's sister lent it to us. I want you to use that.'

They were going to drill open his head in the morning so I held my tongue, but inside me, oh! that shameful, grinding mutiny. I loved my own camera, its scratched black body, a certain inky tremor that winked on the sunken pool of its viewfinder as I raised it to my eye – *my* eye, this unofficial, peripheral eye of mine; but I disciplined myself, I applied the discipline that is missing from Patrick's version, and I submitted. There was no point in explaining to him that the flash would bleach their faces and give them red dots for pupils. Natalie fetched the camera and the children, and Patrick arranged the pose with gestures and quiet orders: himself and Natalie side by side on straight-backed chairs, and the two kids bracketing them, leaning on their parents' shoulders. It was an easy shot to take. Their mood stilled them, and they looked into the camera with identical expressions of formal apprehension. The children moved out of frame, and I took the second one: Natalie and Patrick, side by side, hand in hand, thigh along thigh. Then I stood still and waited; but nobody seemed to remember my suggestion for a third shot, so after a moment I put the lens cap on, and handed the camera back to Natalie.

'Patrick,' said Natalie, as she zipped up the case and the children wandered away, 'tell your dream. He dreamt last night about an angel. The angel of death.'

I looked sharply at him, and he laughed. Patrick had

that rare thing, a mirthful laugh. He always liked to recite
my old dreams, as comic turns, but I had never heard him
relate one of his own. I never thought of him as that kind
of person: I never thought of him as a dreamer.

The shabby walls, whose plaster was so thickly encrusted with the worm-casts of damp that it might have been
French brocade, struck me then as beautiful, as original,
because of Patrick's illness and the danger he was in.

'My dream,' he began mildly, taking his time, 'this
dream which my wife has so histrionically interpreted,
was that I was in a pit. Not a wet pit, but a dry one, with
sides of bare earth tamped hard and packed. Really it was a
lion's den.

'The lion was nowhere to be seen, but I could feel it
somewhere nearby, and I was crouching there, waiting.
Waiting for the person to come who would save me from it.

'And then a figure appeared on the rim of the pit,
looking down at me: a black man, tall, with shining skin,
and eyes that were slanted and Asiatic. He was dressed in
splendid robes, very magnificent, and on his head was a
kind of turban, a great feathered head-dress. He was even
more terrifying than the lion. He was mighty. He was . . .
in majesty.'

The breaths we took were not sudden, but quiet, and
thorough. This was not the kind of dream-telling after
which one asked, 'And *then* what happened?' Patrick kept
his eyes on the weave of the tablecloth. His eyes seemed
further apart, and he held his mouth slightly pursed, as if
restrained by modesty from saying more.

He leaned over and turned up the volume of the radio
which had been too low, all afternoon, for anything to be
audible except the occasional hushed wave of applause;
and the music we now began to hear was hardly more
emphatic.

'A string quartet,' I said. 'That's comforting.'

It was still light. Sparrows were hopping about in the branches of a tree outside the window, and rain, earlier, had collected in the up-turned leaves with their frilled edges. In different spots, now here, now there, a load of rain would become too heavy for its leaf, and the stalk would suddenly sag and let the water pour straight down in a quick stream.

'I like a quartet,' said Natalie. 'It's like a family. Or a conversation. One speaks, then another; then the other two join in.'

'No – listen,' said Patrick. 'It's a quintet. It's the one with the two cellos.'

'Two? Are you sure?' I said; but before Patrick could argue, the music did it for him. It gathered itself in a powerful intake of breath: it paused in a quivering silence: and it exploded.

Now I could hear the extra cello, the point of it, what it was there for.

It dropped through a rent in the net and plunged away into the darkness, crying out. It groaned a warning: it prowled, it ranged, it lay in wait. It was the bad dream of the quartet, brooding, ravening outside the fold, and its argument was doubt and panic, a desolation as yet unlived.

'Yesterday, for the first time in twenty years,' said Patrick with his foot on the bottom stair, 'I tidied my desk. I found dozens, scores of postcards from you. They're in bundles, next to the dictionaries, if you want to read them.'

'Oh, please don't keep them,' I said. 'I bet they're awful.'

'Awful?' he said. 'I may never have answered them, but you went to the trouble of writing them to me; they mean something. Surely you don't think I'd chuck 'em out?'

'You won't like them,' said Natalie as he disappeared round the stair landing. 'I had a look. They're like out-of-date magazines that you read at the dentist. Full of false and inappropriate enthusiasms.'

'I'll burn 'em,' I said recklessly, 'while he's away. Do you think I should?'

I looked at Natalie's face, in the liverish light that came through the glass panel of the front door.

'It won't make any difference,' she said. 'That's the idea of yourself you've given him, and nothing you do now can shift it.'

She was leaning against the wall with her hands behind her and her head on an angle, so that no single footstep of Patrick's, as he shuffled across the floor of the upstairs room, would escape her attention, or go unheard.

I was already rolling mincemeat into balls and shaking them up in a paper bag of flour when I heard the front gate screech and slam. Living so close to the hospital, they could walk there in ten minutes, carrying in Patrick's old satchel only a toothbrush and a copy of *King Lear*. The children were allowed to accompany them as far as the corner, and by the time they slouched back in I was making a salad, the meatballs were sizzling in oil, and three potatoes were toiling in the pot. The boy went straight to Patrick's chair and sat in it. The girl squirmed in under my arm at the stove; with my left arm round her I could feel her hasty heartbeat, and smell the sourness of her thick, damp hair. We kept our eyes on the contents of the pan and said nothing, but as the hot fat shrank the meatballs, as they wallowed and hissed there in a cluster, small and grey, shrivelling in the heat, fissures opened in their floury surfaces, and oozed a thin, bloody fluid.

Patrick's books were coated with creamy dust, and wedged so tightly into the shelves that I broke a finger-nail working the bundles free. The postcards. So many! I squatted on the matting with my shoulders between my knees and fanned the pictures out like a pack. They came from everywhere – Exmouth, Port Vila, Munich, Santa Margherita, Fort William, Ipoh, Ocean Grove – from the paper shops and museums and railway stations of every city or township I had ever passed through. Miramont-de-Quercy, Zahedan, Wilcannia. Augsburg, Campagnatico, Rangoon, Bendigo. Paris, yes – a copper sunset behind the Eiffel Tower, Brassaï's *Couple fâché* with lowered eyes and backs to the café mirror. And always Melbourne, Melbourne, Melbourne, over and over the same photo in glaring greens and reds, of a tram, huffy, blunderous, manoeuvring itself with pole akimbo round the tight corner where Bourke Street enters Spring.

My will was iron. I did not turn one card over, I did not read one word. I told the cards by instinct. My regrets were organised in advance. No verbal evidence was need-ed to show the difference between my life, this career of blind staggering, and the way that Natalie, even while speaking to me, had kept her head cocked for the sound of her husband's foot shifting on the floor of the upper room.

It was night in the yard, and the sky was high now, and cloudless. That special smell of cities – warmed bitumen, and the plants that stubbornly grow in spite of it – sweetened the air as I crouched over four bricks I had set up to shield my little fire from breezes. I offered the cards to it one by one, holding them by their corners with the words facing away from me. While the Australian ones burned with reluctance, being coated in a transparent layer which peeled back at leisure, the foreign ones took to the flames as obediently as if made to be incinerated. The neighbour's dog, jingling its chain and uttering grunts of anxiety, paced up and down the length of the fence, but the neighbour himself was heedless of my drama. He tuned up his bouzouki out there and began to play and sing to himself, thoughtfully, his voice moving in unison with the single notes as he plucked them: a melody, slow and deeply rhythmic, from somewhere I had never been.

'What are you doing?' called the boy from the kitchen door.

'Getting rid of some rubbish,' I answered.

He approached the fire in his enormous, unlaced running shoes, with his sister behind him. He liked me, we had shared a room and conversations before sleep on my visits since he was small and our mutual modesty was exquisite, but he was his father's representative tonight and he was demanding an explanation.

'They're only postcards,' I said, 'that I sent to Patrick when I was young and foolish.'

'Did he say you could burn them?' he asked sternly, standing over me.

'Not exactly,' I said, 'but it's my right, you know, to take them back.'

'Not without his permission. You sent them to him with his name on them. Therefore they belong to him.'

'Legally, perhaps,' I said, turning a tram so the flame could seize its sparking pole, 'but morally I believe I'm in the clear. He may own the cards themselves, as objects, but I own what's written on them; and anyway he knows the words by heart.'

'Ah,' said the boy, his father's son. 'Copyright. I suppose it's all right, then.'

'But what about the pictures on them?' said the girl hoarsely, pushing past him. 'He doesn't know those by heart. How can a person learn a picture by heart?'

'Your father's head,' I said, 'like everybody else's, is a vast gallery of pictures. Nobody will ever know what pictures your father has inside his head.'

They laughed, but their brows were in knots, and they glanced behind them to the yellow rectangle of the kitchen door.

'Not even Mum?' said the girl.

'Not even Natalie,' I said.

The membrane of light bulged and burst to disgorge their mother, walking, taking steps, coming out to the bonfire where the last of the postcards was turning brown at the corners and curling into a writhing tube. She saw what I had done. She smiled; she squatted down beside me without speaking, and with a stout twig began to rake out the ashes.

Next morning everything I saw, in the streets that passed and pierced the hospital, was sharply shimmering. Capped and aproned girls flung open rows of shutters. An ambulance, silent, slid into a discreet bay and yawned there. Two pretty junkies rattled a stroller down the path to detox, while their baby, bounced and flopping, grizzled feebly with no hope of ever being noticed or comforted. What was that singing? Was there a choir? Palmtrees were clacking their hard fans above the roof tiles, boomgates floated and sank, a dog stood open-mouthed in awe before a lawn sprinkler, and every wrist that passed was manacled in plastic.

I kept moving. Something in soft soles was keeping pace with me wherever I walked, padding along silently behind my left shoulder. I walked and walked, with the thing moving smoothly behind me, and as I walked I rehearsed Patrick's version of me, the rubrics under which he had long ago marshalled into a cast-iron curriculum vitae the evidence I had so conscientiously provided: sad girl; problem with her father; full of anger; nympho; self-destructive; unstable; hyper-sensitive; a failure at marriage; unfeminine; man-hater; lost soul.

Was there a way to wipe it out? What if it happened today? I thought of Patrick, shorn and mapped with dotted lines, lying face down on a table. I imagined a foot, clad in a soft slipper shaped like a shower cap, approaching the switch of a drill. What if the surgeon should lose his way, and broach the box of bone where Patrick's official grids were stored? What if, with his savage light-tip, he should isolate, clip out and finally excise my file from the bee-chambers of Patrick's memory? Then, at last, could I spring away free into newness of life?

I went round through the garden of Occupational Therapy, along the front of a red brick wing where tranquillised people sat sombrely in a row on a dark verandah, and up a flight of stone steps towards the windowless side of a building whose exterior was studded all over with cement hand- and foot-holds. Halfway up to the eaves a young man still wearing a canvas back-pack was flattened like a spider, legs parted wide and belly to the wall, gripping and treading, clawing, gathering balance in stillness, then swarming again across the surface of the sun-warmed bricks. I heard his slow, controlled breathing as I passed below him, and took in my own stomach muscles the strain of his spreadeagled position.

I found Natalie in the waiting room of the intensive

ward. She was sitting with upright spine in an ugly dark armchair, knees together and hands folded in her lap. People were smoking and walking back and forth, whispering in pairs, keeping their voices down in front of straining children. There were no windows and the air was blue. Every now and then the lift door would open with a soft dragging sound and display its lighted interior like a scene on a little proscenium stage: a family hand in hand, a bald girl in a cotton gown, three medical students white with fatigue.

I pulled a chair round to face hers, and sat on it. Natalie was not the kind of person you touched. She recognised my shoes and raised her head.

'He's in there,' she said. 'In a few minutes we can go in.'

'Oh, not me,' I shrank back. 'You go. He'll want you.'

'Come in with me,' she said. 'You're his oldest friend. It'll mean a lot to him.'

We sat face to face, staring anywhere but at each other. Natalie was breathing hard.

'They let me in while he was coming out of the anaesthetic,' she said. 'He was deathly cold. Green, like a corpse. His whole body was in shock. They were wrapping him up in silver paper. He looked mad. His eyes were crazed. He was waving his arms, and raving.'

People in the room drew away from us, except for one girl, a fat teenager in stretch jeans and moccasins, who took hold of a chair and dragged it across the carpet to where we were sitting. She placed it three feet from us, at an angle but well within our field of vision, and lowered her large bottom on to it; then, with her forearms along the rests of the chair, she fixed us like a judge or a witness and, flicking her eyes from face to face as we spoke, absorbed our words with unabashed greed.

'Have you ever,' I blurted, 'wished that someone you loved would die? So that the record of all your crimes and failures would be obliterated?'

Natalie gave a gasp of laughter. The fat girl caught her breath and sat forward, letting her mouth fall open.

'Look,' said Natalie. 'The only person in the world with a full inventory of your crimes is you. You can burn things, wish death – but the past is still the past and you're still the same person.'

'I know,' I said. 'I know you must be right. But –'

'But what?' said Natalie.

We were both shivering. The fat girl's eyes were on my face, waiting for my lips to move.

'But what if he forgets everything?' I said. 'What if it's all up to me? He was my first real friend. Everything I ever knew about friendship I learnt from Patrick.'

'Oh, don't start that,' said Natalie, closing her eyes. 'You're worse than he is. Can you imagine how many times I've heard all these tales? You can't *know* how desolating I find that kind of sentimentalism.'

'But listen,' I said. 'He *did* things for me. He was *faithful* to me. He was *there*. He bailed me out of the lock-up. I was in a cage in the back yard of the police station and I saw him coming through the gate. And once a doctor put drops in my eyes to dilate my pupils, and Patrick took me by the hand and led me home.'

'All right,' said Natalie. 'That's enough.'

'He sent me the money for an abortion,' I ground on.

'Stop now,' said Natalie. 'Shut-up.'

'I didn't even know which bloke it was. I wrote to Patrick in Sydney – I hadn't even *seen* him for two years – and he sent me fifty quid the next day. In pound notes. In an envelope. No questions asked.'

'Yes,' said Natalie. 'Yes.' She leaned forward with

her elbows on her knees: I could see her teeth. 'But what *I* want to know is – what did *you* ever do for *him*?'

'I can drag it back,' I babbled. 'He thinks I've forgotten it all – but I can dredge it up. All of it, if I have to – if he can't remember any more.' I began to bawl. 'I'd lie at the foot of his bed like a dog,' I said, 'if it would do any good. Tell him that, Natalie.'

Natalie stood up.

'*You* tell him,' she said. 'Tell him yourself.'

The intercom on the wall next to the ward door spoke a name and Natalie ran to answer, putting her mouth right up against the metal; then she beckoned to me. I followed her in. She had a way of walking which suddenly seemed to find its purpose: she put her feet down firmly, but with a light spring, as if her knees were never completely straightened. She was ready for anything, with this walk. Anything at all would find her ready for it.

The air in the ward was dense with anxiety. Entering it was like wading against a surf of rhythmic moaning, whether human or mechanical I could not tell. Down the aisle between the two rows of beds trod Natalie, lightly and quickly. I saw the first body. That's not him. The head, shaved and with a bloody modess pad clapped to the back of it, was turned away from us in a hard, unnatural position: dead, an Auschwitz victim, someone who had perished in agony. I kept moving but Natalie stopped. She *stopped*. Wildly I tried to read the name on the clipboard. It was Patrick.

He was suffering. He was crying out. A nurse rushed to him with an oxygen mask: he rolled to grab at it and the force of his in-breath seemed to suck it on to his terrible face; then, seeing us over its rim, he tore it away and reached out his left hand to where we stood, two of the *women in his life*, gaping with shock and fear at the foot of the bed. We were tripping over each other to defer. Frantic, Natalie pushed me: 'Go on!' I blundered to the side of the bed and seized his hand. It was warm and very meaty, but it was not my place to go closer, to approach his face, his wounded head. I kissed his hand, squeezed it, and laid it down for Natalie, who took hold of it as I scrambled out of range. He fought to speak to her, her ear was against his face, but his grunts were swallowed in the weird soughing that filled the ward, the sound of the room itself labouring for breath.

Natalie backed away and I fell into step behind her. She was almost running. The big door flopped shut after us, and the waiting faces lifted and swung in our direction like a shoal of satellite dishes. I looked at the clock. We had been inside for barely a minute.

'What was that noise?' I jabbered. 'I heard a noise.'

'I didn't hear it,' said Natalie. 'I block out everything.'

She kept walking fast, barging towards the elevator. She certainly did not need me, but I hurried in her wake, and down in the lobby she paused long enough to turn her blank face towards me, and nod.

'I'm going home,' she said. 'Don't come. I'm going home.'

I stood still, to let her get away from me. When she had become a member of the crowd, I walked slowly, on chalky legs, through the lobby of the hospital.

It was cool there. The hallway was wide and clean, and the floor was made of green marble tiles that shone. I looked up at the stained-glass windows. All I could make out was a figure standing with its arms spread wide and its bare feet balanced, low down in the frame, on what looked like a stack of sandbags. No: they were clouds.

I thought I would have something to eat, somewhere. And after that I had better find myself a hotel.

I tried to walk briskly towards the door; but some-body was standing in the shadow of the huge sandstone pillars which supported the entrance porch. It was a child in a cape, a little boy.

He was hunched over from the waist, working with ferocious concentration on a black metal object he was holding in both hands. His head was bent over his task, but as I walked towards him I could clearly see his face in profile, and trembling with shock and distress though I was, my steps shortened of their own accord, for I felt that I knew him, that in some book or gallery I had seen his picture, or a picture of somebody like him. Out of respect I placed my feet more lightly on the marble floor; and just as I drew level with him he straightened his spine, raised his head, and extended his gun arm towards me in a slow, vertical arc. I saw then what he was: I recognised him. I stood still in front of him. I presented myself: for he was no longer playing. He was here on business, acting on orders. He was a small, serious, stone-eyed angel of mercy.

A VIGIL

KIM'S FATHER was supposed to come down from Queensland or wherever he lived to straighten her life out for her, give her some good advice, pay her uni fees and so on, or even take her back up there to live with him. He promised he'd be there in June, for her birthday, but for some reason he couldn't make it by the date. Then it was going to be August, then September. She was hanging out for this. She stopped going anywhere, in case he turned up while she was out and the others in the house let him get away without giving him her message, to make himself at home and wait ten minutes. First she used to sew, till the machine broke down, and anyway the whine of the motor was starting to make her nervous. Then she drew, or wrote for hours in her diary. Then she read, lying on her bed in a worn-out old nightie, nibbling at the ends of her hair, but she said the books she was supposed to be studying were so boring that she kept dozing off.

Then things got to the point with her where all she could do was sleep. Awake, whatever she heard threw her into a state of nerves: the wind when it bumped, a bird in a tree outside the window, the water rustling down the gutters when the council workers opened the hydrants. Her fearfulness filled Raymond with impatient scorn, and relief that he was not after all the most hopeless person he knew. The morning a truck poured a ton of blue metal chips down in the lane outside, he came back from the kitchen and found her on her knees in the corner with her head in the dirty clothes bag. He thought of laughing, till he saw that her eyes were bulging. There was a primary school behind where she lived. She couldn't stand the noise the kids made in the yard at playtime, their screaming. It made her grind her teeth and blow her nose till it went red. 'Somebody must be hurting them,' she whispered. 'They're hurting each other.'

'You're stupid,' said Raymond irritably. 'That's a _good_ sound. Aren't kids supposed to be a good thing? You shouldn't freak out over something that's _good_. What's the matter with you?'

By October, though she lied about it, she was swallowing day by day in threes and fours the pills she got from her mother and sleeping the time away buried so flat in the quilt and pillows that when he came in he had to feel around to make sure she was still there.

'Get in,' she mumbled, too doped to open her eyes. 'Less go to sleep.'

The nightdress was twisted up round her waist and her skin was loose, like old sacking. She had about as much life in her as a half-deflated dummy, but without complaint she opened her legs, and he kept his face turned away, to avoid her breath. She grunted, that was all, and when he rolled away she made a limp effort to attach herself to his back; but she was a dead weight that could not hang on. Her arms' grip weakened and her torso fell away. The cool air of the room shrank his bare spine. She snuffled, and a light rhythmic click began in the open membranes of her throat. He would have got up straight away except that the tick of her breathing matched itself briefly to his heartbeat, and at the moment of focusing on the leaves outside the glass his mind lost its grip on the edges of the furniture and slithered away into a comforting nest, a sty of warm webs and straw. Then the parrot screeched, in somebody's back yard, and he woke.

He raised himself on one elbow and looked back over his shoulder at her. She was only a small girl, with small bones, and her head too he had always thought of as small. Wandering round the city, the day after she had first dragged him home from a party where he was lurking sourly in a doorway, always too old or too awkward, always wearing the wrong clothes, he had found himself fitting words together in the part of his mind that no one knew about: he practised remarking casually, 'She's buttery', or 'She's well-toothed'; but he never fell into conversation with anyone who looked interested in that way of talking – Alby certainly wasn't – and now her face, like any drugged sleeper's, was as thick, stupid and mean-ingless as a hunk of rock. He saw that there was nothing special about her; that he was superior to her after all. She was damaged goods. The pills were not to blame. The pills were doing him a favour by reminding him of something he had always known was in her, in any girl that age who would do what she did with him, and you could tell by the moron face they made when they were doing it, all vague and grinning. He imagined, propped there in his twisted pose while his insides congealed again into blankness, how he would describe her in the café if any of them stopped talking long enough. 'She was more out of it than I've ever seen her. Mate, she was' – he would stick out his flat hands, palms down, and jerk them sharply apart – '*out* of it. This gig's over. People who can't get their shit together should just go and *die*.'

It was late in the day. If he got up now he could make it to the Hare Krishnas for a feed. The girl downstairs was getting ready for work. As she called to her cat, her clogs on the cobbles of the lane made a sound like a tennis ball bouncing. While he pulled on his clothes, blocking out the irritating click of Kim's open mouth, he ran his eyes over the floor, checking for dropped coins, a screwed-up five dollar note, the price of a coffee, anything he could use.

On the boards between the bed and the door stood a pair of heavy black rubber-soled shoes. Their laces were still in bows. She must have yanked them off in her rush back to the big dipper of sleep, and yet they were placed tidily side by side, and although they were months old they still looked new, since the only wear they got was when she walked over to her mother's every couple of days for pills and maybe a leftover from the fridge. All the girls wore these shoes. He felt nothing about the style. He only noticed the shoes because the neat bows jigged a memory which was gone before his mind could lumber round to it: something about laces, something about tying a shoe. He hesitated, then he stepped over the shoes and went out of the room. The door clicked shut behind him. The air of the stairs was thick with the smell of cooking broccoli.

Four days passed before he came back.

He too spent them horizontal, in his brother's boarding house room with his pants unzipped, holding across
his chest Alby's big acoustic guitar and picking at it
tunelessly, or rereading the collection of seventies comics
from under the bed: epic acid landscapes, hulking heroes
in fur leggings, pinheads, VW buses full of frizzy hair, a
stoned cat, girls with huge legs in boots and mini skirts,
and a special way of walking called 'truckin''. That world,
drawn in square boxes and balloons of words, he knew.
The real one he was lost in, but so lost that he didn't know
he was lost. His father was dead, his mother was stupid,
his sister had run away; and as soon as Alby got back he
would be on the street again. He lived untouched inside a
grey casing through which he watched, dully, how other
people behaved, and sometimes tried to mimic them. He
saw that they remarked on the weather, and he tried to
remember to look at the sky, to see if there were clouds in
it. He saw what people ate, and he bought some. He saw
that they talked to make each other laugh, and he dropped
his mouth open to make the sound 'Ha. Ha.' He saw that
when a band played, they heard something; he saw that they
danced, and he tried to lift his feet. His whole life was
faking. He thought that was what people did.

At six o'clock on Tuesday he cleaned himself up and
went out. He passed Kim's mother leaving the Lebanese
take-away with a felafel roll in each hand and a heavy-
looking bloke coming down the step behind her. 'G'day,
Ursula,' he said. She nodded, but the bloke gave him a
dirty look and Raymond dropped his eyes. He got himself
some chips and ate them as he walked to Kim's, stopping

for a look in the window of a secondhand shop that sold things Alby might need: a stringless guitar or a plastic record rack or books with titles like *Chiropody Today* or *Welcome to Bulbland*. The tattoo shop was open. The artist skulked right down at the back, crouching in a burst chair with wooden arms. No thanks. You could get Aids off those needles, though maybe a little anchor, a bluebird . . .

The small concrete yard of Kim's house was scattered with faded junk mail and plastic pots of grey dirt and stalks. He tossed the chip paper against the fence, wiped his hands on his thighs, and pressed the buzzer. She might ask him if it was 'a nice evening'. That kind of talk she picked up from her mother. He directed his eyes upwards and saw grey: a grey sky, grey air. It was not raining. Was that 'nice'? The clog girl opened. Her boyfriend was in a band and once, when he had gone away on tour without taking her and Kim was staying the night at her mother's, the girl, who Raymond believed fancied him, had blundered into Kim's room bawling, wanting an audience for her sob story. She was disgusting. Raymond lay there on Kim's bed, staring up at the girl. He said, 'Oh, go away. Go away or I'll shoot you. To put you out of your misery.' Now, seeing who he was, she turned away without speaking and headed for the back of the house. From the foot of the stairs, before he started to climb, Raymond glanced after her. He saw her shoulder and heel disappear into the kitchen. The bulb hanging there was lit. It swung slightly, and the shadow above it swung too. This he would remember.

Kim's door was closed. There were no voices, and no light showed under it, so he turned the handle and walked straight in. The room was stuffy, and almost dark. He stepped round the low bed, flicked back the curtain and

pushed up the window, wedging it open with a hunk of
chair leg she kept on the sill. Better air came in under the
raised curtain, and at the same instant, in the tree right
outside the room, a bird started to sing. He could see it, in
against the trunk. It was a small bird but a loud one, and it
was shrilling and yelling without any tune, making the
kind of racket that sent Kim into fits. He felt a surge of
meanness. Holding up the curtain with one hand, he
turned his head to watch her wake.

The bed was a turned-over confusion of materials.
Only the crests of the folds caught the light. Where was
her face? Was she even there? This stupid bird! It was
louder than a whole treeful of cicadas and still she didn't
hear it. There was a pale bit of her up between the pillows:
was it a cheek or a forehead? He stood there with one hand
tangled in the curtain, feeling for a nail to hook it back.
It caught, but still the light on the bed kept darkening:
he was straining to make out her face. Outside, the bird
shrilled and thrilled. A bit of her hair had got twisted
across her chin. He pulled his hand out of the curtain folds
and threw himself to his knees on the very edge of the
mattress. It bounced. The smell hit him. Her mouth, half
open, was clogged with vomit and alive with a busy-ness
of insects. His head and torso jerked back as if on a rein. He
made no sound, but across the ridges of his windpipe rushed
the shrieking, the squalling of the bird in the tree behind.

He reeled down the stairs and out on to the street.
It was almost night. The rooflines of the houses sliced a
green and bitter sky. Bells tinkled in showers and somebody was feebly panting, but otherwise the soundtrack
had shut down. He kept walking, bumping the shop
windows with his shoulder, dragging the soles of his
rubber thongs. He blundered past a man sharpening his

fingernails on a red brick wall, a bare-faced waitress swabbing terrace tables, a busker unpacking a saxophone in a doorway. He was heading for Alby's, if Alby's still existed; it must, it must, and he travelled slowly, trying to keep himself unfocused, for if he stayed submerged long enough he might surface at last flat on his back under Alby's scratchy grey blanket and open his eyes to see Kim standing crossly beside the bed, trampling Alby's comics with her heavy shoes, scowling at him and biting the split ends off her hair. But the night went on and on, and he ran out of vagueness. It gave out on him. He came to the end of it, and then he knew that nobody on earth, nobody he would ever hear of or meet had the authority to rescue him from the cold fact of what had happened; and yet, as he slunk along the avenue where the mercury vapour lights flushed and whitened, he gazed with stupid longing at the line of spruikers outside the porn clubs, kings of the pavement, big fast-talking dangerous boys in long black overcoats and greasy little ponytails who moved him to awe as angels would, they were so tall, so graceful, so inky with unused power.

He was shoving his spare shirt into a bag when the knock came at Alby's front door. What day was it? Sun was shining. It felt like afternoon. He opened the door and Ursula was standing there. He looked quickly behind her for blokes, but she was on her own. Her face under the sunglasses was fatter, and she was dressed in black.

'Get in the car,' said Ursula.

A taxi was waiting at the kerb, with the door open and the motor running. He hung back.

'Do up your fucking shirt and get in the car,' she said. Her voice was hoarse and she smelt of grog, not beer, something stronger and sweeter. His legs weakened. He had not spoken for two days and he could not speak now. He followed her to the cab. As she climbed in ahead of him, he saw the gold chain round her ankle.

This was one of the few taxi rides of Raymond's life and he was worried that the driver, an Asian in a clean white shirt, would think he was a bludger or up himself for taking a cab at all instead of public transport, and also that he might think he had something to do with this puffy, purple-faced moll who tore in cigarette smoke with all her back teeth showing and kept letting out panting noises and wiping under her sunglasses with the bottom of her dress. She had a flagon of sherry in a plastic bag between her feet and every few minutes she bent over, tipped it sideways and took a swallow. Raymond sat with his hands clasped between his tightly clenched thighs, and kept his eyes on the shiny headrest in front of his face.

The place, when at last the taxi swerved off the freeway and followed the signs to its gates, looked more like a golf course than a cemetery. It was vast, bare and trim. At the end of its curved black road they came to a garden, and in it, a building. Ursula shoved him out, pushing the wrapped flagon into his hands, and he stood there sweating while she paid the driver and the taxi drove away. At the mouth of the chapel some people in a group turned towards them and stared. Raymond thought they were looking at him, but it was Ursula they were watching out for, they were waiting for Ursula to arrive. They must be her friends from before; they were old hippies with grey curls or beards, and the women had hair that was long and stiff, or else cut short like boys', showing their wrinkled eyes and foreheads. One of the men was tall and bony, like a skeleton, with a shaved head and rotten teeth; his hands were tattooed. Ursula kept a tight grip on

Raymond's elbow. To the people staring it might have seemed that she was using his arm for support but in fact he was her prisoner, she was yanking him along beside her in a shuffle, in at the chapel door, through a cluster of whispering girls with massed hair and black bodies, and right up the aisle to the empty seats in the front row.

Yellow light fell from long windows at the sides. More people, not many, were waiting in the seats, and someone was playing one of those organs that quiver automatically. Ursula was different now. She was trying to act normal. Raymond heard her put on a voice and say to the woman on her other side, 'What a lot of people have turned up!' The woman tried to put her arm round Ursula's waist, but Ursula went stiff, and the woman, with an offended look, took her arm away and moved across the aisle to a seat further back. Raymond sneaked the flagon under the seat and pushed it out of sight with his foot. As he straightened up someone tapped him sharply on the shoulder. He jerked round. A woman in the seat behind leaned forward and spoke to him in a furtive way.

'What? What?' he said in confusion.

'I said, you were Kimmy's boyfriend, weren't you?' said the woman. She slid her eyes over his face, ears, hair, neck.

'No, no,' he jabbered. 'Not me, no, it wasn't me. Friend of the family, I'm a friend. Of the family.'

His head was shaking itself like a puppet's. He turned his back on her and hunched his shoulders up round his ears. In the front row there was no protection. He could not fold or bend his legs enough; his feet were enlarged, gross, dirty.

The music stopped and a man in a suit stepped uncertainly up to the front and stood against some curtains, facing the people. Raymond did not know whether

they were supposed to stand or sit. He glanced behind him
for a clue. A couple of the girls were scrambling to their
feet, one bloke dropped on to his knees, but most of
the people stayed seated with stiff, embarrassed faces. The
man out the front said nothing, gave no orders. He did not
appear to be in charge: no one was in charge. Raymond
realised that nobody here knew how this thing was meant
to be done, that nobody here was going to stand up and
say the words that would save them.

Then he heard, in the uncomfortable hush, a squeak-
ing and a gliding, the sound of small wheels. Ursula's nails
sank into his arm. The curtains at the front were nosed
apart and into the empty space where the weak man in the
suit was waiting rolled, on a metal trolley, the wooden
box with Kim inside it.

Ursula stood up, dragging him with her. Her fingers
bit into his inner elbow; and now out of her mouth
horrible sounds began, ugly and ridiculous, the noises that
bad singers make when they work up to a solo: woh, woh,
woh, she went, blank and gaping, gobbling for breath.
An old woman darted across and seized her shoulders with
both hands but Ursula flung up one arm and knocked her
away. In the same movement she struck off her own
sunglasses which dangled from one ear and hung half
across her mouth, revealing two swollen bruises: her eyes.
Out of these sore slits poured a gaze that hit the end of the
coffin and bored right in. Ursula at that moment could see
through wood.

She turned on Raymond with a crazy mouth. He
fought to break away but, like the shrilling of the bird
outside the window, Ursula's howling, this horror, exploded and stuffed the universe, paralysed him, swallowed
him whole.

Then the bald skeleton with tattooed hands stepped

right through the commotion in his heavy boots and put both arms round Ursula from behind.

'Let go,' he said, right in her ear, working at her hands, rubbing at them, getting his thumbs under their grip. 'Urs, it's me, Phil. Come on, Urs. It won't help the little girl now. Lay off the poor bastard, Ursula. Come on, let him go.'

He unhooked her claws and Raymond stumbled back. A rush of murmuring women with handkerchiefs and skirts flowed into the space where he had been, but in the second before they engulfed her he saw her one last time, with her back against the bald man's chest, rearing, her arms pinned up by his grip on her two wrists: her face was a demon's muzzle, sucking in air before its final plunge into the chasm.

Raymond got to his feet in the corner where he had been flung. The air in the ugly chapel settled; the coffin hummed behind him. He could not look at it, but he felt it vibrating in the yellow air, rippling out waves that pressed against his back and propelled him down the aisle towards the door. Ankle-deep in crushed garlands he crossed the porch and stopped on the step of the building, swaying and hanging on to the sides of the archway. He slid his head out into the garden. The last of the cars was pulling away. He heard the sponge and pop of its tyres on the bitumen, saw the blurred hair-masses of the girls packed into the back seat, smelled the exhaust that shot out of its low muffler. It swung round the curve in the road, and was gone.

He let his knees buckle, and sat down hard on the step. He was empty. There was nothing left inside him at all. He crouched there on the chapel's lip, rolling up his shirt sleeve to inspect the site of his bruises. If he could work out where he was, if he could find his way to the gate, he was free to get out of here, to drag himself away.

So when the heavy boots came crunching towards him across the carpark, although the skin of his skull tightened and a thousand hairs grew stiff, he did not raise his head. Maybe it was the gardener. Maybe it was the first person arriving for the next funeral. He kept very still. He made himself narrow. He waited, with shoulders clenched, for the boots to pass.

They halted in front of him. In his stupor and weakness, Raymond fixed his eyes on them. Never in his life had he really examined or considered the meaning of what anyone wore on their feet. The boots were very worn. They were black, and old. They met the ground with leisurely authority, and yet their Cuban heels gave them a lightness, a fanciful quality that was poised, vain, almost feminine. The man whose boots they were, from whose footwear Raymond was trying to read his fate, breathed steadily in and out. He was in no hurry. Still Raymond did not raise his eyes.

At last the grating voice began. 'So you were the one, were you,' it said. 'You were the one who was fucking her.'

Raymond made blinkers round his face with his cupped hands and kept his eyes on the boots. 'No, mate,' he said. 'Not me.' He hardly recognised the sound of himself. 'Oh, I knew her, sure. Sure thing. I knew Kim. Everyone knew Kim. She was a nice girl. But I only came today because Ursula, because her mother wanted me to.'

The boots shifted, emitting a faint leathery squeak. 'Bit old for her, weren't you?'

A whiff of cigarette smoke dropped to Raymond's level and spiked the lining of his nose. 'Listen, mate,' he said, cupping his eyes, keeping his eyes down, 'you've got the wrong bloke. It wasn't me. I don't know who she –'

'Anyway,' said the man, moving his weight on to his left foot. 'She's dead now. No point worrying who was up who. Is there.'

'This is right,' said Raymond. 'Nothing can help her now.'

Over in the garden beyond the carpark a bird uttered three notes of a mounting song, and fell silent.

A butt landed with force on the black ground beside the boots. It lay on its side, saliva-stained, twisted, still burning; Raymond could not resist, at last, the urge to reach out one foot and perform the little circular dance of crushing it. Still he did not look up.

'There is one thing, though,' said the low, harsh voice above him. 'There's one more thing that has to be done. For the girl.'

'I have to go, actually,' said Raymond. He drew in his feet and placed his hands on the step as if to stand. This movement raised his gaze to the knees of the man's black jeans: the cloth was beaten, necessary, seldom washed, carelessly pulled on: as flexible as skin. 'I think I'll get on home,' said Raymond. 'I have to find my brother.'

'Hang on,' said the voice, patiently, firmly. 'You can't leave yet. I want to show you something.'

The boots took two steps back, then another two, then two more. The garden, until now blotted out by the hugeness of the boots, the legs, the voice, spread suddenly into Raymond's frame of vision. This he did not want. He did not want movement, noise, softness; he wanted a permanent berth inside his grey casing.

He raised his chin to argue.

Where one man had been standing, there now were two. Raymond sat in his crouched posture, head back, on the threshold of the chapel. His lips parted to speak, but he could not properly see the two men's faces, for the afternoon sun hung exactly behind their two heads which were leaning together ear to ear, calmly regarding him, calmly waiting for his next burst of excuses; and these died in his mouth at the sight of the corona of light whose centre was their pair of skulls, one furred with yellow hair, one shaven bald as ivory.

The two men stepped apart.

'I know who you are,' said Raymond to the bald man. Again his own voice rang oddly to him, as if his thoughts were forming on his tongue and not in his brain. 'Are you her father?'

'Hardly,' said the bald man, and laughed. 'Don't be a dickhead *all* your life.'

The men looked at each other, swung their heads to take in the moving garden, then fixed their eyes again on Raymond. They're crims, thought Raymond. They've been in the nick. The one with hair was dressed in ironed grey trousers and a maroon blazer with gold on the pocket. He must have a job at a racecourse or out the front of a tourist hotel. He wore boots as well but cheap brown ones, hard-looking, though polished. He glanced at his watch. His hands too were tattooed, with bitten nails.

'Come on, Phil,' he said to the bald man. 'The next mob will be on my back at four.'

The bald man, catching Raymond's eye, clicked his tongue and jerked his head sideways. 'Hop up, pal,' he said. 'We want to show you something.'

Raymond got to his feet warily, brushing the seat of his pants.

'Tsk,' said the man in the blazer, to himself. 'People don't care *what* they wear to a funeral these days.' He took a toothpick out of his blazer pocket, jammed it between his back teeth, and clomped away along a narrow path that skirted the chapel's outer wall. The bald man pushed Raymond lightly between the shoulder blades, and himself trod close behind. A freckled man in a towelling hat passed them and went tramping away across an enormous lawn, wheeling a barrow and whistling with raised eyebrows and cheerful trills. All three men greeted each other in an old-fashioned way, with grimaces and clicks.

Raymond's legs were still hollow and shaky; but as the men marched him Indian-style along the pathway, not speaking, moving forward with apparent purpose, he began to relax. Maybe this wouldn't be too bad. These men, like uncles, had taken him in hand. He turned to glance at the bald one, who winked at him and nodded. It was a public place, after all. What could go wrong? Maybe he could drop his guard and walk like this between them, single file. It was not so dangerous. He could slide from one thing to the next, and the next; nothing much would be expected of him, the rest of the day would roll by as even the longest of days do, and by the end of it he would have got a lift somewhere, would have walked somewhere, would find himself somewhere, under somebody's roof, maybe with people, maybe on his own; yes, all this he could handle. The worst was over. He turned again to the bald man, and almost smiled at him.

The man in the blazer veered off the path and plunged into the dense strip of hedge that separated it from the building's side. Between two bouncing bushes of blue flowers he rustled his way, spitting out his toothpick, and with key outstretched unlocked a little wooden door marked *Private*. He held the springy green branches apart for them with turning thrusts of his shoulders; they joined him, pinned against the wall by whippy shrubbery; he went ahead, and one by one they stooped and stepped through the little door, on to a narrow staircase that led them into the underworld.

The shock of it.

Raymond propped on the stair with one leg in midair. Above him the door slammed. The bald man coming close on his heels down the ladder would have cannoned into him, but took the strain with his thighs, and Raymond felt, instead of the weight of a heavy body landing against him, merely a dexterous, light brushing. He lurched down the last step.

Here they had not heard of blood or colour. It was a land made of dust, of chalk, of flour. The walls and floor and ceiling were grey, the air was grey, and as his gaze cleared and crept deeper, he saw that the receding alley of huge ovens was grey, that the workers who moved silently away between them were grey. The only sound was a low, steady roaring.

'Like it?' said the man in the blazer. 'This is where we work.'

'He runs the place,' said the bald man. 'He's the one who gives the orders.'

The man in the blazer, flattered, gave a naughty shrug. His hand closed round Raymond's aching upper arm, but gently, and urged him forward step by step until he stood, trembling and dumb, bracketed by the two men, in front of the closed door of the first furnace.

'Where is she?' said the bald man. 'He won't want to be kept hanging about.'

'Look up there,' said the man in the blazer, and pointed. 'She's next in line.'

'Ah,' said the bald man in his grating voice, with satisfaction. 'Ah, yes.'

A slot opened high in the grey cement wall, thirty yards away, and out of it, strapped to an elevated conveyor belt, flew the coffin. It dashed down and round the tilted track, skimming fast and cornering suavely on its slender arrangement of rails.

'Yep, here she comes,' said the man in the blazer, giving Raymond's elbow a little squeeze. 'Here comes your girl.'

A single pink posy was still clinging, by an accidental twist of sticky-tape, to the coffin's lid. As the box slid smartly into the last turn of the track and came to a stop beside them at the furnace door, the flowers lost their purchase and sailed in a brief, low arc to the floor. The man in the blazer bobbed down for the bunch. He took a sniff and tossed it over his shoulder into a barrow, while with his other hand, in a smooth movement, he checked a number on the coffin's end and made a mark on a list behind him. He raised his arm in a signal.

The oven door opened.

First, a square of colour: a blossoming, the relief of orange flames. Then a colossal blast of heat which evaporated the moisture off Raymond's eyeballs. He staggered, and the bald man caught him by the arm.

'Steady on,' he said. 'You'll be right.'

Behind them the man in the blazer was deftly unbuckling the straps that had secured the coffin to its sled.

'Here,' he said to Raymond. 'Take an end.'

Raymond's mind had abandoned his body. He obeyed. He turned front-on to the coffin and reached out both arms, but the man in the blazer winked at him and wagged one finger, tick tock, right in his face.

'Uh-uh,' he said. 'Bad posture. Bend those knees, mate, or you'll fuck your back.'

Raymond bent them. His muscles quivered. He slid

his fingers under the narrow end of the coffin and got a grip. The bald man played no part in the operation, but stood close by, watching, with his arms folded mildly over his chest. The man in the blazer took hold of the broad end, and nodded to Raymond. They straightened their legs. So light! The box floated up to waist level.

'Little scrap of a thing, was she?' said the man in the blazer. 'Weighs no more than a feather.'

The coffin hovered slant-wise across the open pop-hole in the furnace door. The heat was tremendous: their eyes squinted, their heads involuntarily turned away, their tongues dried in their mouths.

'Back up,' said the man in the blazer. 'We'll slip her in head-first.'

Raymond shuffled backwards and to one side. The man in the blazer screwed up his face against the blast and flexed his legs just enough to give him leverage. Then, in a series of manoeuvres so rapid, dainty and accurate that in three seconds it was done, he flipped his end of the load on to the lip of the furnace slot, darted back and, nudging Raymond out of the way with his hip, shot the coffin straight through the door and on to the shelf of flame. The door clanged shut. The heat faded. The man took a folded hanky out of his blazer sleeve and mopped his neck.

'A bloke,' he said, 'would be a mug to wear a tie in this line of work.'

Something hard pressed against the backs of Raymond's knees, which gave. It was a chair. The two men stood one on either side of him, each with a hand resting lightly on his shoulder. Like a monarch between courtiers, he sat facing the grey door of the grey oven. When he began to sag, to faint, they held him gently upright, keeping his spine against the chair back. The wrist watch of the man on his right ran madly in his ear.

'Sorry about the delay,' said the man in the blazer. 'We have to squirt a bit of oil on to the head and torso, to get them going. But the feet only take a few minutes.'

'The feet?' whispered Raymond. His teeth, his lips were dry: they rubbed against each other wrongly, snagging and missing.

The bald man, whose shaven skull had flushed a delicate pink, looked down at Raymond with sudden interest.

'You want to see?' he said. 'Open up that door.'

They raised Raymond from the chair and half-pressed, half-carried him forward to the furnace. The other man waved, and the door clanked open. Raymond's cheeks clenched of their own accord, turning his eyes to slits. The heat inside the cavern was so intense, so intent that all he could see was a working and a wavering. The men supported him tenderly, pointing him towards the square of liquid orange.

'I can't –' he said. 'I can't –'

'Yes, you can,' said the bald man urgently. 'Look now.'

Something in there was wrinkling. The small end of the coffin, fragile as an eggshell, was crinkling into a network of tiny cracks. While Raymond stared, greedy in his swoon of shock, the panel collapsed; it gave way to the swarming orange argument, and where it had been he saw a dark-cored nimbus of flame, seething, closer to him than an arm's reach. Its twin centres, their shod soles towards them, were her feet. In the passion of their transfiguration they loosened. They opened. They fell apart.

He could manage only his neck. The rest he let the two men deal with, and their tattooed hands went on holding him together. The long tube of the coffin now lost form. Pouf! It fell softly in upon itself, her last shelter gone. Deep in the fire he made out a humped, curved lump, and beyond that, rising, a denser clod, her head. He opened his mouth to cry out, but the wetness needed for speech was sucked off the surface of him by the oven's impersonal breath.

The furnace door slammed. He tottered like a doll. They lifted him backwards and placed him on the chair. While his seared skin loosened and turned salty, he hung by the shoulders from the men's restraining hands. He drooped there, sightless, beside himself, his own hallucination. Was there music? Someone was whistling, stacking the notes in jagged steps and executing a long and detailed flourish: a knot cleverly tied, Kim's shoe, the brass eyelets in a double row, the impossible twirl of her fast fingers lacing; a man's voice grew in song, then the fires roared uninterrupted, while near his ear the watch chattered, a tiny hysteria headlong, never arriving, never drawing breath.

'And again,' said the voice.

He half-raised his head, a dog ready for its next beating, and they bore him forward.

The grey door was open. Raymond looked in. The fire and the heat were barely a shimmer in the cavernous air. There was no colour anywhere, except for the maroon blazer cuff in the outermost corner of Raymond's view. The furnace floor was covered with ordinary ash, and on this desert bed lay scattered in a free arrangement three or four long bones, pale, dry-looking, innocent.

'There,' said the man in the blazer. 'All finished now. You can go home.'

They turned him and unhanded him and dropped him on to his own legs, side on to the cooling furnace.

'Go on,' said the bald man. 'Show's over. Buzz off.'

He stuck his hands in the back pockets of his jeans and jerked his rosy skull in the direction of the ladder.

'I don't know where I am,' said Raymond. He shuffled his feet in the grey dust of the floor. 'Which is the way?' They would cast him aside: and there was no one left in the world but these two men.

'Go on – get out,' said the man in the blazer. He bent down and picked up a long piece of wood. Raymond flinched, but without even looking at him the man shoved the head of the rake through the furnace door and began to drag it harshly across the shelf where the bones and ashes lay. The bald man leaned his chin on his companion's shoulder and plunged his eyes deep into the oven where the final disintegration was taking place: the ash tumbled down, as the teeth of the rake ground back and forth. It tumbled down through the grille and crumbled into the under chamber.

'Where do I go?' said Raymond. He felt the words cross his lips, but the voice was a child's. 'How do I get home from here?'

The bald man could not extricate his attention from the graceful behaviour of the ashes. He spoke absently, staring into the furnace where the other man's rake was accomplishing its task. He sighed. Then, with the slow resoluteness of a dreamer waking, he lifted his chin and turned on Raymond eyes as inhuman, blank and depthless as those of a figure carved in granite.

'Home,' he said, 'is the last place you need to go. Don't bother. Don't even go back for your things.' He flexed his arms and shoulders, and let them drop. The ripple of it ran down his torso. His joints were oiled with wakefulness.

Raymond stared. He hung on his own breath. 'Who are you?' he whispered. 'What's your name?'

'None of your business,' said the man. 'But you know where to find me, now. I'm always here. Always on duty.'

Raymond feasted his eyes on the man: his dark limbs, his worn boots, his shining ivory skull. He felt a terrible urge to approach. He longed to offer his forehead to the touch of the bald man's tattooed hand. Appalled, he saw his own grubby foot move out into the narrow space between them; but without taking a step the man was suddenly beyond his reach, balancing easily on the ladder with one arm raised to the latch of the high trapdoor.

'You'll be right,' said the bald man in his low, scraping voice. 'Things'll be different now. Just get out of here and start walking.'

He opened the trapdoor with a quick twist of his up-stretched hand, and leaned back from the ladder to make room, resting on Raymond his calm stone gaze.

Raymond stood in the dust and looked up.

An unbearable diamond of evening sky hovered over his head, scalloped and sprigged at its edges by dark foliage. Air gushed through it, smelling of cut grass; and out of the fresh leaf-masses, there poured down on him a light, nervous, persistent whirring, a multitudinous soft tapping and chewing, a vast and infinitesimal cacophony of insects living, living, living.

Raymond shut his mouth. He reached for the jamb with both hands, planted his feet – one, two – on the steep steps and, helped by a violent shove in the small of his back, hauled himself, flailing, through the shrubbery and out on to the staggering lawn.

COSMO
COSMOLINO

*S*UPPOSE THERE were a woman once, not long ago or far from here, whose husband came home one night and stood at the door to make a simple statement. Voices were raised. Kitchen utensils struck walls and spewed their contents. So quick! Janet lay on the sofa. What was the point of weeping? He was already gone.

The euphoria which followed lasted, oh, a month. All her senses had perfect pitch. Crowds parted at her approach, old men and boys and babies smiled at her in the street, waitresses spoke to her with a tender address. Milky clouds covered the sky. A warm dry wind blew all day, and the leaves changed colour.

This is not so hard, thought Janet. I can do this. Why do people make a fuss?

For years she had made herself so flexible that she

hardly felt a thing. Forgetting was her greatest skill. But now she noticed that the passing of time began to hurt her. Wherever she looked she saw the fleetingness of things. Mend as she might, clothes wore out. Things broke. Paper came briefly into her possession, was scanned or scribbled on, then screwed up and thrown away. Even the black mist that her fingers left on a café counter evaporated before the cup could reach her lips. It was painful to watch an old woman – and Janet was only forty-five – stumble unshepherded down the back steps of a bus while an energetic young one, admired by all the passengers, bounded aboard through the front, holding out her money. To see a couple of any age lean towards each other across a restaurant table caused Janet's stomach to fracture like an egg.

She looked at herself in a shop's long mirror and saw that she had grown crooked. Her right hip was higher than her left, and the opposite side of her top lip had developed, as it were in compensation, a bitter upward twist. If she placed two fingers against the outer point of each cheekbone and gently raised the skin, her jaw-line smoothed out, her upper lip lost its tense and radiating lines, and she saw a version of the girl she had once been; but the only thing that could take the years out of her face now was surgery, and the vanity of that she scorned.

She scorned many things. All she believed in was the physical, the practical, the stoical. Bite the bullet, she said. Plug on, one foot in front of the other and keep going. She had no children. Her family was scattered. She was too proud to take advice or sympathy: to a woman like Janet, nothing is more enfeebling than *pity*: and so she fell out with all her friends.

It was already years since she had severed herself, with rough strokes, from the demanding work she had been trained for, and had arranged her life so that she could earn a living without needing to leave the house more than two or three times a week. She could turn her hand to most things an old-fashioned typewriter was used for. She could review, she could edit, she could sling words around grammatically into sharp little pieces for fashion magazines, weekend colour supplements, and the glossy publications found in the seat pockets of domestic airlines. She was known for keeping a deadline; and if anyone asked, she called herself a journalist.

So she lay on her bed and read. She sat at the table in her upstairs room and tapped the keys. At night she would open the blind and lean out when the pub on the corner of the avenue was closing, and watch the real people going home with gaiety, some singing as they slung their legs over saddles and pedalled away, their fitful dynamo lamps blossoming on the dark surface of the road. And sometimes, now, in the empty house, she heard her own footsteps hurry past on the other side of a wall, her own voice, more girlish, laughing in a closed room. Unwelcome memories of happiness rustled behind her or pounced from doorways. She remembered being the youngest person present, being a student with a job: how it was to tie on an apron and slap together sandwiches in a shop, taking orders, chiacking with the customers; to have sore feet from standing up all day to serve; and later, the surprised pride of being on a payroll and a promotions list, of belonging to a union and knowing where she fitted into her society. She remembered the pleasure of being driven to work on sunny mornings by a bunch of older colleagues from the staffroom, married men with shaven cheeks, viyella shirts, maroon ties: the tonic, laundered smell of the car when she climbed in with her newspaper at the pick-up point near the start of the freeway.

Janet was not a mother, but she was a natural aunt. Her friends' children had loved her: she could not work out why, she was so brisk with them; she paid them so little attention that whenever she did speak the wildest of them sprang to obey her.

'Ah no,' she used to say, stroking the polish on to her toenails, 'I was a feminist. What if I'd had a girl? I would have felt it my duty to dress her in overalls and force her to play with Lego. Lego is the reason why I never had children. I hate going into houses and seeing those little bits of plastic scattered all over the floor.'

The real reason, which nobody knew, was that at thirty, between lovers and contemptuous of her own romantic fantasies, she had presented herself so plausibly to a gynaecologist that he agreed without demur to perform on her a tubal ligation, and did so within forty-eight hours. Janet came to in a hospital bed with a parched mouth, a clamp in her scabbing abdomen, and a terrible sense of having been rushed, rushed past herself into a future with no outcome. Somebody should have argued with her, somebody should have stopped her: but who? She was *beholden to nobody*, and that was her proudest boast. An old woman in the next ward was laughing, deep unstoppable harsh spasms of it, not crazy laughter but a response to something genuinely funny. Beside Janet's head lay a sandwich. Feeble with pain she peeled off its top layer and found inside it a tiny sliver of tomato which lay on her tongue, refreshing her, while she passed out.

Her house, bought with a windfall as deposit twenty years ago in a suburb not yet fashionable, was a two-storey corner terrace, one of those narrow and yet imposing Victorian arrangements of rooms which have been likened, by the disobliging, to railway carriages. 'Every room has a room off it,' chattered a visiting child to its mother, 'and every room with a room off it has a room off *it*.' It was littered, at the time when this story begins, with the detritus of many a failed household. Janet knew that one day she would have to hire somebody to put it in order, or else sell it and buy herself a hard, bright little apartment on the other side of the river: but in the meantime she retreated before chaos, closing doors as she went, leaving timber half-stripped and plaster unpainted, until only in the kitchen and her bedroom was any kind of order maintained.

In fact the house had always been her liability. In the seventies, when collective households regularly formed and crashed, when teaspoons had holes drilled in their bowls to frustrate the passing junkie, when cooking was rostered and bands practised in the bedrooms and tooth-brushes like icicles hung by the wall, it was demonstrated to Janet many a time that property is theft. Households exploded or collapsed, friends quarrelled and parted forever, the police thundered on the door at five a.m. and hauled the junkies away, and the one left behind in the echoing house, picking up mess off floors scarred by the repeated dragging of heavy club chairs, was always the hapless owner.

Take the wrong tone at breakfast, said Janet, and you were *laying a heavy trip*. Mention the mortgage payments on pension day and you were a slum landlord, the last worm on earth. People stopped talking when you entered your own kitchen; the word *my* could cause sharp intakes of breath round the teapot. What were we thinking of, in those days, said Janet. For all our righteous egalitarianism we were wild and cruel. We had no patience: our hearts were stony: our house meetings were courts of no appeal: people who displeased us we purged and sent packing. We hated our families and tried to hurt them: we despised our mothers for their sacrifice.

Some of us, said Janet, fell into the gap between

theory and practice, though we called it overdose, or
suicide, or falling asleep at the wheel. We had not learnt
the words with which to speak of death. 'Poor Chips,'
whispered the last of the household children, a little girl
whose head bristled with a hundred tightly yanked plait-
lets, holding Janet's hand in a bleak crematorium chapel:
'he died by *loneliness*.' They sat in a pew, dry-eyed and
desolate, listening to the ideological ramblings of a con-
temporary with scum on his lips who knew of no comfort
to offer, no blessing to call down, nothing useful or true to
say. The gods had long ago been mocked and forgotten.
Nobody prayed.

And the house, *Sweetpea Mansions*, with its foolishly
fanciful name worked in bossets and bulges on an old brass
plate beside the door: it jinxed her. Perhaps the commu-
nards, departing at the end of the seventies with armloads
of collectively purchased kitchen-ware, had had a point
after all; or perhaps it was not Janet's ownership of property *per se*, so much as the breezy, impatient confidence
it gave her, her irritating refusal to adapt her *bourgeois
individualism*, that made her so unclubbable, and later,
so unwifely.

Unwifely women, even independent ones with property, do marry, as Janet did at forty; and her husband,
a kind and comical man for whom, though she was too
distracted to express it, she felt real tenderness, real *liking*,
Janet's husband did his best. He tried. But at last he
became sad, and lost heart. Janet had no talent for intimacy. She did not know how it was done. Privately she
thought of it as *knuckling under*. She had thrived, before,
on drama, on being treated badly: it enlivened her. Her
husband, who wanted to be good to her, could never seem
to get her full attention. The chess set he gave her was

flung into an upper room. The ukelele he brought home from Vanuatu lay forgotten and dust-choked under their bed; and in the end, after five years of wandering in the complicated moral landscape of such a marriage, when he tripped the landmine which buckled the horizon and hurled them cartwheeling across it, he picked himself up, half-stunned with sorrow and relief, and limped away to a girl whose hair and teeth gleamed behind the rolled up window of a waiting car, leaving Janet sprawled there on the sofa, holding her breath while the back gate slammed and the motor roared and the beetroot soup dribbled down the wall. She lay and stared up at the familiar cracks and mouldings of the ceiling, its chubby plaster garlands and upside-down cornucopias of ambrosial fruits and flowers. It was all still there, enclosing her. She had the house, and the house was all she had.

Is it any wonder, then, that at such a juncture a woman like Janet should put on some lipstick and a clean pair of white socks, take the tram downtown, and outlay a small fortune for a haircut so savage that, walking home, she saw herself reflected in shop windows as a skull?

Now consider Maxine, who lived in a shed and called herself a carpenter. Although she had little training and no worldly ambition, she was in the grip of such a powerful urge *to make* that she barely slept. Ideas came swarming through her, and like many people who labour in the obsession of solitude she lacked the detachment to challenge them; yet when pressed in company she never lost her temper but argued round and round with a serene unshakable courtesy. She expected good of everything, she thought the best of the world and against all evidence was full of trust. Auras, star charts, chakras, the directing of energy and rays, the power of crystals, the moral values of colours: these phenomena were her delight: they guided her.

No one would buy her furniture. It was too outlandish for ordinary houses, being devised out of scavenged objects or pieces of native timber that she spotted deep in the scrub and crawled in after, with her little bowsaw, to cut and drag home. She *carved uncouth figures on the heads of sticks*; she wandered by lakes, and out of fallen branches would fashion, to celebrate the spirit of the place, a strange and delicate bench which she would plant up to its knees in the shallow ripples; then she would tramp away in her boots, leaving it to contemplate quiet water.

Open one of Maxine's cupboards and its interior would be decorated with threatening runes, or motifs and insignias you could under no circumstances incorporate into your practical life. Her tables were carved with hollows which prescribed the exact spots where your plate and glass must stand, and her chairs, while stable, tore at your stockings with their seats, or had flyaway backs which gestured towards the ceiling with all the authority of a diva's final note: so rhetorical that while the air was still vibrating you hesitated to resume your conversation.

For money she took jobs where she could find them, scrubbing, mowing, ironing for women who went to work in shoulder pads. Alone in their cavernous kitchens Maxine ate standing up at the stove, out of a greed that was almost spiritual: she ravened in a saucepan with butter running down her chin. Her terrible bush of frizzy hair she attacked with combs, clamps and clips, all of them helpless against the vehemency of what sprang from her head.

Vehemently, too, each night in her crowded shed with its line of tomatoes ripening on the sill, she dreamed of digging and discovering, of vegetables loose in the soil, of a bush covered in red flowers that bloomed on the very edge of a whistling chasm; and over and over she dreamed of a baby, a male child which, giddy with gladness, she took upon her knee and dandled, stroking his limbs, his plumpness, rubbing her face against his delicious temples; he permitted it; but nothing she did could lift him out of his mood of discontent. He sat on her lap by the high window, this anxious monarch with his crown and sceptre, and looked out over a landscape of hazy fields, of orchards, towns and forests; a mighty, polluted river wound across his prospect, and up and down its breast long barge-like vessels toiled in silence, laden down with cargo and trailing wakes of oil.

For dream sadness there is only art; and so the next thing that Maxine constructed, using the curliest and strongest twigs stripped under cover of night from the trunk of a neighbour's tortured willow, was a trembling cradle, smaller than a shoebox, lighter by far than any human babe could be; so light that the lightest puff of wind could set it in motion, lilting it on its dainty rockers. She placed it in her doorway and stood gazing at it. The same movement of air that shifted it lifted one corner of a curtain; as fleeting as the skirt of a running child it caught the edge of her eye in the darkening shed, and her heart was suddenly growing too high in her ribcage for her to catch a breath. Was it already too late?

But suddenly, in autumn, that season when the angle of the light changes and without warning one thinks of the past, when at mid-afternoon even the most carefully groomed garden is chilled by the meditative scraping of a cricket, Maxine lost her shed.

A fortnight's notice was all she got, but though news of the property sale chagrined her she held no grudge against her landlord, for she believed that everything was

meant, that she was responsible for and had in fact initiat-
ed all the events and conditions of her life; and she had no
idea that her landlord, with whom she was on nodding
terms as she passed his windows on her way home to the
bottom of his yard, was in the habit of taking his friends
on visits to her shed while she was out working for the
rent. They stood at the door, the last group he would
usher, with their hands over their mouths or in their
pockets, watching him pick his way nimbly to the bed-
side. He beckoned them to follow. 'And look, look – these
are her little slippers,' said the landlord, but his mockery
held a note of fondness, even of respect, though he scarcely knew it; and when he held up for their amusement the
fantastically titled tracts she kept beside her bed they hung
back, reluctant to disturb the demeanour of the furniture,
its silent, dignified postures, the shivering of the tiny
cradle. Like a shrine in honour of a god whose name they
had forgotten, the dim shed quietened them: it made their
own city seem foreign.

Maxine, thinking of leases, bonds, and the hiring of a
truck, increased her hours of labour by taking on a new
employer, and waited for her next lodging, or the path
towards it, to take shape.

Late one morning of her shed's last week, while she
was down on her hands and knees in the house of this as
yet unseen stranger, scrubbing at a stain on the hall carpet,
a wind sprang up and unsettled the street. She heard the
boom of air in chimneys, the venetians' brisk tattoo;
plastic bottles whispered on the rim of the bath. Maxine
lengthened her back to glance towards the narrow panes of
the front door.

The sky looked dry, bright and empty. She was
intent, passively alert, but the sounds confused her.
Had the council workers opened the fire hydrants? Were

dead leaves beginning their seasonal journey down the gutters? Or was it the letter sliding under the door, the step on the verandah? Had somebody called for her? Had her moment come?

Upright on her knees like a pilgrim she crawled to the front door and opened it. There was no letter on the step, and nobody on the verandah, but down at the gate, half obscured by the fronds of the unclipped hedge, stood a man in dark glasses.

His arms were flung out wide. His right hand lightly touched the gatepost. His knees were in the act of straightening, and the outline of his tightened thigh muscles showed as powerfully through the cloth of his trousers as if he were a gymnast who had just that second landed after a manoeuvre on the bar. Even the sinews of his feet, bare but for a brand-new pair of thongs, were bright with tension. Could he be the one? The one for what?

Maxine scrambled up in such haste that her blood did not keep pace, and the street outside shuffled its cards before her eyes. She grabbed the door frame to steady herself, and in the few beats it took for the black edges on things to disperse she saw a kind of tremor behind the man's shoulders, the large relaxed furling of a flag from which the wind has withdrawn itself.

Her head cleared. She craned her neck to see what was on his back, but he brushed a path through the waving hedge strands, and stepped on to the property; there was nothing behind him.

'Good morning,' he said. He stopped halfway up the path, holding a cardigan folded over his forearm and tilting his dark-lensed face up to her.

'Hullo,' said Maxine. 'Are you looking for somebody?'

'As a matter of fact,' he said in a meek but confidential voice, 'I've been sent.'

Maxine clasped her hands under her chin and rolled up her eyes. The sky was peachy with autumn: in her relief it seemed to swirl. 'Sent,' she said. 'Thank heavens.'

'Halleluia,' he said casually, looking round him. 'This is a very lovely house. I expected it would be. But these leaves. Shouldn't somebody take a rake to them?'

The timbre of his voice sent shots of energy coursing through her.

'I will,' she said eagerly. 'I'll do them as soon as I've finished inside. Would you like to come in?'

She made a sweeping gesture of welcome, but he did not respond. He stood on the brown and yellow tiles of the path, waiting.

'Don't you want to ask me some questions first?' he said. 'I mean who I am, who sent me, and so forth?'

What? Interrogate? Demand credentials? She made an impatient movement. 'You can tell me that later. Come into the house.'

Still he stood without moving. Some formality had not been observed: what could it be? Perhaps she was rushing him. This must be what men meant when they said to her *You are rushing me, Maxine*. She took three proper breaths, and began again.

'Where *do* you come from?'

'Ah – that would be telling.' He smiled. 'You'll have to work harder than that.'

'Is this a game?' said Maxine, taken aback. She had no sense of humour, she was not playful, but if that was what he wanted, she would make the effort. 'All right. Who sent you?'

'Look at me,' he said. 'Have a good look. Don't I seem familiar?'

The sunglasses bothered her. Would it be cheating to ask him to take them off? What were the rules? The trouble was that nothing about him so far rang a bell, nothing at all. Again she felt that her heart was fixed too high in her chest. This was not a game. It was much more crucial: a test, like the exams we face in dreams and have forgotten to prepare for. She let out a nervous laugh.

'Don't you recognise me?' he said. 'Don't I remind you of someone?'

Perplexed, Maxine rubbed the crystals of her necklace. She wished she had bought the pocket stone after all, the four-dollar one that *unified every aspect of life.* A false move now might ruin everything.

He was young. He was tall. In the power of his teasing his thin shoulders seemed to widen. His hands were invisible, clasped under his neat cardigan. How fresh he looked, almost beautiful, smiling there on the checkered path and waiting for her to take the plunge! A grand confusion of possibilities blossomed in her head. Was he a son, from another incarnation? Was he her father, come back on second thoughts to bless her? Was he her imaginary brother, her male self, soul's husband, cosmic twin? Was he an angelic being of the kind that comes in paintings offering a single lily, the flower whose contemplation furnishes all that is required? Or was he simply the bearer of the key to a shed?

'I'm sure this is terribly important,' she said, 'but just for the moment I don't seem to know quite what to say.'

He looked down and laughed: a pleasant sound: a voice with a crack in it, like music. Oh! she trusted him.

'Don't worry,' he said. 'It'll come to you. I hope this won't seem forward – would there be anything here to eat?'

'Of course. Come in!'

'Thank you. I've been on the road a while.'

Maxine imagined a peppering of galaxies, a tremendous trajectory along the star lanes. She saw a stony track among palm trees, a low horizon fading under a sky of pure green; and at night a woollen cloak wrapped round, the deep chill of a body sleeping on sand. She glanced at his thongs. They were pristine, utterly unmarked by travel. But he was already past her and through the front door, stepping carefully over her cooling bucket, and forging on into the body of the house.

Now if a house can be bruised, this one was. Its height and depth were still imposing, but its windows, propped open with lumps of wood, had to gasp for breath, and plastic bags nested in the branches of the trees outside them. The garden behind was derelict, wild with shrubbery and composed of moribund clods. The bicycle in its shed had grey pancakes for tyres. Indoors, the planet lamps bowed their heads in corners and over the table, and dusty runners lay discouraged in the hallways, drained of the energy to slither, as rugs should, along the floors. Had its enfilade of hollow rooms ever been counted, ever been tamed and put to use? The heart of the house was broken. It ought to have been blown up and scraped off the surface of the earth.

But houses as well as their owners must soldier on: and what would this pair of lost souls, already off on the wrong footing with one another, charging down the hall towards the kitchen where perhaps a heel of dry bread awaited them, a scrap of cheap Camembert lying shamefully on its face – what would they care about the building's history? All they saw was roof, walls, floor. This was what they needed. Why ask questions? Why search for more?

'This house,' said the young man in the darkest part of the hallway, 'is rather large.'

'I know,' said Maxine with a blithe laugh, skirting round him where he had paused to stare up at the framed pictures askew on the walls of the stairwell. 'I haven't even *seen* all the rooms yet, let alone cleaned them.'

He gave her a strange look, but she pranced by with the fingers of both hands shoved deep into her uncontrollable hair, fishing out combs and stabbing them into its tangles which now he saw outlined in a fuzzy halo against the light of the doorway she was approaching, the entrance to the central room of the house.

He followed, sniffing her wake with dread, but it was untainted by perfume: it smelt like wood or glue and he wondered why. He wondered too whether this was a car-stripping neighbourhood, whether he should offer to go round the corner to the shop for a couple of pasties, whether he could take a quick look round upstairs by asking to use the toilet, and whether she was the modern angry type of woman – whether he should time his announcement with care, or just open his mouth and blurt it out.

She bounded in four steps across the central room and out through another door on its opposite side, but he resisted her pace and stopped in the middle of the carpet. Even with his sunglasses on, his eyes began to water and he had to screw up his face. Was *this* the place? The autumn light in the room was dreadful. It bounced in brutal sheets off a large white table that stood right under the window; shafts of it shot out on sharp angles from the backs of white-painted wooden chairs and swam in the curves of white cups, white plates, a white teapot. What he saw and squinted at was a blinding mirage of spotlessness, and yet for all its blaze the room was grubby. The crockery, shoved into piles, was stained with lipstick and gummy with dregs and crumbs; and the chairbacks showed the grey fingerprints of newspaper readers and chip eaters. On the wall near the kitchen door something dark red had exploded, dripped and hardened. All this he registered not in detail but as a general discomfort, a falseness under what proclaimed order; but he did clearly see that the table itself was pocked and snicked. Nailheads broke its surface, and down the length of it ran a deep groove that someone long ago had tried to plug with spackle; where the stuff had dried out and crumbled he saw the thicknesses of white paint that caked the timber.

He laid his right hand on the left breast pocket of his shirt. The little book was there. It comforted him, and he did not need to open it to find the phrase for this alarming room which, though it pulsated with light to the point where furniture levitated, was only a white-washed tomb, a whited sepulchre.

'There's nothing here but bones,' cried the woman gaily from the kitchen. She appeared in the doorway with a flat dish in her hands, holding it out to him and beaming like a housewife on a label. 'An old carcass. Do you want to have a pick at it?'

If only she knew how desperate he was. Not for the food – that he could scrounge anywhere, he was not proud – but for her gesture: the offering, the direct gaze, the smile. Self-pity swarmed through him. He kept his eyes on the dried bones and breathed slowly and evenly. At last he looked up. Maxine saw her own reflection in his lenses: a dish thrust out, behind it a shiny nose, a fading smile, a bush of hair.

'Is it a bit too awful?' she said. 'Sorry.' In shame she lowered the plate.

He put out both hands to reassure her.

'Thank you,' he said. 'It will do very nicely.'

She laid the dish on the white table and they sat down facing each other over its pitiful contents. So extreme was the light that the shrivelled remains of the chicken seemed about to dematerialise in it: the bones bleached as they stared at them.

'It *is* awful,' said Maxine, with sagging shoulders.

'It's *awful*.'

'Never mind,' said the man. 'We'll manage.'

He hung his cardigan over the back of his chair, pushed up his cuffs, and seized the bird's poor ribcage in both hands. With one wrench he parted it.

'I thought so,' he said. 'A little bit of stuffing left inside.'

Carefully he divided into halves the scraps of meat and seasoning, and passed her a share. With their whole faces tightened against the light they gnawed on what was there. They ate without speaking, without looking at each other. They had no manners. They put the food into their mouths with their bare hands, swallowing herb twigs, sucking dry shreds of flesh out of every crevice.

The meal was short. When the food was gone they wiped their mouths, cheeks and fingers on two dirty serviettes that lay among the debris, and sat face to face, each with one elbow resting on the table and one hand cupped round the temple nearest the source of the light.

Uncertainly Maxine took up the game.

'You would eat better than this where you come from, I suppose.'

The man laughed. 'Don't be so sure of that,' he said.

'Where *are* you from?'

'Oh, it's a fair way from here,' he said, lowering his face. 'Quite a long way north.'

He would not give an inch, behind his dark glasses. Was there a way to charm it out of him? But she had long ago lost the feel for that. Nothing about him stirred her memory. She could not strike a note off him. She drew blanks, whichever channel she tried. And yet he kept his face, with its twin eggs of green glass, fully turned towards her with a sort of candour, passive, half-smiling, patient. What was he waiting for?

'Would it be all right if I looked around the house?' he said at last.

She was out of the room and round the foot of the staircase before he could pick up his cardigan. Still half-blinded, he wandered into the dark hall with relief. The pictures on the wall meant nothing to him as he mounted, with his thongs slapping lightly against his soles, except that they were cock-eyed on their hooks, knocked skew-whiff by the shoulders of someone running past them. These women who *skip*: at *her* age. On the landing a single high-heeled shoe lay gaping on its side against the skirting board. He averted his eyes, hoping there would not be underwear. Maxine was already at the top. She hung over the railing to watch him plod after her. She was racking her brains. For a messenger, a courier of import, he was certainly taking his time.

On the upper floor, closed doors stood to attention. Under each one slid a slice of light as flat as a sheet of paper. The young man in his glasses perceived this as so much geometry, but Maxine noticed the scars on the timber and the skeins of fluff that drifted across them, and remembered guiltily her work, the long contemplations that housework brings – but first she must be given her news. Why was he holding back? She turned to him in a surge, but he spoke.

'And will you show me inside the rooms?'

She stared at him. How would they ever get to the point? Impatience ran its sharp currents down her legs and she hopped from foot to foot. But he stepped closer to her, and stood almost touching her belly with the backs of his hands. His cardigan hung from his bent arm, a little screen that covered the front of his trousers. She stopped her jigging. A smell she had forgotten emanated from him, the stab of sweat that stiffens the cotton it dries on. She looked up at him. Under his dark glasses he was smiling.

Ah – so it was not a shed. It was to be *this*. The trembling cradle tilted, the corner of the curtain rose and fell. Something throbbed, low in the cup of her pelvis.

'Only a glance,' he said. 'I wasn't expecting anything quite so – '

'Anything so what?' she said faintly, taking a long breath of him and feeling the strength leak out of her legs.

'So sort of grand.'

'Come in here,' she said. She floated to the nearest door and pushed it open. He lowered his head and without hesitation entered the room. Maxine followed.

It was ordinary. What mystery can survive the lunch-time mood of houses? Ordinary clothes, emptied of limbs and torsos, sprawled on an ordinary unmade bed, and the room was thick with silence. Its window was closed, the holland blind was drawn, and the air was exhausted and motionless, muffling the smallest sound: their breathing, the brush of an arm against its body, of thigh against inner thigh. Maxine's legs had turned to sponge. At his elbow she waited for him to put down his cardigan and open his arms; but he was staring at the sheets. He was thinking of the dank foam rubber strip in the back of the panel van, the scrub patch beside the highway, the shallow sleep through which again and again the road trains smashed, shattering his dream and jerking him upright, gasping and sweating. Behind him the woman was talking.

'What?' he said.

'I said, how did you know where to find me?'

'Oh ... I had the address,' he murmured. His eyes tangled among the folds of the quilt and pillows.

'I've been dreaming about this,' said Maxine. She sat down on the edge of the bed. Looking up at him under her explosion of hair she began to unlace her boots. The room was dim. Were his eyes slowly closing? They were both in a kind of swoon.

'Mmm,' he said vaguely. 'People remember their dreams, I'm told. Specially women.'

For a second she was jealous – how quickly bad habits sprout again – but of course this was his job, his task in the universe. It was mighty; it was nothing personal. She was aware of a smooth internal softening, a preparation by her body of all its organs, glands and passageways. This is much better than *love*, she thought, doubled up over her feet with her head at knee level. I was wasting my time when I used to be always falling in love, listening to their ideas about what I should be doing and making. I ought to have been a nun. I ought to have locked myself in a tower to build and think until the angel came for me; but now he's found me and I'm ready for him. By tonight he'll be gone and I'll have what I need and be free again: after all it is not too late. Her left boot was off and she started on the other one.

He was almost asleep on his feet, but he could hardly push her aside and lie down, in spite of the smell of cotton rising from the bed. It was stuffy: he needed air. He mooned across the room and zipped up the blind and the sash. The freedom of the street below flowed in, clearing his head: a boy cursing on a cruising bicycle, a tram chattering across the intersection a block away, and just outside the room a mass of loose and light-filled foliage shifting easily in the air as it moved.

He pressed his palms against the sill and leaned out into the slow leaves. Craning to the left along the flank of the house, he could glimpse a strip of wild back garden, and right at the bottom of it the rusting ripples of an outhouse roof. This was all right. This was very, very nice. He could take any amount of this.

A bird called in the tree, a brief warning stab. He recoiled, then forced himself to hang over the ledge and search for it. There it was; he saw the bead of its eye, right in against the trunk. Only a dove. A pretty little head and pearly feathers. It was not horrible. But he hung there, staring at it, his back cold with sweat; and the noises of the street and the tree's rustling filled his ears, so he did not hear the footsteps pounding up the stairs, and his back was not protected when the owner of the house, swinging her bag out ahead of her, strode into her own bedroom.

'What? Who let you in – Do you *mind*?'

A woman on her back on the bed. A total stranger with her head between the pillows – barefoot, and arched to pull off her tracksuit pants – and a man leaning out the window – so casual – but as the bag flew through the doorway his head came round over his shoulder with its mouth open to speak; and though the daylight was behind him and his eyes were hidden by an unfashionable pair of dark green glasses, she knew him at once.

The shoulder pads rose to ear level. She stamped her foot.

'Not you, Alby! I changed my name. I got *married*, for Christ's sake. What the hell are *you* doing here?'

Maxine saw the man turn, register, and flinch. Her hips dropped to the mattress. The virtue went out of the day. It was the world again: only the world.

Hot-faced, she pulled her trousers back up and crawled off the bed, gathering her discarded socks and poking her toe into the mouth of her still-warm boot. For the first time in all these years of solitary walking and working Maxine noticed, eyes down and fingers twirling the laces, how ugly were the shapes into which her feet had mould-ed the leather. I am middle-aged, and I have not looked after myself, she thought. Angels and archangels do not call for women like me.

Behind her at the open window the man began pon-derously to explain himself.

'I'm not Alby,' he said. 'I'm Alby's brother. Alby

can't come yet. He'll be down soon. But he's the one who sent me. I've got a message for you, if you're Janet. Alby sends his love. Love to you, Janet, from Alby.'

'What's your name?' said the householder sharply.

'My name's Ray.'

Maxine caught her breath. *Ray*. She dared not look up, in case she had heard it wrong. Again she had judged too quickly and given up too soon. With deliberate slowness, controlling her breathing, she doubled the bow of her second boot and got up to face the staring woman in the doorway. Their eyes met on the level.

'And I thought *this* lady,' the man went on pointing at Maxine's back, 'well I thought *she* must be *you*.'

'And will somebody please tell me,' said the householder, hands on hips, 'who she *is*?'

'I'm your new cleaner,' said Maxine. 'I found the key under the brick, like you said on the phone. I've already done three hours. It's going to be quite a big job.'

'Ah,' said the householder. The anger went out of the shoulders of her black linen jacket. 'So you're Maxine. You're not what I'd expected, at all.'

Thus they were accounted for. Three such people, in the same room. Nobody spoke. But a nameless breeze slid across the windowsill from the autumn afternoon outside, and brushed each of them in turn as it passed into the house, moving, it seemed, in strands. Those lovely words, *it seemed*! Already the room was gentler. Janet lowered her bag to the floor and dropped it. Maxine raised her palms to flatten her woolly hair. Ray bent his arm so that his cardigan returned to a polite vertical.

All at once he spoke.

'To tell the truth,' he said, 'I'm a bit desperate.'

The women turned to hear him. They stood side by side.

'I've been unemployed – well, unemployable,' he said, 'for a long time. I'm trying to change. To change myself.'

Janet studied him. Fat chance. A born loser. Just like any number of spongeing no-hopers arriving from the north in thongs. Something about his feet, however, pale and archless and pathetically lacking in experience, made her suspend the blade.

'Don't you ever take off those bloody glasses?' she said.

'Oh,' said Ray. 'Sorry.'

He let them slip down his nose and drop on to his chest, where they dangled on a woven cord. Ah yes, Janet knew the type. She was familiar with those cow's lashes, the lids that slid with maddening slowness up and down over the lowered, watery blue globes. She recognised in him another broken-spirited, obedient poor bastard, weak in imagination, lacking in drive, a wimp in whom the flame of life burned low; the sort that battens off the mother in a woman and ends up driving her berserk. Her judgement crystallised, and with a grimace she turned aside – but Maxine stood breathless, under her starburst of hair, lit up with wonder and renewed trust: she was witnessing at last the uncovering of the messenger's eyes.

Astonished, Janet paused – and that was her mistake, for the look went flashing from Janet to Maxine, from Maxine to Ray, and now Ray turned it, unmodulated by his glasses, straight back on to the mistress of the house. It struck her like a blast of sound: it rocked her. His pupils were bottomless black. The gaze with which he fixed her was as egoless, as scouring, as unblinking as a baby's, and the responsibility it heaped on her was as total. No! She felt the tiny fingers latch on, their knuckles whitening with the force of their grip: the feeble flesh, the tender skin, the still unhardened bones – edible, devourable, but *one did not.* She took one big step backwards, but it was too late. The story had already begun.

Downstairs, Janet pushed the ravaged dish of chicken bones to one side and rolled the match-stick blind halfway to the sill: but the kick had gone out of the sun. The clouds passed over. It was afternoon.

'Look,' said Janet across the table. 'The house is too empty. I hate the house to be so empty. It's *wrong* for a house to be so empty when there are people with nowhere to sleep.'

'That,' said Ray, 'is a very moral attitude. Most unusual.'

'Moral?' said Janet. 'I'm only moral because I'm unhappy.'

She gave a short laugh, but he saw that she meant it. A grey film lay over her, and her face, despite bright lipstick, was webbed with shadows. Maxine said nothing. She could not take her eyes off Ray; and besides, from lack of practice she had forgotten how conversations were conducted, and had become the kind of person who sits smiling, smiling, and occasionally uttering a non sequitur or a meaningless exclamation – 'We-e-ell!' or 'So-o-o!' or 'Uh *huh*!', making people jump and stare. Now she picked up the wishbone and held it out to Ray. He shook his head, so she snapped it herself, looked confusedly at the pieces, and slipped them into her tracksuit pocket.

'It's moral, yes,' said Ray. 'But you wouldn't want just anyone to move in, would you?'

'Of course not,' said Janet smartly. 'No dope freaks, no drunks, no woman-haters. No politicos, no hippies. Above all, nobody in a band. Otherwise, I'm not fussy.'

'Would I do?' said Maxine, focusing suddenly. 'I don't know anything about drugs or politics.' She gave a brilliant, dippy smile. 'And I'm sort of floating, domestically, at the moment.'

Janet shrugged. 'The place is big. We wouldn't have to see each other, if we didn't want to.'

There was a short pause.

'I did notice,' said Ray, 'that there was a shed. That would do me.'

Maxine sat up straighter.

'The shed,' said Janet impatiently. 'You're worse than your brother. Why do you class yourself so low? This dump's full of empty rooms.'

'I fancied,' said Ray, 'that the shed might be cheaper.'

'What?' said Janet. 'Surely you're not going to offer to *pay* me, for God's sake. I'd be pretty pathetic if I couldn't offer people a roof. For a couple of weeks. Or so.' Again she laughed, *ha*, a chopped-off sound.

'I don't want any favours,' said Ray stiffly. 'I can pay my way. And it's only till Alby gets here. Alby and I have got plans. Major plans.'

'Alby,' said Janet, 'was always big on plans. Don't hold your breath, if you're waiting for Alby.'

Ray looked offended. He went to speak, but Maxine butted in. 'Did you say a shed? Is there a shed out there?'

'Do *you* want it?' said Janet. She made a gesture of indifference. 'What would you do out there?'

'Make things,' said Maxine. 'I make things out of wood. And if it was all right with you, I could even sleep in it.'

'Take it,' said Janet. 'Be my guest. But there's no power. It hasn't got a proper floor, or anything. And I'd have to find myself another cleaner.'

'Oh,' said Maxine, rolling up her eyes and placing her hands over her cheeks. '*Oh.* I knew today would be special. I can hardly believe this.'

'What's so special about a shed?' said Janet. 'It gets cold out there. No one's ever *lived* in it.'

'Sheds are what I like best,' said Maxine. 'I had a good one, but I've lost it. The cold doesn't bother me. I'm always happiest in a shed.'

'Is it because of the noise?' said Janet. 'Do you have music on while you work?'

'Music?' Maxine's face clouded. 'No. Not music. Not me.'

'Music's all right,' said Ray. 'Some of it. But you have to be careful with the words. Most modern music's just . . . well, it can be dangerous.'

Maxine looked at him anxiously. But the music of the spheres? Or is it all silence, out there?

'Toss for the bloody shed, then,' said Janet, turning away. 'It's all the same to me.' It was not. She wanted other people to be breathing all night under the same roof, but she was too proud and sore to ask.

'It's against my beliefs to gamble,' said Ray. 'Let Maxine take the shed. I'm grateful for any shelter. I'll take whatever I'm given.'

Oh, come off it, thought Janet. 'Don't worry,' she said sourly. 'You won't have to sleep anywhere near *me.*'

He reddened. Maxine gazed at him, entranced.

'Listen,' said Janet. 'There's a couple of rooms upstairs. Take your pick. I haven't even been into them for years. I'll show you. See what you think.'

They followed her up, this time averting their eyes from her open bedroom at the top of the stairs. They paused in the upper hall and swung right, obeying the instinct that guides people to the best part of a house; but Janet put out her arms like a guide.

'No,' she said, and herded them in the opposite direction. 'Not those. They're stacked with junk that people never came back for. The big front one's where the kids used to sleep. It's a mess. The roof leaks. Houses sort of crumble. I used to try to keep up, but it's not much fun on your own. One of these days I'll get round to it.' She heard herself apologising, and closed her mouth.

Towards the back of the house, beyond the bathroom, things became less impressive. The floorboards of the narrow passageway were dried right out, long grey splinters had been torn from them, and the architraves had lost their grip on the walls and slouched this way and that, showing electrical wiring through the broken plaster. The visitors paused.

'Dark up here, isn't it,' said Ray.

'Were these the maids' quarters,' said Maxine, 'in the olden days?'

Janet pushed them on into the hall. 'I haven't been past the bathroom for ages,' she said. 'It's a part of the house I prefer to pretend doesn't exist.'

The first door was locked. 'Some dill took off with the key,' said Janet.

'Maybe it's haunted,' said Maxine. 'Maybe someone had bad dreams in there. Or a spirit came and made them toss and turn all night. So they cornered it, and locked it in.' She rounded her eyes and bit her bottom lip.

Ray placed his hand over his breast pocket. 'You can't lock spirits in,' he said. 'Or out. Believe me. There are incubi, and succubi. It's no joke. I know what I'm talking about. They come and go as they wish. There's only one thing that can control them.'

In a minute they would start reminding each other of *The Exorcist*. Janet cut across them. 'Actually,' she said, 'if you must know, it was Alby who slept in there. When I didn't feel like company.'

She hustled them past it.

The second of the three rooms was little more than a cupboard, filled to the roof with a tower of old cardboard cartons; a rope of cobweb connected the light-flex to the corner of the window frame. Quickly they withdrew.

Janet threw open the last door and they looked in, elbows touching. An empty socket hung from the ceiling, a bedspread was hooked over the window, and on the bare lino lay a stained single mattress, headless, with one shoulder stiffly twisted.

'Pooh,' said Maxine, turning aside.

'The last person to crash here,' said Janet to Ray, 'was your brother's horrible friend Chips. Remember him? That's probably why it pongs.'

Ray blinked. 'Chips died,' he said.

'I know,' said Janet. 'He OD'd. We all turned out for the funeral. Alby took it hard.'

'That was a couple of years before Alby was saved,' said Ray. 'He's got a resource, now. In these matters.'

'Was your brother sick too?' said Maxine. Did angels *have* brothers?

'No sicker than any of us,' said Ray. 'More of a slave than a sick man, actually. But Chips,' he added solemnly, 'was a poet.'

'Crap,' said Janet. 'He was a whinger and he wrote it down. That's not poetry.'

'I wouldn't know about that,' said Ray. 'About what's poetry and what's not. Alby liked what he wrote, that's all.'

'Well I didn't,' said Janet. 'And I didn't like Chips. He was a sleaze-bag.'

'Gosh, that's tough,' said Ray, mildly.

'Tough! Listen – that bastard used me. He treated the place like a flophouse and then went round putting shit on me behind my back. We only let him in the *door* because he was with Alby. Alby had style. But Chips was a log and a manipulator.'

Ray shrugged. He pursed his lips. 'Alby may have had "style",' he said, 'but it didn't save him from making a mess of his life.'

'Anyway,' said Janet, 'I should have known Chips would be trouble. His head was the wrong shape.'

She laughed to herself, a sound that made hairs stand up on Ray's neck. At his elbow Maxine too let out a laugh. Janet picked it up smoothly and ran with it.

'From the side,' she said, catching Maxine's eye, 'his head resembled the pickled onion from the very bottom of the jar.'

She advanced into the room with her face screwed up, and without looking at the mattress sank her elegant shoe into its ribcage, its raised shoulder; she shoved and kicked at it until it peeled back off the lino and flopped its sagging spine against the skirting board. A wave travelled off the mattress's under-side and reached Maxine and Ray at the door, a staleness that must have once been stench but now was faded, dry and weak; barely able to offend.

'Even in life,' said Janet, hands on hips, panting, 'he had no backbone.'

While the air settled in the room nobody spoke, but Janet felt the play of their eye-beams between her shoulder blades, and was ashamed. As always, shame made her angry. She looked at her hands, although she had not used them on the mattress; she wiped them on the sides of her skirt, examined them again, then turned and pressed between the two watchers, out into the hallway and back along it to the bathroom. She went in and closed the door with a sharp click.

'Boy,' said Ray. 'Is *she* snaky.'

'Is your name really Ray?' said Maxine. How long was it since she had stood so close to a man? She had forgotten how small she was. Her shoulder would have fitted neatly into his armpit. 'I mean – have you got other names as well? Or do you always call yourself the same thing?'

He looked down at her, not listening.

'I think I'll accept,' he said. 'Just while I get my bearings – till my brother comes for me. He'll be here soon. Wait till you meet Alby. He's pretty talented. He's had his problems, of course – but he's a really special bloke. We've taught each other a lot. Yes, I think I'll stay a bit. How about you?'

Was this the invitation? 'I'm not like Chips,' said Maxine, thrilled and bashful. 'I don't drink or write poetry. And I own a lot of stuff.'

'Take the shed, then,' said Ray with a magnanimous gesture. 'I'll choose myself a room. That's what she said.'

Softly on his thongs he turned back to the first door in the shabby back passageway. Maxine followed him. He rattled the brass handle, using it to lift the door in its frame and shift it to left and right, but it would not give. They stood still. Then Maxine rose on tiptoe and ran her fingers along the top rim of the doorframe. Dust tumbled off and sprinkled Ray's hair and shoulders: but when she held out her flat palm, there was a key on it.

'How did you know that was there?' said Ray.

'It was peeping,' said Maxine.

He stared.

'I mean I saw it,' she said hastily. 'Peeping over the edge.'

He looked up at the frame, and down at her. Then he took the key out of her hand, and examined the lock.

'Don't you think we should wait for Janet to come back?' said Maxine. 'Ask first?'

'I want to see my brother's room,' said Ray.

He rubbed the key against the material of his hip, and slid it into the lock. Maxine bent her knees, to watch. Pressure, withdrawal; press again with lightness; a flutter, a wrist-flick and a tug; a daintier push. While his other hand rolled the brass knob in unison, the key turned, and the door swung open.

Inside, behind it, there was nothing at first, only darkness and dead air, but gradually, as if waxing into Maxine's field of hearing, there came from low down near the floor a fast, rhythmic sound, something metal, something going like mad. Before she knew she had moved, she found herself behind Ray like a pillion passenger, hanging on to his waist. She felt his back go rigid, then relax. Was that her heart, or his?

'It's all right,' said Ray. He reached round the door jamb, flicked the dud switch on and off, and slipped out of her clutches into the dark brown room. 'It's all right,' he said. 'It's empty.'

How on earth could he not see it? It stood on the wooden floor behind him, in the corner just inside the door, where the light from the hallway poorly fell: an old-fashioned alarm clock with three blunt stumps for legs and a bell like a Prussian helmet. Its face, a faithful little moon, was turned up to her, its hands were spread to plead innocence, and its inner mechanism emitted without ceasing the rapid ribbon of blows called the passing of time.

But as she opened her mouth to call out the wonder of it, the silver ticking spread along the walls of the room, became a drumming, and was drowned in an ample and agreeable rush, as if water somewhere were gushing in sudden release.

Ray swung round with his arms wide, floating in the darts of daylight that pierced the blind.

'How could he have got a wink of sleep in here?' he

said. 'Those pipes are prehistoric. I think I'd better take the end one. The one that was Chips's.'

Before she could point or warn, he had stepped past the clock and shepherded her back into the hall, pulling the door to behind him.

In the bathroom, Janet turned off the taps and opened the window. She knew she should come out and face whatever needed to be dealt with next, but instead she shot a look at her haircut in the mirror, and turned away from it, appalled, to sit down on the wooden lid of the still groaning lavatory. She was hiding. These weirdos. Why do I always collect them? It must be my fate, to be depended on by lost souls. Just for the time being, though, she could put up with them. For a little while. Until they took what they needed, got fed up with her bossiness, rounded on her, and shot through.

From the sloping street under the window rose the cries of home-going schoolchildren, their passionate, breaking voices. She squeezed her eyes shut and doubled herself up over her knotted arms. It was a good sound, she believed with the part of her that still believed anything; but it hurt her. She knew why, and there was nothing she could do about it. It was much, much too late.

The dark column shifted into position, near her left shoulder. It did not touch her. It formed and fluttered there, further behind her than her glance could have reached; and it waited.

Apart from Maxine's tools and furniture, there was not much to be transported; it was all done in a morning, with the absorbed and practical cheerfulness which at the establishment of any household sweeps away misgivings. The furniture, when it came, filled Ray's panel van like an excursion of handicapped children, some supine and passive, some eagerly upright but exhibiting at the windows bizarre body language which snagged the attention of pedestrians and left them puzzled and staring.

'What do you make of her stuff?' said Janet to Ray on the back verandah, while Maxine, fifty feet deeper in the unreconstructed garden, trotted backwards and forwards outside the shed's gaping double doors, hands clasped under her chin, engrossed in the fresh arrangement of her creations.

'Her stuff?' said Ray.

'Her work. The chairs and cupboards, and so on.'

'I haven't formed an opinion,' said Ray. 'Yet.'

'Just at first glance, though,' said Janet. 'How does it strike you?'

'Oh, I don't know whether I can really say, at the moment.'

She glanced at him, surprised, impatient. 'Not even off the top of your head?'

Sweat broke through the skin of his armpits. 'I'll have to examine it much more carefully,' he mumbled. 'I'll have to become accustomed to it, and get acquainted with her . . . theories, before I can offer an opinion.'

'I'm not asking for a final judgment,' said Janet. 'Just an impression – you know, a gut reaction.'

Dumb, he stared at her.

'What I mean is,' said Janet, more gently, 'do you *like* it?'

'Like it?' he repeated.

'Is there any of it that you – that you sort of feel good about, when you look at it?' She was speaking in words of one syllable, as if to a child.

He closed his mouth and turned away towards the garden, his thoughts struggling behind a cloud. Again she looked at his feet and saw the pathos of them, how unguarded they were, how feebly shod.

'I'll tell you,' he said in a rush, 'if you really want to know. Her stuff gives me the creeps.'

Relieved, Janet laughed, then lowered her voice. 'Why?'

'Look,' he said. 'I'm not very sophisticated, right? Anyone can see that. I haven't had much education. I'm not a talker. But I do know one thing. I know the difference between right and wrong.'

Janet fixed her eyes on Maxine's little figure down there at the shed doors, beyond the mossy lattice and the old tomato stakes: rapt, unconscious of scrutiny, she came and went keenly in her faded flannel shirt and running pants, clasping and unclasping her hands under her chin, hesitating for long moments with her explosive head of hair tilted to one side, pressing a forefinger across her pointed lips, then, with both arms outstretched, dashing into the shed again and out of sight. Janet felt the back of her neck prickle.

'How the hell,' she said, carefully keeping her tone steady, 'how can *furniture* be right or wrong?'

Ray stepped closer. 'What she's got out there,' he said, 'is not just ordinary furniture. It's got things *carved* in it. Signs, and special holes and pictures.'

'You mean slogans?' said Janet. 'Or decorations?'

'No,' said Ray. His hand crossed his chest and felt for the book buttoned into his shirt pocket. 'Kind of magic. Superstitious beliefs. And I saw the books she reads. Scary stuff. Cosmic. Don't you know what I mean?'

'Oh, it's probably just New Age,' said Janet. 'A lot of people are into that, these days. They seem to believe in everything all at once. It's not very discriminating. But it's pretty harmless, isn't it?'

'Harmless?' said Ray. 'You think that stuff's harmless?' He wrestled with the button of his shirt pocket and pulled out a small black book. 'It's all in here,' he said, riffling the cigarette-paper pages with his thumb. 'I can show you. It's crystal clear, in here.'

'Put it away,' said Janet. 'Here she comes.'

He obeyed. They tu...... Maxine was ploughing up the garden towards them, smiling enormously, carrying something tiny on her two extended hands.

'It's a cage,' hissed Ray. 'Look, she's built a cage for a rat, or something.'

'Shut *up*,' said Janet. 'Just calm down.'

'Look,' said Maxine, stopping below them at the foot of the verandah. 'Look what I made. It's my favourite.'

She held it up to them so that a rocker balanced delicately on each palm.

'See?' she said, beaming. 'Can you tell what it is?'

'Oh,' said Janet. 'Oh, look.'

She stretched out her hand and brushed the cradle lightly with one finger. A tremor ran through it and on into the air. Janet sighed.

'Oh, Maxine,' she said. 'It's lovely. Look,' she said, turning to Ray. 'See – how beautiful!'

He tried, he really tried to see it with them, to see it as they wanted him to. He urged himself to respond, he stared at it with fierce willpower, but before their avid, demanding smiles his whole intelligence went numb. In vain he applied himself. His store of remarks was empty. Into the space between him and the object, this arrangement of twigs, this box-like contraption on skis, there rolled, in the form of a dense fog, the idea of himself *looking at art*. The women waited, with their eyes on his stiffening face, then, embarrassed for him and disappointed, they looked away. With his whole body he felt Janet's allegiance shift. The river swung away from him and he was high and dry, bereft again and foolish, on his own.

For consolation he brought his thoughts to bear on

their plainness. Maxine's skin was papery, Janet's nose was red, and both of them had something middle-aged and hard about their mouths: unloved, unkissed. He did not need these two ducks. *Ducks*, he thought. They were waddling away from him, waggling their smelly tail feathers, swaggering down the yard and bumping their folded wings as they went, lowering their blunt beaks over the empty cage, quacking and clucking together as if they had known each other all their lives.

He flopped upstairs to the room he had chosen, Chips's old one, which he had swept, crouching soberly with Janet's pan and brush, then mopped, having to apply severe push and pull to the encrusted lino. The mattress he had lumped to the tip and dumped, not without raised eyes and a brief murmur in memoriam; and now on the dull green floor he spread his strip of foam rubber and on top of that his sleeping bag, khaki, aired for once, and flattened. He lay down on his back and took out the book. The nubbliness of its black cover soothed him. He opened it at random.

And the Babylonians came to her in the bed of love, and they defiled her with their whoredom. Uh oh. Try again. *And he brake in pieces the images.* Better. Once more. *There shall no evil befall thee, neither shall any plague come near thy dwelling.* Good. He closed his eyes, keeping his finger between the pages. Maxine's piece of art, the twig thing. Now, away from them, he could think about it. Really it wasn't such a bad little job, a box, a cage, a cot or whatever, though what all the fuss and sighing were in aid of he didn't know, it was only a couple of scraps of wood fixed together and was that supposed to be art? Also it was hard to separate his picture of the thing itself from the awful smile behind it, the toothy gash in the face of

someone whose eyes were spinning in her head. How old
were these two women, anyway? Same age as Alby –
forty-five at least, ten years older than he was. *And* they
looked it, in spite of the bottles in the bathroom, the
muck they must have slapped on themselves over the
years. He was after someone younger. Someone he could
. . . influence, and educate, now he knew what to teach.
Someone innocent. A virgin. *Were* there virgins, any
more? He turned it up in his book. *A garden enclosed is my
sister, my spouse; a spring shut up, a fountain sealed*. Oh, stop.
Not to be used like this. He shoved the book into the hood
of his sleeping bag, and tried to scour his mind. Sternly; be
stern. He herded his thoughts back to the young girls on
the church steps with their families: their horsy cruppers,
their dry hair scraped back, their skirts, their pink and
yellow jumpers, the way they stood close to their fathers
and glanced about them with meek and stupefied faces.
Chantelle, Casey, Tiffany and Stacey. One of them was
meant for him. What he should do was marry. What he
needed was a bride. The idea of having to play a part in a
public ceremony made him go dead all over, and grimly,
to punish himself, he stuck with it, wielding it to discipline his thoughts away from these afternoons in rented
and borrowed rooms, to send them briskly down lanes to
the back doors of factories, to the gnashing confusion
of construction sites, the damp concrete of supermarket
loading bays. A job. *A job*. He looked at his watch. It was
twenty to five in the afternoon, that terrible time of
day for the unemployed, when all hope of a fresh start
is lost and everything shrivels, loses colour and slides
gravewards. He had himself under control now, and sat
up on his bag, disoriented, sorry for himself, homesick for
something he had not yet found.

And that was when he heard the bird. *Here*, after all this travelling, outside even this ivy-clogged, broken-corded, sunless window. It started on the same note as before, as always, with no trilling or quavering, and worked its way drearily up a scale of six, where it stuck, but instead of hitting the seventh and eighth notes to round off a proper tune, repeated the fifth and sixth ones over and over again till Ray was nearly tearing out his hair. It refused to – it was too stupid to – he did not know the words to describe what the bird's song withheld from him.

Downstairs in the kitchen, Janet stripped off the rubber gloves and put out her hand to the tap. Gripping the metal, she heard from outside in the garden a bird's clumsy stepladder of notes, vibrato-less, unresolved, and felt her own skeleton fold itself up like the spokes of an umbrella inside its loosened covering of skin. Behind her left shoulder a fissure opened in the room's density. I will die. I will die and leave nothing behind: I will be forgotten.

The back door swung open and Maxine stepped in from the verandah in her rubber shoes.

'Hullo,' she said shyly. 'I was out there working, and I thought I'd – Oh, pardon me!'

Janet looked up from the sink. 'What?'

Maxine stared past her, then gave a small, embarrassed laugh. 'I must be tired,' she said. 'It's only the apron. Hanging on the cupboard door.' She shoved the heels of her hands into her eyes and rubbed harshly. 'Is it all right if I make myself a cup of tea?'

'Feel free,' said Janet. 'You live here, don't you?'

She let go of the tap and reached along the bench for the kettle. It was a quarter to five, the hour when children burst into kitchens blank-eyed and mindless with hunger, when schoolbags crash against skirting-boards, when music starts and for ten minutes the house is jostled from within by its own unruly future. The fridge motor, whose purr had been the only thing holding at bay the daily end of the world, cut out. Between the kitchen and the sound of traffic a block away where the tramline ran and the big trucks thundered northward, a chasm opened. The house shifted on its foundations, redisposing its emptiness.

'I wonder,' said Maxine vaguel*j*, 'what that little bird is. That sings. Out there.'

'You heard it too?'

'I thought it lived at my old place,' said Maxine, 'but it must have followed me here.'

'I hear it sometimes,' said Janet, holding the kettle under the dry tap. 'Don't you know what bird it is?'

'No,' said Maxine. 'And I've never seen it. But it tries to sing around this time nearly every day. I made up a name for it.' She laughed, a sound more like a sharp sigh.

'What?' said Janet. 'What do you call it?'

'It's silly, I suppose,' said Maxine, 'but I call it the failure bird.'

She was pale. The way she stood with her hands hidden inside her bunched-up cuffs made her look tiny and stiff-armed, like a wigged doll propped on a shelf in a toyshop.

'Have you got any children?' said Janet suddenly.

'No,' said Maxine.

'And is that something you . . . regret?'

'For a long time,' said Maxine, coming forward, still holding her cuffs closed from inside, 'I thought it must be my destiny not to. But now I'm ready. I've got the message. By the end of next summer I'll have one. I *have* got pretty pressing money problems – but I've made up my mind to, and everything else seems to be falling into place.'

Janet tried to smile. 'That's nice,' she said. 'And you've got a bloke? It's all lined up?'

'I think so,' said Maxine. Two red dots appeared on her cheeks. 'That is – unless *you've* got plans for him, of course. In which case I'm quite prepared to wait. To wait my turn.'

'Who on earth do you mean?'

'Him.' Maxine dropped her head back and pursed her lips at the ceiling.

'You mean Ray?' said Janet. She turned on the tap. Water crashed on to the floor of the kettle. 'You mean you've arranged it? Already?'

'Not in so many words,' said Maxine with a laugh. 'I wasn't quite sure myself, till I heard his name. But now – here we are – and living in the same house, thanks to you!' She shot back her cuffs and spread her hands in a gesture of wondering beatitude.

Janet swallowed. 'And – Ray does know about this, I suppose?'

'Perhaps not with his conscious mind, yet,' said Maxine. 'That depends on the number of his incarnations.'

'Sorry?' said Janet.

'Oh, everybody,' said Maxine, 'at *some* stage has to do a spell on earth.'

'On earth?'

'Yes – on this particular level.'

'I don't quite get it,' said Janet, hanging on to the kettle handle.

'I know it sounds strange, at first,' said Maxine. She repositioned her feet on the floor, preparing to expound. 'See – angelic beings aren't necessarily aware of their status.'

'Hang on,' said Janet. 'Let me get this straight. You're talking about Ray? The bloke upstairs?'

'Yes,' said Maxine. 'Who else?'

'And you're telling me there are angels who don't *know* they're angels? And that Ray's one of these?'

'Well, he's made it pretty clear to me,' said Maxine, 'that he's been sent.'

'Tsk. How could he *not* know, if he's been sent?'

Maxine smiled. 'Who knows what they are?' she said. 'Do you?'

Janet made an impatient movement. 'You've lost me, I'm afraid.'

'Look – don't get me wrong,' said Maxine. 'I'm talking about a being pretty low down in the hierarchy. Once you get to a higher echelon – to archangels, the ones that everybody's heard of – well, they're much more likely to know exactly what they are and what their mission is. I'm not important enough to be noticed by one of those. I'd be satisfied with a novice. I could even be a learning experience for him – a beginner could easily be led astray. By human passions. There are things here that are very hard to resist. But I don't imagine Ray will stay long. He'll do the job – as soon as he realises what it is – and then he'll be on his way. The universe is large. I can't expect an actual *relationship*.'

Janet set the kettle on the stove. Sliding the lid into place, she saw the water inside it trembling in concentric rings, and not for the first time she doubted whether any force existed which could warm this chilled, heavy mass, let alone bring it to the boil and transform it into steam. If I can't believe even *that*, she thought, in spite of its having been proved to me daily all my life, how the hell am I supposed to live in the same house as this – this –

'Tell me, Maxine,' she said, straightening up from the lit stove and flicking the dead match at the bin, 'is there anything at all you *don't* believe in?'

The brightness went out of Maxine's face. She thrust each hand into the opposite cuff, dropped her bushy head, and presented herself again at once, flushed but still beaming.

'There's sure to be,' she said. 'I suppose there must be, mustn't there!'

In the next room something gasped and shuffled. They looked up. Coming at chest height through the thickening doorway was a bird, a tiny blue and yellow thing with dotted gills, flat-breasted, smug, helmeted and beaked, its claws neatly clamped to the extended and quivering forefinger of Ray.

'Help,' he croaked. 'Help! *Emergency*. Get this thing off me. Quick, someone – get it *off* me.'

His teeth were showing right back into his cheeks and his eyes were sunken, as if soot had been rubbed into their sockets. He gave a shrill laugh.

The kettle began to tick and shimmer.

'I can't,' said Janet. She hid her hands behind her. 'I'm hopeless with animals.'

Maxine glided forward. Her leathery hands shot out of her sleeves. One forefinger stroked the budgerigar's blue bosom, and the other offered itself as a new perch on to which, while she clicked her tongue and kissed the air, the little creature took two brisk steps, whirring and settling its plumage; then, as she raised it gently to the level of her eyes, it fixed her with an expressionless gaze, opened its tucked-in beak, and peeled off a trill of such relaxed and thrilling inventiveness that they forgot to breathe out.

'That can't be the same one,' whispered Janet. 'The one we heard before.'

'Of course not,' said Maxine. '*This* is a *real* bird.'

'I opened Chips's window,' said Ray, 'and it flew in. I thought it was going to bash itself against the walls. I've got a thing about birds. I hate them to touch me.'

'But he's yours now,' said Maxine. 'He came looking for you, and he found you. You have to take him on.'

'No way,' said Ray. Fervently he shook his head. He was trying to smile, but his forehead shone with sweat. 'No way known.'

'Yes!' said Maxine. She approached Ray with her bird hand out in front of her. 'Come on,' she said. 'How can he hurt you? You're a hundred times his size.'

'Its feet are scaly,' said Ray, backing away. 'I felt them. Look at those holes in its beak. They can fly in your face and peck you. And don't they have lice or something?'

'Ray,' said Maxine. 'Take him.'

'They make a mess!' he cried. 'They do their droppings!' His back was against the cupboard.

'Ray,' said Maxine. '*Ray.*'

Her hair fanned out round her head. She was so close that he could make out each fierce lock where it sprang coiled from her scalp; but closer to him still, enthroned on her finger, sat the bird, unblinking now and virtuous, so subtly caparisoned in ripples of grey and cream, riding so smooth and high, that he might have been an emperor erect upon his chariot.

Through the curved kettle spout slid the first tuft of steam, stirring the throat of the whistle. It groaned, choked, then cleared itself and gave voice to a flawless shriek. The bird exploded into the air, releasing a jet of shit. It cannoned off the ceiling and plummeted. Maxine was ready. She darted across the room and swooped to seize it where it struggled, half-stunned, to get airborne; but Janet leaned past her and threw open the back door, and before Maxine could clap her hands around it, the bird gathered itself, flashed along the lino, and shot across the doormat out into the dusky garden.

Janet twisted the knob of the stove and the kettle died.

Maxine, sprawled half across the doorstep, got to her

feet and slowly closed the back door. The sleeve of
her check flannel shirt was streaked with birdshit and her
tracksuit knees were stained. Pointlessly brushing, she
turned to face the others, expecting to see them as they
usually appeared to her when they were together: two lost
souls, two rectangles jarring each other with the jagged
light fields they radiated; but in the breathless calm that
followed the shrieking they showed new to her, fresher,
more vivid. Ray was solid dark red, ah yes, death, a bird
outside a room and a body, something he could not speak
of which had terribly shocked and frightened him, poor
angel; and Janet (if one could ignore a blip the colour of
verdigris, a rent in her aura low down at four o'clock, a
rupture neatly stitched but impossible to hide) would have
been almost presentable for once, except that behind her
left shoulder reared a column, more intense than the
dimness of the evening kitchen, seven feet tall and shadowy as smoke: *a lord of terrible aspect.*

These matters Maxine had learnt not to speak of.
Now she dismissed them, firmly but with respect, and as
they faded she arranged her features into what she hoped
was a suitable smile, and moved forward into the room.

'Well!' she said, lifting her chin with her clasped
hands. 'What sort of tea will we have? Ordinary or
camomile? There isn't any milk.'

So now three people lived at the house, though nobody
could have called it a household: why, they were still
barely acquainted, keeping as they did to their own
quarters where they brooded over their private histories,
their disciplines, their fantasies and intimations about one
another. They never sat down to share a meal. Each of
them ate separately, guiltily, in haste, shovelling it down

in a kitchen corner or bowed over a newspaper at the white table, bogging in without grace or pleasure, as if the need for nourishment in company were something to be ashamed of, a weakness.

But the twig cradle, left by Maxine on the corner of the kitchen bench, on the mantelpiece or the edge of the bath, could sweeten the atmosphere of any room in which it found itself. Eyes were drawn to it and rested there, talk faltered and thoughts turned dreamy, for it was always in motion, responding with insect-like frissons to air currents that were imperceptible to humans. A single word uttered, a note sung at the other end of the house would be enough to set it off. It was so small: what kind of being could it contain? Only an imagined one, a baby conceived and born on a puff of wind; and having read in one of her cosmic pamphlets that anciently the Amazons, when they had fallen out with their neighbouring tribe of impregnators, would open their loins to the wind in the hope that the seeds it carried might inseminate them, Maxine paid close attention to the weather.

It was the season of winds. Air hissed all day and all night long, tremendous, sharp and dry. It travelled in off the northern grasslands, the stony rises, the mighty basalt plains, barrelling furiously down freeways, rolling empty cans in the streets, stripping the foreign trees, pressing back dark foliage in which the globes of lemons shone.

Though the shed had its back to the source of the wind, its timbers let the breath through in filaments and slivers, and Maxine lived in oceans of air: by night she floated on streams of it, a foot above her bed; by day, anchored only by the metal tools she worked with, she bobbed on its currents. The rhythm of her saw, the deliberate placement of her hammer blows inserted wedges into the balance of her housemates' sleep. If at an inconvenient hour she ran out of suitable timber she simply pulled apart something previous. Nothing but the cradle was precious to her: it was real art, and though one day it would have to leave her, she would be proud to let it go.

Ray kept well away from the shed. He hated the loony gestures of the furniture, its bossiness, the way Maxine would shape a table to enclose the sitter at it, trapping him like a baby in a high chair or a schoolboy at his inkwell. He was afraid of her driven, absent-minded serenity, and worst, of the way she seemed to have him targeted for something, mooning over him whenever they met in the kitchen, in the yard, or outside the bathroom, asking him batty questions about his travels and his past lives. Dreamy, fanciful, tolerant, she existed beyond the reach of the order which Ray believed, more and more urgently, he had been sent here to impart to them, his mission: for to him the women were crackers, both of them, a pair of wretched lost souls, worse than orphans.

'Haven't you got any family?' he said one night at the white table, where Janet sat working out her tax and Maxine sharpened her whittling knife, while he sombrely and self-consciously tried to mend the seam of his tobacco-coloured trousers.

'Mine gave up on me long ago,' said Janet.

'All gone,' said Maxine, 'somewhere.' Out of her hair sprouted the ends of coloured binding thread which, using her head as a third hand, she would thrust into its mass while she worked. 'But I think I was married, once,' she said, with a high, silly laugh. 'In America.'

'What do you mean, you *think* you were,' said Ray.

'I've forgotten his name,' said Maxine. She pushed aside her stone and seized a hunk of wood she had by her. 'I suppose I should track him down and get a divorce, or something. One of these days.' The blade entered the grain and peeled back a fine curlicue. 'But where on earth can he be? And who?' Again she cackled, privately.

Disapproval froze Ray's face into a block. 'I don't see,' he said, 'how you could have forgotten something like that.'

'You'd be surprised what women can forget,' said Janet. 'Have *you* ever been married?'

'No,' said Ray. 'But I'm familiar with the pain.'

They looked at him with interest, then away to their tasks.

'And,' said Maxine, carving with skill, dropping peelings on to the spread-out newspaper, 'have you ever seen an angel?'

Ray stared. Maxine glanced up at him with a peculiar, thin-eyed expression of concentration. She looks *cunning*, thought Ray. This was not the way he had planned to begin on the important subjects. He shrugged, up-staged and discontented, declining to answer.

'I've seen the devil,' said Janet casually. She closed the accounts book and put the lid back on her pen.

Maxine snickered. Her hands gripped and fondled the butt of wood with sympathy. She touched like a blind person, lacking all sense of decency and with the same inward, voluptuous grin.

'Where,' said Ray.

'In Brunswick,' said Janet. 'He ran out of a shop as I was walking up Sydney Road. He looked straight at me.'

'How did you know it was the devil?' murmured Maxine, turning the lump of wood against the blade with a slow, deep pressure.

'By his face. It was tight and smooth, and he had a kind of brutal expression. Brutal and vain.'

'I can't stand vain men,' said Maxine. 'Specially the

ones with those bushy moustaches. Men with moustaches never give way to you on pedestrian crossings, have you noticed?'

'When I say "the devil",' said Janet, 'of course I don't really mean "*The Devil*". I mean he looked evil. Know what I mean? He made my hackles rise. He was probably some sort of crim. Full of bad vibes.'

'Do you want to know, by the way, Janet,' said Maxine, 'what I see in your aura?' She carved on with slow diligence. 'I see that in a previous life you were tortured. If you don't mind my saying so.'

'Tortured?'

'Yes. For your religious beliefs.'

Janet snorted with her mouth shut, but Ray saw her eyes brighten: she paid full attention.

'And I tested it, too,' said Maxine, carving, carving. 'Remember in the kitchen last week you asked me what kind of wood I made the cradle out of? And I said "*Tortured* willow"? In a very clear voice? Keeping my eye right on you? Well – you froze, over there at the sink.'

Janet laughed outright, but Maxine kept on working, with her shoulders hunched and her eyes on the stub of wood.

'So,' she said, 'that's why you don't want to believe in devils or angels. Your painful experiences have made you very, very sceptical.'

Janet glanced at Ray. He had pushed his sewing away, and something was hardening round his mouth. She too closed her lips firmly, and controlled herself. After a moment she spoke, too loudly.

'And what's that you're making?'

'Oh, I'm just practising,' said Maxine. She was concentrating her gaze on the wood, but her mouth was curved in a good-natured smile. 'Keeping my hand in. So that when an idea comes to me, I'll be ready.'

A quietness fell. Then Ray spoke. His voice had darkened, as if something were stuck in his throat.

'The devil,' he said, 'is worse than *vain*. The devil's worse than anything you can imagine.'

The only sound in the room was the gentle dropping of the shavings.

'You've got a bit of a nerve, haven't you?' said Janet. Her tone was conversational.

'What?' said Ray.

'Telling us what we can or can't imagine.'

'I'm talking,' said Ray, with difficulty, 'about suffering. Real suffering.'

'You don't know me,' said Janet in a light, tight voice. 'You don't know either of us. You don't know what we've done, what's been done to us, what we've lost. What gives you the right to tell us whether or not we've "suffered" enough? Enough for what?'

The wind bumped in the chimney and felt its way along the side of the house.

'I may not know you yet,' said Ray. 'But I've been watching you.' He spoke ploddingly and with care, looking her right in the eyes. 'And one thing I see, Janet, is that your life is ruled by anger.'

Janet snorted again. 'What *is* this,' she said. 'A campaign? Now *you're* starting on me!'

Ray pulled the book out of his breast pocket and laid it down on the table between them.

'I better tell you now,' he said. 'I probably should have told you before. I know Jesus. Jesus is my personal friend. And I believe he's sent me here to tell you about him.'

Maxine held her knife in one hand and the wood in the other, like a diner interrupted between mouthfuls.

'Jesus didn't send you here,' said Janet. 'Alby did.'

'Alby's saved too,' said Ray. 'Alby is guided by Jesus in everything he does. Alby's saved from the slavery of sin, and so am I.'

'Bully for you,' said Janet. 'And don't give me that jargon. Speak for yourself.'

'So you deny the workings of the spirit?' said Ray, clenching his jaw and keeping one hand flat on the black book.

'The spirit?' said Janet. Her mouth twisted into a bitter hook. '*I've* had spiritual experiences too, you know.'

Ray leaned forward to her across the table. He was shaking his head. 'You can't be too careful with those,' he said. 'Specially if you've done a bit of acid, or meditation.'

'What – you mean you're going to *warn* me?' said Janet. 'You are incredible. You really are.'

'They can come from the devil,' said Ray. 'Believe me, Janet – they can.'

'*This* is what I can't stand about you bastards,' said Janet. She was holding her volume low, but her cheeks and nose began to flush. 'You've got it all sewn up. Would it occur to you to *ask* me about my experience, before you dismiss it out of hand? No! It wouldn't even cross your mind!'

Ray's fists and forehead tightened. 'But you've got to *test* the spirits,' he said.

'P'raps she did,' said Maxine anxiously. 'You haven't asked her.'

They ignored her. Ray was flustering open the pages of his book.

'It's in here,' he said. 'Listen – "Beloved, believe not every spirit, but try the spirits whether they are of God:

because many false prophets are gone out into the world".
John four one.' He clapped the book shut and raised to
Janet a justified face.

Janet stiffened. She puffed up. With alarm Maxine
saw the air round her smooth-cropped head begin to spark
and crackle.

'You should *ask* her, Ray,' said Maxine, but Ray, deaf
with zeal, bored on.

'The devil's everywhere,' he said. 'Not just at Brunswick one day and somewhere else the next. He's *everywhere*.
He's here with us right now. He's all around us, prowling,
looking for a way to get in.'

Janet spread herself back on her chair. 'And by what
process,' she said, pointing with a theatrical flourish at her
own chest, 'does he enter? How exactly does he get *in*?
To *me*, for example?'

Ray's eyes were fluttering with strain. He cleared his
throat. 'You won't like what I'm about to tell you, Janet,'
he said. 'On the breath.'

'Hoh!' said Janet with a rough laugh. 'We're all
damned, then, aren't we! What hope have we got, as
organisms? None, it appears. No hope.'

'No,' he said. 'No. We've got no hope "as organisms". But in the spirit there is hope.'

'Don't *preach* to me, Ray,' said Janet. 'I am not
interested in hearing you *preach*.'

'Why not?' he said doggedly. 'What makes *you* too
special to hear the word? "To be carnally minded is death.
But to be spiritually minded is life and peace". Romans
eight six.'

They were breathing hard, staring into each other's
faces. Ray kept swallowing; white showed all round
his irises.

'You can't *split* matter and spirit,' said Janet between

her teeth. 'How can you *split* them? It doesn't make *sense*.'

Flinching and flickering, Ray held her contemptuous stare.

'Jesus can smash through all those structures,' he said. 'I feel sorry for you, Janet. You're clever. You've been to uni, and that's going to make it harder for you. Because another way in, for the devil, is through the mind.'

Janet threw back her head and uttered a savage guffaw.

'Fuck you, then, Ray,' she snarled. She crashed her fist on the table: Maxine's whetstone leapt like a toad. 'All I've got to recommend me, apart from my body, is my mind. So fuck you, and fuck the devil!'

Maxine jumped up, leaving her knife spinning on the tabletop, and bolted out of the room. They heard her boots pounding away across the verandah and thudding down on to the concrete.

Cold air from the open kitchen door rushed round the corner and flooded into the room. It brought Janet to her senses. With an effort she reined herself in, dropped her eyes, and sat back. She put forward one hand and stayed the revolving knife.

'Now look what I've done,' she said stiffly. 'Sorry. I saw red. I'm sorry I spoke to you like that.'

Ray nodded.

'I shouldn't have bellowed,' insisted Janet. 'That was rude. I lost my temper. I'm sorry.'

He lowered his face again, and raised it.

'I said I'm *sorry*,' said Janet.

'Yes,' he said, getting to his feet and leaning forward on his hands across the table. 'Yes, but I'm right, aren't I. You *are* a slave. A slave to anger.'

'*Oh!* Haven't you got any manners? Can't you accept an apology?'

'And you use your anger as a social weapon.'

'Ray. I'm warning you. I refuse. I refuse to be bullied and interrogated here. In my own *house*.'

He swallowed again, with a loud gulp. 'Your house is very nice,' he said, 'and it's kind of you to let us live here. But your house won't save you. None of that will save you.'

'I won't have it.' She heaved herself upright. 'I refuse. Get off my back!'

He held up both hands, palms towards her, and strained his squinting face sideways as if to ward off a blow.

'And I'm not going to hit you!' she shouted, jumping back from the table. 'Not on one cheek *or* the other. How dare you? How dare you set me up?'

The back door crashed shut, and round the corner from the kitchen came whirling and skidding Maxine, Medusa-haired, carrying on her outstretched hands the twig cradle. She braked short of the table, laid the thing on it, and tiptoed back to her chair.

The cradle stood on the thick white paint, between the nest of shavings and the dense black gold-edged book. It stood obedient, exactly where its maker had placed it; but it shuddered with such violence, poised on its fragile rockers, that the antagonists were shocked; and they paused, and lowered their hands and shoulders, and drew closer to the table, and stood by it with their fingers folded, until they were breathing steadily again and the air in the room had stabilised; and then the cradle too became calmer. It became serene, and its movements refined themselves into its customary gentle tremor, barely a quiver, merely a sign that there was life and breath in the room where it was standing.

Even an angel, in our hostile world, needs all the help it can get: so Maxine did not relax her vigilance, and when one lunchtime, browsing high in the stacks of the state library, she opened at random a volume on pagan British mythology and found herself face to face with a drawing of an ancient doll known as a *bride*, she felt the tingle of meaning, and prepared herself to act.

Footfalls, giggles and whispers rustled like bats in the dome of the huge, star-shaped reading room, but Maxine was deep in the scholar's account of the little doll and its powers. She examined the drawing for a long time, moving her lips as she turned it this way and that; then she slid the fat leather tome back on to its shelf and walked down the stairs, out through the portico, and home along the bare elm avenues and bluestone lanes to her shed.

She heaved the door open and stepped down on to the packed earth floor. The furniture, tranquil or nonchalantly gesturing, paused in its colloquy and froze; Maxine bustled in and cleared her work bench with one sweep of the forearm.

In the milky light from the four-paned window she fossicked in her basket of wood scraps, palpating the little nubs and knoblets, and chose a good-for-nothing bit left over, a gnarled and knotted chunk about as big as an egg.

Then, standing at the bench with all her materials and scraps within reach, she began to whittle. She was in form and it was easy; but for the dreamy pleasure of it she worked slowly, spinning it out, every now and then holding up the nub to the light from the open door to match it against her memory of the diagram.

First she shaped the nub into an eyeless, mouthless head, then hollowed out its neck to accommodate a thick bunch of dry grass stems that she wrenched from Janet's garden; these she crammed in deep and made snug with a ribbing of coarse thread. Next, by parting the clump several inches further down, she formed two legs and thus, between them, a little grassy cunt. The legs, bound with criss-cross gaiters of twine, were footless, ending freely in enormous, untrimmed sprouts of grass.

Now, half an inch below the wooden head, she lashed at right angles to the torso a second clump of dried stalks, with a couple of turns at the axis to make a firm cross-shape. She tidied each end of the horizontal grass-hank, then grabbed her scissors and chopped the fringed ends off blunt, leaving two handless wrists.

Inward-eyed and breathing through her nose, she gripped the creature in her left hand and groped behind her for a strip of cloth, an old piece of skirt, a rag – but everything her fingers touched was square and hard; so she shoved the grass cross into the waistband of her tracksuit and trotted out of the shed into the crisp afternoon, roving her eye-beams short and long over the disorder of the garden, seeking a garment for her bride.

What she spotted, flapping pleasantly among the towels from a wire rigged along the back verandah, was Ray's old Texan shirt. It was a faded cobalt blue, embroidered with lariats, cacti and desert roses, and it fastened with heavy pearl and metal snapstuds which clacked like teeth with the wearer's every move. It had worn thin in Chips's service, and then Alby's, and Ray, ill-favoured dag that he was, had salvaged it unbeknownst from Alby's rubbish bin when he had tired of it, and had been hoarding it ever since. Ray knew the shirt did not suit him. He was much too plain and prim to carry it off. Even secretly in the bathroom, scowling and pouting before the mirror, he could not live up to its casual, rakish manliness; but maybe when he got round to finding a job and saving some money ... maybe by next summer ... And meanwhile, one of the women would unpeg it and iron it for him; and one day he would have the nerve to put it on and walk about openly in it, offhand, powerful, showing his neck and forearms, exactly like his brother.

In Maxine's busy hands the sleeve came away from the body as cleanly as if they were waiting to be parted. Three sharp rips, and in no time she had wrapped the bride's lower parts in a skirt of faded blue cotton, and swathed its wooden head in a pointed riding hood which dropped to its waist and concealed its stalky bosom.

She ran back to the shed for needle and thread, pulled her little stool out through the open door, and sat in the air cobbling the frayed shirt pieces together and stitching the strip of cuff with the mother-of-pearl stud, as a fetching touch, under the bride's chin to fasten the hood.

She held it away from her with both hands, to look. Was it finished? She propped it against a tuft of grass that grew not far from the shed door, and squatted on the ground in front of it.

It looked weird, leaning there. Its proportions unnerved her: it was only inches tall and yet, though its legs ended in wild bursts of unclipped stalks, so like a human figure. Maxine's calves began to go numb and her scalp to itch, but she stayed stubbornly in frog position, condensing her gaze on to the faceless nub inside its hood. How was this done? Would there be a message?

A breeze swooped over the shed roof and shook the grasses at the bottom of the yard where she crouched. Half-hypnotised, left behind like a surfer by a wave, Maxine let her eyes follow the air-gust's progress up the length of land towards the house. It crossed grass whose pale and flattened fibres were parted by the edges of smashed bricks; it passed a vegetable patch where stakes staggered and seedheads died blighted by their own stiff-ness; it threaded itself through the holes of a crumbling lattice fence that sliced the yard in two; it pressed on over a mattress of wavering nasturtiums, and eddied on the tree-shaded grey concrete by the gate –

– but how dark and shrunken it suddenly looked, the house end of the garden. Was it an eclipse? Dropping to her knees, Maxine tried to focus. She could hardly make out the verandah, the rubbish bins, the torn shirt on the wire – and what was that sound, that huge booming and rumbling coming, that deep and mumbling roar?

Her forehead weighed too much. It was dense, as cold as a dish. It longed to press itself into the dirt before the wiry stalk clumps of the bride. Down she went, like a vomiting child urged forward over the porcelain by its mother's callous hand – but even as this large force pushed her shoulders down, she strained her head up and kept her eyes fixed on the wimple of blue cloth through whose slit the bride's tanned, implacable face narrowly showed.

Maxine breathed out, out, out. Her lungs were almost empty. The sky was bellowing. Her chin touched ground, the dirt parted for her, the stiff twigs feathered her nostrils – and the plane's shadow skimmed over and was gone.

The weight lifted from Maxine's shoulders. Breath with its welcome sweetness swelled her chest. Her head cleared, and she raised it to the bride, still hoping for a sign – but somebody laughed outside the fence, and a bunch of schoolgirls went scampering past, clapping in rhythm and vigorously chanting a song.

The bride toppled to the left and keeled over. Slowly, slow, it executed a quarter cartwheel, hesitated, and came to rest, balancing on one chopped wrist.

Maxine sprang up. The distant bins stood in perspective, respectably daylit. But the sun was covered. The sky was gaberdine. The colours were colder, and on the tip of a branch, a leaf wagged.

Again she propped the bride, jiggling and settling it

into the grass tuft. Again, while the girls' chant faded, the bride listed sideways and made as if to fall.

Maxine caught it. Her eyes glazed and she clawed at her hair. The feet were wrong. How could she expect it to stand, if she hadn't made it a proper pair of feet? But realistic feet would destroy the look of it. The burst of stalks was its beauty, what made it different from the one in the book, what made it *hers*. No, she would not clip its feet. She would fix it to a wall. An inside wall, in case of weather. The inside wall of the shed.

In she ran. Above the low bed in the corner she whacked into the timber wall two nails, a thumb's width apart, and hooked the bride up by its armpits. She twitched at it till its spread arms and the flaps of its garment settled, hiding its means of support. It poised above the pillow. Maxine, with her feet among the blankets, saw that the bride's grass-bursts were what kept it in position. They were rocket-blasts of energy. When the stars swung into auspicious configuration, that energy would gush into her. She would be fertilised, she would flourish, she would crop.

It was three o'clock.

Cheerfully she hopped off the bed, collected her keys and a rubber band for her hair, and set out on foot to clean a small but fiddly house on the other side of the freeway.

The afternoon, left in the garden with the remains of the shirt, swung quietly down towards evening.

At four-thirty the temperature dropped, then dropped again. Presently the sky cleared, leaving a few bobtail clouds to float upon its purity. The failure bird, that auto-didact, arrived in the tree in a fluster and would have struck up its earnest, unmelodious scale: but there was no one home to hear it, so it perched glumly on a twig, whirring its feathers, and peered about it with a dull and desperate eye.

Just at dark, Janet came trudging through the gate. On her way across the verandah she unpegged the dry washing, out of habit, and gathered it in. She slung it into the ironing basket in the corner of the living room, then swept the newspapers into a pile, switched on the lamp, and went upstairs to her room.

Anyone with half a heart can learn to sleep alone and like it. Mornings have their own metabolisms, and the working day will take care of itself. No – the hard thing about living alone is having no one to report to at the end of the day, no witness for a re-enactment of one's mortifications and snappy rejoinders, one's heroic endurance of the intolerable. For that there must be a household, and this was only a house.

Besides, there was really only one subject that Ray felt driven to talk about, and in the company of people who showed no interest in it, he was restless, sombre, at a loss.

The women, however, squandered language. If Ray did not take his turn at speech when it was offered, they exchanged expressionless looks and went galloping past him, scattering words from their gaping purses. 'Today,' Janet would say, 'I passed the biggest, grandest, most magnificently, beautifully and generously tremendous oak tree I've ever seen in my whole life. I felt like prostrating myself before it.' Goose-flesh coated him, as it did when Maxine got going, veering out into her phantasmagorical theories about toxins and purifications, luxuriating for hours in her own indecisiveness about which cure to apply

to her many-fold, elusive and delicious ailments. 'Naturo-
paths,' she would say, 'treat everything as the whole
digestive system and the this and the that and the other
thing, so it's all *slightly* this or that.' Cramps seized his
stomach and wrung it like a rag. He sat in silence, finger-
ing his little black book.

'Why are *you* so forlorn, Ray?' said Janet. 'Hey!
Forlorn! That must have something to do with *verloren*,
German for *lost*. Do you feel lost?'

Know-all. Skite. She was clever all right. She knew
plenty of words, where to find out more, and how to fix
them together correctly: she made a living out of them:
but she was empty. She had nothing to say. Whenever he
brought out his book and laid it on the white table she
would stand up abruptly and prance out of the room, or
put on a record and turn up the volume, flashing him a
mean, sidelong smile. The music was noise to him, fat
ladies warbling, orchestras on the rampage, some idiots
twanging bits of string and tapping on a tin; the cradle,
dumped on top of a speaker, would vibrate as madly as a
leaf in the wind; but he liked to watch Janet listening,
because she looked so silly.

She would adopt special, sensitive expressions during
the slow bits, stretching her neck, pointing her lips like
a beak, breathing in sharply through her nostrils, and
making her eyebrows into an inverted V of anguish, while
in the fast bits she would nod in a stern rhythm, frowning,
as if the music belonged to her and she had personally sent
down instructions about how it was to be played. Sometimes when the record ended she would put on a little act
of breaking out of a spell, pretending to have been so
swept away that she had forgotten the existence of the real
world (including him); she would suddenly shake her head
to clear it, widen her eyes in a pantomime of confusion as

to her whereabouts, then, with an affected smile, feign recognition of her own living room. These performances caused strange tingles to occur in various parts of his person: runs of dislike, pity, a strangled desire to laugh that made his mouth feel unnatural.

'Wasn't that *won* – derful,' she would breathe, pressing the back of one hand against her forehead. 'Enough to restore your faith in the human race.'

'No point having faith in the human race,' he said doggedly. 'There's only one thing to have faith in. One man.'

'Oh, shut up,' she said, and dropped it cold.

He had seen the shadows on her face. He knew that emptiness. He too had been scoured. But the moment had not come, and while he waited for it, he contented himself, as weeks passed and the weather chilled and he still had not found a job, with copying out scriptural quotations for her and leaving them propped against the sauce bottle or the empty fruit dish on the bench. She began to use her education against him then, to shield herself from what he obstinately believed he had been sent to tell her. *My soul shall boast in the Lord* she batted back with *Not every one that saith unto me, Lord, Lord, shall enter the kingdom of heaven*. He persisted with warnings and threats: *Beware of false prophets, which come to you in sheep's clothing, but inwardly they are ravening wolves*; and *Every tree that bringeth not forth good fruit is hewn down, and cast into the fire*; but because of the hours he kept, dawdling, waiting for word from his brother, and using the delay as an excuse, she got the upper hand. Back through the Old Testament she ranged, busily hunting up mocking rebukes: *Go to the ant, thou sluggard: consider her ways, and be wise. As the door turneth upon its hinges, so doth the slothful upon his bed.* Often he was still in his sleeping bag when the sheet of paper slid under his door. At first he would roll over and seize it eagerly, always hoping for a letter from Alby, for news of when he would come, for reassurance that he had not dropped his bundle and gone off the rails again; but it was always only her reply to his sally of the day before, dashed on to the paper in her merciless, legible hand, nothing crossed out or corrected, peremptory as a memo from an irritable superior.

He let his side of the duel lapse, but still the messages came, spiky, malicious, their meaning perverted by lack of context, and presently he read fewer and fewer of them, then only one in five, and by the time her tone began to shift he had stopped reading them altogether, and merely gathered them up and dropped them, still folded, into the council bin near the corner shop, to withhold from her the satisfaction of finding them in the kitchen rubbish: and thus he missed *It is better to dwell in a corner of the housetop, than with a brawling woman in a wide house*, and *Let me set a morsel of bread before thee*, and *Let us reason together, saith the Lord*. Janet copied these things and pushed them under his door, but when he would not bite she became bored and scornful, and despised him for a wimp; the game was over.

Given this domestic stand-off, then, how, and to whom, was Ray to announce, when the day came, the stunning news that he had at last been hired? That, standing in slime in front of a foreman who was holding an orange mug of tea in one hand and a Boston bun in the other, he had wanted to burst into a whining protest, to show his palms with their innocence of calluses, to make the bloke see his mistake and send him packing back to his natural habitat, the dole office? Already, spongeing back to the street in his thongs, Ray felt the leash of his shortened freedom get a grip on his neck and start to choke him.

Winter fell on them overnight. They hardly knew which was worse, the wind or the rain, and while they sat on their hands in front of the grate or poked kindling sticks between its bars to enliven the sullen logs, the splendidly mantelled fireplace sucked heat straight out of the wood they had chopped and sent it whirling up the chimney to disperse under the low sky.

There was no heat in the shed, but Maxine dragged out extra jumpers and thicker socks, and while she worked on, uncomplaining, she would glance up, from time to time, at the bride, implacable on the wall. She respected it. She greeted it formally on waking and retiring; she turned her face up to it while she meditated; she hummed tuneless, wordless little ditties in its honour, and invented special sequences of gestures with meanings she could not have explained; and before too long these rituals, like most observances, lost their freshness and became automatic; but still she performed them, absentmindedly, out of habit.

Ray's new steel-toed boots came home so caked with mud that he stepped out of them on the back verandah, leaving them disposed in a more casual V than they ever adopted when his feet were inside them, and slid about the house in socks. Secretly Janet thought better of him when she could no longer see his weak-looking, broken-arched feet, but Maxine missed the sight of them, their vulnerability, for to her they were beautiful, and familiar from the paintings she had seen in books or at the occasional travelling exhibition from Italy, wonderful old pictures in which angels, cool or warm, calmly took their places in human dramas, wearing sandals whose complicated fastenings and slender soles, designed only for ether, were never meant to be distorted by walking, or sullied by contact with the earth.

'Are your poor feet sore?' said Maxine from the table, as Ray hobbled in across the ugly carpet. Usually, when he came home at this hour and found her waiting for him, doing nothing, just sitting up brightly with her hands folded and the cradle rocking in front of her, he walked straight through and upstairs to the bathroom, to avoid her; but today he could hear water brushing in the pipes. Janet must be having a shower. He was stuck.

'Not sore,' he said. 'Just tired. I'm not used to it yet.' He sat down opposite her, with his face averted, and pulled a newspaper towards him.

'Used to what?' said Maxine fondly. 'What do you do out there, exactly?'

'I do what I'm told,' said Ray, blindly turning the pages. 'It's a factory. A warehouse. In a paddock full of thistles. I don't know what they're doing to it, and nobody else seems to know either.'

'Couldn't you ask someone?' said Maxine.

'Oh, nobody asks *questions*,' said Ray. 'They hire you from the neck down.'

Maxine melted with sympathy and respect. 'How do you mean?' she murmured.

'It's like this,' said Ray wearily. He pushed the paper away. 'On my first day they gave me a crowbar and told me to chip the cement off this floor. I started doing it the way they showed me, but it was *slow*. Sometimes I'd get the corner of the crowbar under it and be able to sort of lift it, but usually I could only get about an inch up at a time. My hands got all torn – see? Anyway, after lunch the foreman came to check up on me, so I said, "Look – do you mind if I only do about this much every day? Because it's kind of laborious." And he yelled at me. He said "Laborious? You're a bloody labourer, aren't you? It's *meant* to be laborious!"'

'Laborious,' whispered Maxine. 'Mmmmm. I bet they're really glad they hired *you*.'

She did not get it. Ray sat still, slumped in his fatigue. But Maxine was gazing at him, tilting her bushy head to one side, and with a pleasant surprise he noticed that she was still waiting, that he was actually being listened to, or would be, should he care to speak. Her face had become rounder and younger while he told his tale, and her lips were gently closed, as if not needing to restrain a single interruption. He felt his own face go soft with shyness.

'Anyway,' he said, 'I went on chipping away, all by myself in there, and after a week a different foreman came to me and said, "You can stop doing that now. They've decided to knock the whole building down."'

Maxine neither laughed nor spoke. She merely went on looking at him, with moist and shining eyes.

'And now,' he trailed off, 'I don't know whether they're pulling it down or not.'

She listened.

'At lunchtime,' he said, struggling on, 'I sit by myself and read my book.'

Still she listened.

'It's cold out there,' he said. 'The wind comes tearing across the paddocks.'

He felt the suction of her silence.

'The other blokes sit in a shed,' he said, 'scrapping and gambling and throwing food around. They don't take much notice of me.'

Her eyes were giving out a brown fog of devotion: her face was swarming. He felt giddy. He was conking out; he was losing shape; he was sinking into the swamp of her attention. Maxine drew a long, romantic sigh, and suddenly Ray was stabbed with complete desperation. I'll have to grow a moustache, he thought. I'll have to start drinking beer. I'm lonely. My loneliness is unbearable.

'Are all jobs like this?' he burst out in a cracking voice. 'I don't know how long I can stand it. Is this what jobs are *like*?'

Brilliantly, Maxine centred herself. She reached out and took his hand, cross-wise, as if they had just been introduced. 'Tell me, Ray,' she said. 'What's your sign?'

He jumped, and went rigid, but she had a firm grip on him, palm against palm, a man's grip. 'My what?' he said.

'You know,' she said. 'Your sun sign. What the magazines call your star.'

'Oh no,' he said with a groan. 'No, not that stuff. I don't –'

He tried to withdraw the meat of his hand and leave her with only the fingertips, but she hung on.

'Why not?' she said, glowing at him from under her corona of hair.

'That's astrology,' he said. 'That's satanism. The devil comes through that kind of thing.'

Maxine laughed. 'Oh, Ray,' she said, massaging his hand with both of hers. 'Ray – you may not believe in it. You may doubt its power. But you can't make it not exist.'

He jerked his hand away, and she let it go without a struggle. He clenched it into a fist in the air, then forced it to relax, and laid it flat on the table. All the tiny hairs of his forearm were standing on end.

'It's all right, Ray,' said Maxine, leaning back in her chair. 'You don't have to pretend, with me. I know why you're here. There's no hurry. At least now we've shaken hands. I think that goes quite far, don't you? Psychically? A handshake?'

Even with his secret palm pressed against wood he

could remember the hands that had kneaded him. They were tough, seamed and warm. They would not take no for an answer.

Hunger struck the house-dwellers at different times and with different desires. If there was more than one of them eating at the same time, it was purely by chance. The women did not care. They were content with little where food was concerned, and could dine, standing up at the fridge door, on a raw carrot and a lump of cheese every night for months and never notice the sameliness. But Ray, out of a sober longing for what he had only been told about, wanted things to be done more formally. At night-fall, while Maxine swept up the day's sawdust in her shed and Janet sat in front of the television smartly taking notes for her next article, he would be drawn to the bleak kitchen like a spirit haunting a place where it had once been nourished, and would loiter there in the gathering dark, dissatisfied and morose.

One evening he drifted in and came upon Janet rummaging through the cupboards.

'We should be congratulated,' she said. 'We have achieved a totally snack-free kitchen.'

'We could take it in turns to go to the market,' said Ray, 'instead of living like this – bringing things home at random.'

'A *roster*,' said Janet. 'How passé. You can't be serious.'

'*I* could go,' he said.

'When men do the market,' said Janet suavely, 'there is blood on the inner walls of the fridge.'

Ray opened it and stood staring in at the old vegetables that drooped through the wire shelves or lay sadly in mounds below.

'But I'm always hungry,' he said. 'Look at this wastage. Couldn't we make soup? Isn't there something called stock?'

'There is such a thing, yes,' said Janet, keying open a tin of sardines and beginning to squash them on to a stale biscuit.

'I read in the paper,' said Ray, 'about these pots that stand on the back burner and never get turned off. People chuck all the scraps in there and it keeps on cooking for generations.'

'That's in France,' said Janet. She leaned back against the bench and took a large bite. 'You won't be here long enough. Anyway for that you need a servant. A mother, or a wife.'

'I don't see why,' said Ray.

'Because, my dear,' said Janet, muffled by fish, 'someone has to *be* there. To keep an eye on it.'

'What about Maxine?' said Ray. 'Isn't she out in that shed most of the day?'

'I wouldn't dream of asking her,' said Janet. 'A classic stockpot is a *major domestic commitment*. I'm amazed you can't see that.'

Ray dug in. 'Alby's got a stockpot,' he said, sliding his eyes her way.

'*Alby*?' said Janet. She stopped chewing and her mouth dropped open. 'Is Alby *married*?'

'No,' said Ray. He squatted down in front of the fridge and with two hands parted the hopeless vegetables. 'But he's got a stockpot.'

'Well. Now I'm really struck dumb,' said Janet. She sounded almost good-humoured. 'So Alby's got a stockpot, as well as life everlasting.'

Ray pulled out a plastic jar with a red cap and held it up to her. 'Do you mind if I eat this?' he said. 'This yogurt?'

'Go ahead,' said Janet. 'I haven't had the nerve to open it. It's been there quite a while.'

He thumbed off the lid. The contents were green and strandy, pullulating with mould. On an impulse he thrust it up under her nose. She reared back.

'Look, Janet,' he said, on his haunches at her feet. 'Here it is. Eternal life. The un-dead.'

Janet had forgotten how it felt to let go: the seizure of the skin across the nose, the dissolve of the abdomen, the warm collapse of an inner barricade. They stared at each other, once their first paroxysms had subsided, with tears in their eyes, shocked and loose-mouthed in the sudden intimacy of laughter.

Ray struggled to his feet. 'That wasn't exactly the truth,' he said, running a cuff across his face. 'About Alby having a stockpot. I was piling it on. For argument's sake.'

Janet started again. She had to turn away, in a kind of modesty; she balanced her forearm along the bench and bowed over it while he waited, grinning, snapping the sides of the yogurt pot in and out with his fingertips.

Presently Janet pulled herself together and straightened her spine into its customary correct posture.

'Surely,' she said with enfeebled lips, 'surely you didn't think I *believed* you.'

'Well he was *going* to get one,' said Ray. 'Him and some people he was staying with, last time I saw him. Fellow-Christians. They were. Or at least they said they were.'

Janet began to laugh again, then stopped. In the glow from the half-open fridge door he saw that the grey film had lifted off her. Her skin was flushed, and her eyes glistened under a brow which had lost its shadowy stiffness and was broadening, as he watched, into harmony with a private, tender mouth.

He dropped the plastic jar into the bin and kicked the

fridge door to with his socked foot. It shut, snapping off the only light in the room, and the two of them stood side by side against the bench in the dark, breathing in and out.

Janet had once read in an account of the Irish potato famine that it takes only two generations for a people to lose its practical skills. In the life of one person, she thought, this process telescopes: it can happen in a season. When she was young she taught herself to cook from books. Although she never cared for it she found it easy enough, even in the big households when her turn came round, to prepare and serve something worth eating, and what the collective children turned up their noses at she got into them by dint of will or trickery. But now, since the night her beetroot soup hit the wall, she had not so much as chopped up an onion. In delicatessens she stood helpless, lacking a single idea to bless herself with, and when approached she would buy in haste the first thing her eye fell on, and go home carrying nothing but a jar of pickled capsicums or a packet of custard powder. She was no more civilised than Maxine or Ray. She too scrounged and scavenged, but in her own house; she ate on her feet and only to stay alive. Pleasure had left her life. What pleasure? There was a sort of gratification in the quick hit of a pasty in a bag, a coffee, a bunch of grapes. What she had lost was the pleasure of serving.

In the bowels of the corner cupboard she found an old-fashioned oval oven-proof dish, still with a lid, but chipped, stained and encrusted along its edges with nameless scum. She pulled it out and stared at it, tickled by a strange and distant sensation, an almost childish pleasure in its chunky shape and unusual depth. It radiated meaning, like an object from a forgotten dream. She set it on the bench, and with painful slowness, biting on the pen which upstairs in her room flew so readily across the pages, she began to make a list.

But it was only when she reached the market and stood indecisively between the counters in the meat section that she remembered what she had used to cook in the dish. Years ago Chips and Alby, forced one day by communal pressure to take the smallest household child along when they went to busk at the market, had let the little girl wander off alone among the delicatessen shops while they strummed and yodelled under the broad verandahs. They brought her home white-faced and dumb, her plaits standing on end, and from that day on she refused to let rabbit in any form whatsoever pass her lips. The older children picked up on this and turned it into an ideological position, one which Janet felt an irritable urge to foil, and many a battle had been fought over the marinated, filleted, minced and poached contents of the oval dish, fought and lost, for not even the greatest chef in the world can hoodwink the instincts of a child.

Today, though, in the bright cleanliness of the refurbished shop, the rabbits lay behind glass on glossy enamel trays, stretched out skinned and headless in positions of full flight. The rabbit seller in a crisp pale-blue overall approached with his eyebrows up, and when Janet pointed, he hooked two of the little carcases with a finger under each ribcage and held them out to her, arranged with a merchant's flourish along his inner forearms. 'Yes,' said Janet. Scrupulously he weighed and wrapped them, and she watched him, so soothed by the intent angle of his head, the seriousness of his attentions, that when she noticed on the wall behind his shoulder a hand-lettered sign that read RABBIT'S AND HARE'S, the apostrophes loosened in her a gush of foolish love for every creature in sight, alive or dead. She could hardly catch her breath for the desire to laugh out loud or break into song.

The rabbit man offering the white parcel grinned at her as if he knew that bliss; but how could he, for she scarcely knew it herself – it must be low blood sugar, some sort of chemical imbalance – and blushing, she swallowed it, holding out the money and feigning sudden interest in a half-open door at the back of the shop, an entry to a darker annexe where something all along had been swaying and swinging in a mechanical rhythm. She stood on her toes and leaned sideways, to see.

It was an old woman, standing between two heaps of corpses and up to her elbows in blood.

Working at speed and with a bitter efficiency, she seized each furry body from the stack on her right and skinned it in a single savage movement, turning the pelt inside out as fast as a dishwasher strips off a rubber glove, then slung the flayed cadaver on to the pile at her left. She sensed the shock of Janet's focus and raised her speechless face to the light. Without slackening her pace she cast Janet a look that was less a greeting than a challenge, a dark flash from under her heavy, blood-flecked brow.

To Janet this was *a class thing*, and out of her guilt she nodded and tried to smile. The skinner's mouth writhed in irony. Janet took her parcel and hurried away. As she came out of the market carrying the meat, the bread, the salad and the wine, the sky closed over and rain began to fall in fat, deliberate drops.

Not only had Janet lost ideas, she found that she had become stupid in the kitchen, and clumsy. The garlic in its papery envelope had softened and turned yellow, the peeled onion spun on the board and would not stand still to be sliced, and when she cursed the knife for skidding on the glistening flesh it repaid her with a stern slash across the fingerpad out of which blood welled and swelled: nothing she did could stanch it. She stood snivelling at the sink, letting the reddened water run down the drain, and listening to the failure bird outside in the garden as it tried with a special, dreary gusto to prop its stepladder of notes among the dripping boughs.

But the blood stopped at last, the dish was slid into the oven; and at seven o'clock, when the rain had settled in for the long haul and Janet had run out the front to empty the wet letterbox of junk mail and then upstairs to position saucepans under all the best-known leaks, she wiped down the white table with an Ajaxed rag and set about making it beautiful: an ironed cloth, proper cutlery and crockery for three, glasses with stems, two candle stubs in silver holders, and even the serviettes that the household children, echoing their parents, had called 'serve-you-rights', pink linen ones with drawn-thread borders, dragged like the tablecloth from the utter bottom of the ironing basket.

She uncorked the bottle of wine, laid the baguette at an attractive angle across the middle of the cloth, and stood back satisfied.

It was seven-twenty. Any minute now the others would walk in. But the room was cold. The fireplace was clogged with ash from days ago. Hastily she brushed it clean, then ran out the back door for wood. There were logs in a pile by the door, but no small stuff and no kindling, and when she put out her hand to the spot where the axe usually leaned, it met blank wall. Maxine. Water was welling in rills over the rim of the choked guttering, dropping a curtain between the dry verandah and the rain-darkened garden. Janet draped a teatowel over her head and burst through.

She had to fight the bolt of the shed, lifting and tugging and favouring her cut finger, before the big door swung open. There was no light at all, but a strange, pleasant perfume, woody, peppery, drifted out of the darkness to where Janet stood, and waiting to be able to see, she breathed it in.

She groped along the wall and found a box of matches on the windowsill. How anyone could live in here was beyond her – a dirt floor, no electric light, a dismal window with bathroom panes – but the peppery scent was seductive and the roof did not leak, and though she saw the axe at once, leaning tidily against a crate, she did not stoop to pick it up. She shuffled forward till her shins were barked by a low table on which stood a hurricane lamp. She put the match to its wick, and holding it high in front of her, stepped into the gesturing forest of the furniture.

A chairback plucked the teatowel from her collar; a table edge jostled her hip. She leaned forward with the lamp and peered between the petrified limbs into the depths of the shed. Along one wall she made out the workbench; on its far end, near a severe-looking narrow bed, the twig cradle, uncharacteristically motionless; and above the pillow, too high and too far in for the lamp to illuminate anything but its general shape, there hovered a little figure, a kind of doll.

Was this snooping? She was, after all, the landlady. She glanced over her shoulder to the dripping doorway, and hesitated. Back in the kitchen the rabbit flesh would have softened by now in hot juices, and loosened itself from the bones. But she took three steps further in, raising the lamp. The doll was spread-armed, like a crucifix, but the tips of its feet were blurred, somehow, and it was partly wrapped in cloth. A trickle of cold ran down Janet's scalp under her hair and into the neck of her jumper. She could not find an angle for the lamp that would show her what the thing was. She pushed forward again, with her elbows out, turning her hips sideways to get past a curved desk, but a footstool snagged the hem of her skirt. She heard the stitches rip and swore out loud, hopping and staggering against the side wall to get her balance: the whole frame of the building shivered from the impact, and with a rustle the doll tumbled off its hook and plunged out of sight into the darkness of the bed.

If anyone came, Janet would be deafened by the rain. She backed out, extinguishing the lamp and replacing the matches, and struggled, with the axe gripped between her knees, to shoot the bolt home. Her head and shoulders were sodden. The rain fell and fell. The garden was bowed under it. As she turned to run towards the back door, she saw the house suddenly as if it were a stranger's and she the traveller: hollow, bleak, forbidding, although it was lit up from door to top: the only shelter between her and the coming night.

Her axe blows shook the concrete of the yard, and in ten minutes a fire was wriggling and popping in the grate, but still the others did not come.

She ran up to her room and changed into a dry jumper. Any minute now the back gate would scrape: it probably had already, while her head was muffled in the woollen folds. In the bathroom, taking her time, she rinsed and dressed the seeping cut on her finger. She brushed the brief feathers of her hair, dashed on a couple of stabs of lipstick which she wiped off immediately on the back of her hand, and sauntered down the stairs, humming an aria.

The room was empty.

But the kitchen was warm with the smell of cooked meat. She turned the oven down while she made a slow and dignified salad, then with gloved hands she carried the brown dish into the living room and placed it on a board right in the middle of the arrangement. She lit the candles, first one, then the other; she blew out the match; she sat down at the head of the table.

Everything was ready. The oven dish shimmered gently, the salad sprouted its oiled green leaves between the dark bottle and the loaf's cubist crust; and Janet, with her hands clasped on the cloth, her lips discreetly coloured, and her brutal haircut beginning to soften, was not only the creator of this tableau but also its central element. What she was offering was herself.

Nobody came.

Still sitting with upright spine, Janet rolled her wrist towards her and looked at her watch. Half-past eight.

The rain kept falling, the closed windows streamed. Its white noise should have kept at bay all other sounds from the world beyond the house; but a tiny burr of anxiety prickled far inside her chest. She began to twist about on her chair. By its intensity she knew that her discomfort had nothing to do with Maxine. It was an attack of night-time waiting for a man, that most demoralising state, which starts at the incredulous, deflating, forgotten dinner hour and can continue without mercy till first light.

Ugh, the shame of it! Every sound that could possibly herald an approach sprang direct into her head. If tyres sponged or hissed, the car must pull in to the kerb and become his. A voice laughing or calling out goodbye at the corner must belong to him. A tram screeching down the metal to the stop must disgorge his running figure. Nothing had changed. She was still the same old sucker. All a man had to do, to put her at his mercy, was to make her laugh. All dignity, all stoicism was lost. Full of self-disgust, Janet lowered her head on to the tablecloth between her knife and fork, and held it there.

And that was how Maxine found her when she came in on her soft shoes and stood panting in the kitchen doorway under a bush of hair studded with trembling droplets.

'Janet,' she whispered urgently. 'Janet. Are you asleep? Wake up! What are you doing? What can I smell? It's so dark in here.'

Janet sat up with a jerk and whirled around on her chair. Her face in the candle-light was creased and red. 'Where the fuck have *you* been?' she cried. 'And where's Ray? Was he with you? Where *is* that bastard?'

Maxine paid no attention. She forged into the room, smiling; her eyes were extra bright. 'Listen, Janet,' she said. 'Nothing can stop me now. I've found the answer to all my money problems.'

'Your *money* problems? Right now I couldn't give a shit about your money problems! Where have you been? The meal's cold. It's spoilt.'

'Have you got a thousand dollars?' said Maxine, looming over the table in her yellow slicker. 'A thousand. That's all you need. It's for a game. Well, they call it a game, but really it's a kind of revolution.'

She had left the back door open and the rain's hiss and splatter drowned all other sounds from outside. The candles guttered in the rush of air. Silent, clenching her teeth, Janet steadied them. She reached for the wine and slopped the first big slug of it into her glass. Maxine pulled out a chair and plumped on to it, elbowing aside the table arrangement.

'*Everyone* from meditation's going to go in it,' she babbled. 'It's called the Golden Aeroplane. You put in a thousand dollars to buy a ticket, and you have to bring two new friends along to the next meeting. Everyone pays their thousand, and every week you go up one rung in this kind of pyramid, and then after a month *you* become the pilot, and you fly out – it's called *flying out!* – with about $8,000 I think they said. It's going to change *everything*, Janet. It's going to revolutionise society's attitude to money. I'm going to invite Ray, too. He'll be able to leave his job. I'm going to borrow most of my thousand, but I've got seventy-five dollars in the bank from a clothes-rack I sold last Christmas. Oh, it's fabulous. It's going to *spiritualise* money.'

She wrenched the end off the loaf of bread and began to tear at it with her teeth. 'I'm starving,' she grunted. She lifted the lid off the cooling oven dish and plunged a hunk of bread into the gravy.

Janet emptied the wine down her throat in one harsh gulp, and whacked the glass on to the table.

'Maxine,' she said. 'Are you completely cuckoo? Can't you see it's a scam? Everyone *can't* win. It's not mathematically possible. You will *lose your money*.'

'No!' said Maxine, fever-eyed, chewing and swallowing. 'It's *guaranteed*. They said! It can't fail. The only thing that can bring failure is negative energy. You should see the sort of people who were at the meeting. They're so generous and idealistic. All their dreams are going to come true. The man sitting next to me told me he's going to put his money into an alternative healing centre, out in the eastern suburbs.'

'Did you have a look in the carpark?' Janet filled her glass again and began to swig from it, choking as she spoke. 'Did you? I bet it was full of Saabs and Volvos. Those people can *afford* to throw away a thousand bucks, Maxine, but *you can't*. Listen to me – listen. You are out of your league. If you do this, you're crazier than I thought you were. You're a barking lunatic.'

Stung, Maxine paused with a piece of bread in her left hand. With her right, keeping her eyes on Janet's face, she stabbed a fork into the dish and brought out a dripping lump of meat.

'No – *you* listen, Janet,' she said, holding the fork over the cloth like a sceptre. 'At the door of the meeting you leave your old self behind. It drops off you, if you let it. Somebody gives you a pen and a name-tag, and you have to choose a new name for yourself. A man near me had his arms folded and a crabby look on his face – like you do right now – and on his name-tag he wrote SCEPTIC. But an hour later, after the two pilots had collected their money and flown out, I saw that man go back to the table and write himself another name-tag. I had a little peep. It was beautiful, Janet. He'd changed his name to HAWKWIND.'

Janet covered her whole jaw with her hands.

'I *was* going to invite you as my second friend,' Maxine went on severely. 'But I see that your scepticism is too strong. Even one guest with the wrong attitude could bring the whole endeavour crashing down. So I'm sorry, Janet. If I'm going to fly out, I'll have to ask somebody else. I just can't take that risk.'

She shut her eyes and opened her mouth to load in the food, but the smell of it brought her up short, and she lowered the fork and peered at it closely in the light of the fluttering candles.

'What am I doing?' she said. 'I can't eat this. It's meat.'

She laid the fork across the nearest plate and looked up at Janet with a shrug and a laugh.

'Since when,' said Janet in a trembling voice, 'have *you* been a vegetarian?'

'Oh, for *ever*, on and off,' said Maxine. She spun the

plate around, to cover the gravy she had splashed on to the linen cloth. 'And I shouldn't be eating bread, either. Someone told me that any food mould can grow on is really really bad for a metabolism like mine.'

'Have a drink, then,' said Janet, with heavy irony. 'At least we can share a glass of wine.'

Maxine shook her head. 'No thanks, Janet,' she said. 'Wine's full of histamines.' She brushed crumbs into a pile with the backs of her fingertips, then raised distracted eyes to Janet's face. 'Where *is* Ray? I can't wait to tell him about this. It'll change his life. Do you know where he is?'

Janet drained her glass again. Then she stood up in her place. Very slowly, drilling Maxine with her stare, she took hold of the bottle and up-ended it over the oven dish. Wine twirled out through the neck and spread in gouts over the surface of the stew. Maxine hunched her shoulders with alarm; she slid her hands under her thighs and sat on them hard. Janet reached out for the bread. She tore the rest of the loaf in half, then, breathing in sharply through her nose, she raised both arms in a grand gesture and aimed her two bread daggers down towards the plundered pot.

She hung there.

In tremendous slow motion, Maxine saw the bat-wings of darkness unfurl between Janet's arms and her torso: she felt herself, in the same yawning slowness, grow wide, and huge, and become omnipotent. Maxine opened her vast mouth. She tubed her lips. She blew. The breath bellowed under the bridge of her palate and across the causeway of her tongue. The candle flames flowed along it like two feeble flags, and went out.

She heard Janet lay the half-loaves down. She heard the rain continue unperturbed to fall. She heard the struggle of the unfed fire to burn.

Invisible, Maxine got to her feet.

'Goodnight, Janet,' she said, with dignity, and strode towards the kitchen. At the door she paused, and said over her shoulder, 'By the way – do you realise that this is the longest night of the year?'

Janet stood in the dark, and made no reply.

The house was quiet when Ray got home, an hour later, carrying a souvlaki in a paper bag. He slid out of his boots on the back verandah and entered on cold feet. There was no one in the kitchen. In the living room the white table had been cleared and wiped. Relieved, he clicked on the lamp and sat at the table to rip open his food, but before the first bite, despite the painful urgency of onions, he clasped his hands and lowered his head; then he sank into the job of it, holding the rolled bread in both fists, tearing at it sideways, gulping the cubes of meat down ragged. His chewing was loud, slow and deliberate.

Like the workings of his mind, thought Janet, lying on the couch that stood with its high back to the room, by the fireplace where only pinkish ashes lay. Before she spoke she let him devour his muck to the end, screw up the bag, and expel a deep, sighing belch; then she pitched the question low, without inflection, so it would roll at him along the floor.

'Where have you been.'

She heard him jump and gather himself, but she did not move. Let him come to her.

He appeared over the couch-back. His hair lay in a tangle of lank tails over his forehead and ears.

'I went to see a film after work,' he said. 'At the Kye-no.'

Janet gave an unpleasant laugh. 'I suppose you mean the Keeno,' she said. '*Kino*'s German, you know. For cinema.'

Ray's smile faded. 'I see,' he said. 'Now we have to know German before we can go to the movies.'

'Oh, don't be stupid,' snapped Janet. 'It won't hurt you to learn something, will it?'

'What's biting you?' said Ray. Drops slid off his hair and down his cheeks; he let them run.

'I,' said Janet, 'have been sitting here for hours, waiting. Like an idiot. Like some bloody *servant*.'

'Waiting for what?'

'I cooked,' she said. 'As requested by you. And you didn't see fit to turn up.'

'Well,' said Ray. With ponderous care he unzipped his jacket and extricated his arms from it. 'You didn't tell me. I couldn't have known. So it's not my fault. But I'm sorry.'

Janet lay watching him, with her hands clasped under her head, not speaking. How lonely he looks, she thought spitefully. He looks as lonely as some old pensioner, in his cheap, shoddy, puffy, ugly clothes.

'Did you go to the movie by yourself,' she said.

'Yes,' said Ray.

'Where are your friends,' she said.

Standing behind the couch with the dripping parka hanging from his hand, he turned back to her.

'Alby's coming for me,' he said. 'He promised.'

'Alby promised a lot of things, in his time,' said Janet.

'He'll be here pretty soon, I fancy,' said Ray. 'He's my brother. He won't let me down.'

'Family doesn't count,' said Janet. 'I said friends.'

'Where are *yours*.'

'I asked first,' she said.

This would be work. He tried to keep his gaze steady. 'I lost them,' he said.

'What – all of them,' said Janet.

'I lost my whole ... peer group,' he said. 'When I was saved.'

'So,' she said with distaste. 'You had "a peer group".'

'I knew some people,' he said. 'Not many. A few.'

He dropped his jacket and rested his hands on the couch-back. Very slightly she drew away; but he left them there.

'Where *are* yours,' he said. 'No one ever comes round.'

Janet laughed through her nose without moving her face.

'Scared of me, I suppose,' she said. 'Scared of my "anger". Like you. Or maybe they think I need to "lick my wounds in private".'

'What wounds,' he said.

'Oh, you don't need to know,' she said.

'What happened.'

'Just another tedious modern tale,' said Janet. 'Another broken marriage. I can't blame him, unfortunately. When you can't find someone to blame, it's worse.'

He stood patiently, in the violent aura of his food. He saw the large shiny earrings lying flat as plates on the cushion, one on each side of her neat little head; and though the holes had been allowed to grow closed, nothing could hide the row of puncture marks along her lobes where the old hippy studs had pierced her.

Janet shoved her feet hard against the couch-arm. 'I suppose,' she said, 'I must seem to you rather pathetic.'

'No,' said Ray. 'Not pathetic, I wouldn't say.'

But her mouth and nose were ridged with white, such was her effort at containment.

'What about the kids,' said Ray. 'They must help.'

'What kids.'

'I thought you said – the ones who used to sleep in the front room,' he said. 'Upstairs.'

'Oh, ask for the big room,' she said, jerking her head left, right, left. 'Argue with me. Don't be so fucking humble. Go on – take the bigger room.'

'I didn't mean that,' said Ray. 'Where *are* the kids, is what I meant.'

'Gone,' said Janet. 'Years ago. They weren't mine in the first place.' Her face was like plaster.

'It's not too late, is it,' said Ray. 'I mean, couldn't you –'

'Hardly,' she said.

Ray stepped nearer and sat down on the couch-arm. 'Do you want me,' he said, 'to . . .'

'To what,' she said.

'Rub your feet,' he said. 'Or something.'

For two beats she regarded him in silence. Her lips twitched and pointed as if in amusement; then she spoke bluntly.

'No.'

Ray stood up and moved away to the end of the couch.

'I'd probably start bawling,' she said. 'Sorry. Thanks. For the offer.'

She hid her feet under the cushions.

'You're not used to comfort, are you,' he said, about to walk away.

'What comfort,' she said.

'There *is* comfort,' he said.

His hand slid across his chest and raised the flap of his shirt pocket.

'No thanks,' said Janet. 'I don't need that.'

He raised his shoulders, and dropped them. 'There's not much else I can offer,' he said.

'It's all pretty bleak, then,' she said. 'Isn't it.'

'I'd like to be useful,' he said.

'Well,' she said. 'You could get me a drink.'

He hurried out to the kitchen, filled a glass at the tap, and carried it back to her, brimming. He held it out, and she lay looking up at him, not removing her hands from behind her head. The bottom half of her face was barely under control.

'What,' she said, with an ugly laugh. 'No lemon.'

The strain of it hurt him. Dumbly he proffered the cold glass.

'Actually,' she said, 'what I had in mind was something a bit stronger.'

'Oh,' he said, 'I didn't –'

'I never drink water,' she said. But she sat up and took the glass from him. 'I can hardly make it go down. Never mind.'

With her hard mouth she took a couple of pecks.

He could not help himself.

'There's living water,' he said, 'to be had. Water that if you drink it you'll never be thirsty again.'

So as not to look at him she forced it down, gulp after gulp; she drained the glass and gripped it in her lap with two hands, staring into it with a kind of ferocious boredom.

'Why should I listen to you,' she said.

'No reason,' said Ray. 'It's your choice.'

'Don't be a wimp,' she said. 'Now's your chance. What do you know.'

Outside in the dark street sirens raced past, weaving their songs. The rain fell and fell, swarming down, as if it would never stop.

He leaned against the wall with his hands behind him. 'I know,' he said, 'that I'm redeemed. That my redeemer liveth.'

'Don't quote the book,' she said. 'You're not the

only one who's read it. What do you *know*. From your *own* life.'

'Some things,' he said.

'Don't hedge,' said Janet. 'Answer.'

'I know,' he said, 'that I'm a sinner.'

'Oh, everyone's "*a sinner*",' she said roughly. 'Surprise me, can't you.'

'I'm saved,' said Ray. 'I've got everlasting life. I'm forgiven.'

'Forgiven for *what*,' said Janet. 'What have *you* ever done.'

She was after his credentials. His gorge rolled. Again he reached to his pocket for the book, but she sensed the direction of the movement and looked up sharply.

'No,' she said. '*Not* that. I'm asking *you*.'

He dropped his hand and shifted, to get his back to the wall.

'I know,' he said, 'about loss.'

'Join the club,' said Janet.

'About weakness,' he said. 'And failure.'

'Nothing special about that,' said Janet. 'What else.'

His thigh muscles began to quiver, as if he were focusing strength in them to lift something heavy.

'You won't want me in the house,' he said, 'if I tell you.'

'I suppose you stole something,' said Janet. 'Is that what it was.'

'Worse,' said Ray.

'Come on,' said Janet.

'I . . . betrayed someone,' he said.

'I have found,' said Janet, 'in fact it is my experience, that people will do anything.'

'There was this girl,' he said.

'There is nothing at all,' said Janet, 'that people will not do.'

'I slept with her,' he said.

'Oh, for God's sake,' said Janet.

'I used her,' said Ray. 'I admired the look of her, you might say, but –'

'But you didn't love her,' said Janet. 'And you think this would shock *me*.'

'I am not trying to shock you.'

'What, then.'

'She died,' said Ray. 'She died, because of me.'

The white table with the lamp on it was an island, a long way away. Neither of them was strong enough to swim that far.

'Do you mean,' said Janet presently, 'that you killed her.'

'She died,' he said. 'She died of loneliness. I didn't try to stop her from dying. If that means I killed her, I killed her.'

He let his knees bend, and slid down the wall until he was sitting on the carpet. His questioner, a bleached mask, floated in the depths of the distant couch.

'I've known people,' she said, 'and I've read about them in books. People who want so much to die that you can't stop them. Their whole life is a long, slow process of self-destruction. Of trying to die. And when they manage to, when at last they do, I imagine it might be almost a relief.'

'No,' shouted Ray. 'You don't know what you're saying. Not a relief.'

'That their suffering is over.'

'Never. Never. Not a relief.'

'Why. *Why*. If that was what she wanted.'

He knew the wall was still behind him, but it seemed

that the room had become vast and hollow, that its boundaries were terribly remote from him and its edges no support to him at all.

'Because,' he said, 'she took part of me with her when she died. Part of me that I didn't even know was there till it'd gone. And I had to try and find a way of getting it back.'

Janet sat bolt upright.

'How,' she said. 'How did you get it back. *Did* you get it back. What did you *do*, to get it back.'

'It's taken me years,' said Ray. 'Years. And still sometimes I feel it slipping away.'

'But *how*,' she said. 'How to even get a *grip* on it. How is this *done*.'

The room contracted round Ray again, fitting itself tightly to the shape of him, squeezing: when Janet leaned down and placed the empty water glass on the floor his eyes were whetted so by pressure that the damp, creased smudge her mouth had left on its rim detached itself from the glass and floated above it. He got to his feet and stood between the arm of the couch and the wall.

'I'm redeemed,' he said. 'That's what it means. The word's got a *meaning*. All my debts are paid. But that's what you don't want to be told. That's the thing that you don't need. Or so you say.'

The light from the table lamp picked up the bone-form of his head, its ridges, dips and dusky hollows. Janet took one of the cushions off her feet and lay down again, holding it in her arms like a shield, pressing it hard against her chest while her eyes ranged over his face.

'That'll do for now,' she said. 'Thank you. That'll do.'

But Ray leaned forward to her over the end of the couch, and she took a breath, for just as his face entered shadow and blurred, she noticed for the first time how the shape of his mouth resembled Alby's: there was something passionate in its raised peaks and deeply indented corners.

'He can break you, Janet,' said Ray in a soft, urgent voice.

Pinned there on her back among the cushions, unable to look away, she shifted her knees awkwardly this way and that, and cleared her throat. 'I can't keep fighting,' she said. She coughed again. 'That'll do, Ray. That's enough for today. For tonight.'

'Listen,' he said, very low. 'Listen. I used to be a piece of shit. Rubbish. Chucked away into the gutter. I wandered round looking for myself in all the garbage. But he *found* me. I'm trying to tell you that I've been *found*.'

Janet gripped her cushion. Their eye-beams collided and tangled. Ray kept going, he kept pushing, hovering over her in the dark of the deep sofa.

'It doesn't matter, Janet,' he whispered, 'if you're full of pride. It doesn't matter if you're *stiff* with it.'

In the fireplace a last spark exploded. All Janet's muscles jumped, and melted. She stared up at him. He leaned in closer. Her arms loosened and fell to her sides; her knees relaxed. The sleek cushion, released, slithered off her breasts and tumbled on to the floor. He reached out both hands to where she lay; her eyes glazed and drooped; a charge of warmth flowed from his approaching fingers and brushed against her skin: and then, in the air above her chest, he clenched his fists. He mimed the seizing of lapels, and he gave two brusque shakes, bang, bang, as hard as slaps. Janet's eyes popped open.

'Don't *pike*, sister,' he hissed through clenched teeth. 'This is *your* chance. *Don't pike.*'

She smelt the meat and onions on his breath. She was

afraid she was going to laugh, or sob; but she summoned up what was left of herself, and shot it at him out of her dry eyeballs.

'*Pike*,' she said in a choking voice. 'Who do you think you are. My *coach*.'

He dropped his fists and straightened his spine.

'No,' he said, from high above her, at a proper distance. 'No, I'm not. I'm nobody special at all.'

She lay. He stood. Their gazes, blown apart, advanced towards each other's territory only far enough to respect the border.

'All right,' said Janet, still breathing shallow. 'I heard you. We'll stop. Drop it now. All right.'

She rolled on to her side and lay curled up, eyes closed, with her hands folded and her thumbs touching her nose, facing the motionless embers. Dismissed, Ray stepped round the end of the couch and turned his back on her, but his feet were unwilling, he had to force himself, and only out in the bare centre of the room did he acknowledge how powerfully his heart was thudding, shaking his chest like a drum and driving the blood right through him so that his whole body focused on her, tight and hard. He heard the little voices gurgling and sniggering in his ear. Go on – go back. What are you waiting for? She's been around. It'll be fun. It won't mean anything. She's ready for it. What's the matter with you? Go back. Appalled, he stumbled away towards the stairs.

But she called after him.

'Put your clean clothes away, why don't you,' she said, invisible behind the high back of the couch. 'There's a shirt that's been in that basket for at least a month. Take it upstairs.'

'All right,' said Ray. 'Thanks.'

'My pleasure.'

Ray got to the turn of the stairs, with one arm through the sleeve of the damp parka, before he shook out the shirt and looked at it. He held it away from him by the scruff of the neck – and saw the violated shoulder.

The bitch – oh, the bitch.

Something he thought he had concreted over and made airtight cracked in him, and split open. Tears spurted into his eyes, and boiling and gasping, he sat down on the stairs with his head in his hands. What's happening to me here? What's Alby trying to do to me? Is this some sort of game, or test? I haven't got the strength for it. Alby should have warned me. I was not prepared.

With shaking hands he folded the shirt as best he could, trying to conceal from himself the rag of it, the outraged seam. Then, laying it on the step beside him, he took the book out of his pocket and raised it to his nose. He breathed in a big draught of it and held its cold edges against his lips.

A shirt, to the saved, was only a shirt. He would never speak about it. He would never complain, never give her the satisfaction – no, in vain might she wait. He would show the world how this was done. He would silently turn the other cheek.

He rolled the folded shirt round the book, wedged the bundle under his arm, and slowly mounted the rest of the stairs to his room. He turned on the overhead light and stood looking into the grim little room with its bare floor and vine-clogged, unopenable window: this cold box he had chosen to live in.

He undressed. His heart was still knocking. He switched off the light and crawled naked into his sleeping bag. He was exhausted, but no matter how he turned and settled, his thoughts would not slow down. He reached out for the book, and thrust it under his pillow. Whenever

he moved, the sleeping bag's slick cover rustled like silk
against his skin. He tried to lie still. His body pulsed out
warmth in surges, and the bag blocked it, collected it in a
layer, and beamed it back to him, a troubling cocoon of
self-longing. You had to be awake to pray, and he was
so tired: in sleep, anything can happen: but he began,
murmuring any entreaty that came to mind.

Janet listened to him plod up the stairs, pause, and head
out into the back wing of the house. Then silence. She lay
on the sofa shrivelling with shame. She had made a
complete idiot of herself; for *hours*. She had practically set
herself up for knock-backs. Even dopy Maxine had wiped
the floor with her; and then with Ray she had let her guard
down; she had shown her hand, like a lonely farm widow
fixated pathetically on her yardman. The thick woven rug
that concealed the rips in the couch-back had slipped down
and was half-covering her legs; she wriggled under it till
it reached her chest. She opened her eyes and noticed, with
a dull curiosity, that two hands were still folded on the
cushion beside her head. They belonged not to her but to
some other woman, one who remembered night words
that might be said and was not too proud to say them.
What were they? She was too old, too old for this. It
would be rhetorical to say *O Lord*. It would be sentimental
to say *Our Father*. It would be humiliating to say *Help me*.
So she lay on her side with her knees bent and her hands
clasped, and she said nothing at all.

Maxine did not need the lamp to find her way: with
practised swings of the hip and shoulder she passed
untouched among the furniture, stripped off her clothes in

the dark, and dived head-first through the tossed hoop of a flannel nightie into her bed.

The clash with Janet was already forgotten. Her mind buzzed busily round the prospect of the golden aeroplane game, this fabulous and timely blessing which fate was holding out to her. I don't even understand how it works! she thought in glee, hugging herself in the dark. It's like trying to understand a chain letter – it's like trying to understand infinity!

This mental sheet lightning that she called thinking could keep her head whirring till all hours of the morning. She brought her attention to bear on her breathing. Its rhythm was haywire, completely off the beam. She set herself to count, three in, three out, then in fours, four, four. Her thoughts kept rolling briskly past her like the carriages of a train, clickety clack, clickety clack; but soon, as she counted and breathed and tuned her breaths to her heartbeat, the carriages dissolved into barges which some large engine much further upstream, too far ahead for her to see, was towing steadily along a canal in a long and flexuous line: the barges made no sound in the water but a gracious shoosh and hush, and their wakes pulsed outwards in a V to ripple against the verge of the canal where Maxine lay on her back in tall, flower-studded grass, under a warm blanket of sun. She sighed, and turned on to her side. Something prickly stroked her cheek. She pushed at it with a feeble hand, and settled herself again. But once more it tickled, pressing its point into the skin under her eye. Vaguely she swatted it away, and slept.

It was the bride.

Since the day of its creation, dust had gathered in the folds of its blue garment, and its grass-bursts, once dynamic, had withered until they were merely brittle.

When blood in a thin red broth flowed again and then again on to Maxine's wads of cotton, she had acknowledged, sadly, that the bride was not as potent as advertised. Her respectful usages ceased; but she had developed a soft spot for her creature, and while no longer venerating it or looking to it for help, she came to dote on it and to think of it as a toy; it did not occur to her to take it down.

Now it had been sprung from its perch, and was sharing her pillow.

Maxine slept on, under the rattling roof of her shed; but her heart was wakeful. Dreams came, and peppered her. She screwed up her face, giggled hoarsely, rocked her head from side to side, but thick and fast they pelted her, in salvos, in fusillades, and each was a variation on the same theme: the baby. She was ready to have it, she was glad, she was not anxious, she was going to have it any minute now, there was the bed, the window was open, the sun was shining, everything was clean and ready, she was alone in the clean bright ready room, the sheet was stretched tight, her helpers had just stepped out for a second to take the air, they were competent, they were cheerful, they were waiting, they would come running the minute she called, it was simply a matter of putting down her tools, she merely needed to stop being busy, all she had to do was lay aside her other occupations, to choose the moment, to acknowledge it, to make up her mind to go to the bed and lie down, to say *now* – and she would have it, out it would pop, she would give birth to it, it would surge out all blind and bloody into the light, it would be born – and she would sing to it sweetly, *Cosmo, Cosmolino,* world, little world, and suckle it and pet it and hold it on her knee and teach it, and soon it would be strong enough to crawl away and sit up by itself in the middle of the room and eat an apple.

Not long after midnight the rain let up. A dry breeze moved in through the propped flaps of Maxine's door. In her sleep she grimaced and laughed, she sang a husky tune; but so insistent was the phantom baby's pestering that at last it drove her out of bed.

Barefoot in her flannel nightdress and still thickly asleep, with one hand reaching sideways to slide along the wall and the other playing in the air in front of her face, Maxine glided through the furniture and past her extinguished hurricane lamp, and stepped out into the rustling sepia universe of the garden.

Her feet were instantly soaked and so was the hem of her nightdress, but she did not feel it. Her fingertips frisked brick, wire, the bark of trees, and while her face, as it parted the air, kept quailing and flinching in dread of a collision or a precipice, her feet were fearless in their steady progress: on and on she went. There was a house, but far, and to get to it she had to wade knee-deep across a paddock of velvet out of which shoved flowers in blunt, buttery clots. Closer in she encountered a cross-current of intense agitation through which she flailed a passage, sweating and hyperventilating, but soon her fingers found plaster, a building closed round her and took the distance out of the air, and though Spanish combs as tough as spiders squatted in formation on the walls, she surged past them up the levels of a massive staircase so brilliantly designed that mounting it was easier than descending: her throat could not swallow rills of laughter at her power and weightlessness.

But when she reached the top, where echoes should have ricocheted off stone, the galleries of the castle were clogged with hostile darkness. She was sure, sure that her eyes were open, but she could not see. Where was the baby? How would it know her, and choose her? How would it come to her? There was no sound.

Ray heard someone laughing. He heard the shuffling of feet. He heard them, and then he heard them stop.

He lay heavily on his back.

Taking great pains, as though he were awake, he worked his way through the rooms of his life, rehearsing the acoustics of each one until the place where he was sleeping came back to him and named itself, the dusty concrete chamber where faithfully, once again, he had laid out his pallet. The great ovens beside him were silent now, and the silence, like the darkness of this room without windows, was total. It blocked his ears and kept his thoughts stuffed inside his skull, where they could form themselves only in an intimate, insanely articulated voice, tight as the ticking of a tiny clock.

She's come back for you. She's come from a long way away. She's been travelling, travelling, always coming after you. She hasn't forgotten you. She loves you and she wants to lie beside you. Her fire's gone out. She's cold and she will always be cold and she needs someone to warm her. Poor girl. Poor girl. It's not so much to ask. It's a long time till morning.

It was wrong, it must be, this visit of the succubus: it was a kind of repeating fit, a nightmare: and yet he could not truly say that he was afraid of her. She was small – only a girl – and she was lonely; and he felt such shocking pity for her. The thought of her sent eruptions of tenderness undulating through him; and at night like this, when the narrow tunic of salvation was off him and his body with its cashmere skin and jutting hip-bones seemed under his fingers so smooth as to be almost pure, almost beautiful, the stone heart woke in him; it became flesh, and lived.

She was stalking nearer, with tentative steps, feeling

her way towards him. Her palm grazed the length of the cement wall, skimming over its protuberances, and her soles brushing the floor (they must be bare, since he had seen her shoes consumed by fire) hardly imprinted the dust, she was so meagre. What form would she take, this time?

'Yes,' he said, whispering so as not to put her to flight. 'Come here. Come to me.'

He heard breathing near him, careful, slow, the little catch in it of her uncertainty; then a voluminous upward rush, and a soft collapse of cloth.

In one sweep he had the bag unzipped and his legs free of it. He gathered his limbs together, preparing to stand, and threw up his arms to her in the helpless dark, but all he found, where he expected her head to be, was a nimbus, springy, crackling, dry. Before his fingers could probe its centre, two hands, hardened by the desert where she had wandered, seized his shoulders and flattened them gently on to the padded bedding. He let his knees go and lay down, with the backs of his hands against the floor. She must be on her haunches now, beside him: her hair stroked him, her breath came and went on his chest as if she could see in the dark and were studying him, making up her mind where to begin.

Elated and aroused, made daring by the intensity of his blindness, he opened his mouth to cry out her name, but a palm harder than his own and smelling of pepper and ash covered it, and at the same instant a moist muscle flitted in spirals down his belly, butted against the root of him, and began in a warm exhalation to flick at him, making him bounce and spring. The air popped with sparks which he felt and heard but could not see; then a leg slid across his hips, and she lowered herself on to him as if he were a saddle, guiding him with her fingers into a swelling cleft where he was swallowed and bathed in a silky grip.

The gag was raised from his mouth and he groaned out loud.

Once, twice, she rocked, three times, five; drew back off him, excruciating, hovering over him, holding only the tip of him and threatening to vaporise; for an eternity she hung there, musing, brooding on the chaos with no sound; then she plunged on him again and like a crude boy he sobbed and let go: he burst into her and felt the convulsion go rippling up the quilted ridges he was held in. He smelt the change in her odour: a new metallic sharpness that soured his teeth like lemon without even touching his lips, and freshened every crevice of his sleeper's mouth.

Speechless, sightless with the desire to bless, he curved his arms round her, he enfolded her; and for the first time she allowed it. She sighed; she murmured; she laid her head with its tickling aura into the cradle of his shoulder. She rested on him. She let him feel the faithful lope of her heartbeat.

Then with a brief, firm pressure on his chest, she broke his grip, raised herself clean off him, and was gone. Air flowed over his belly where she had lain. He shivered, and opened his eyes.

It was a long time since he had let himself go this far without waking at the peak of it; but his body was loose and heavy with a sickly, still-fizzing sweetness, and he was too contented to collect himself for shame. Letting his eyelids droop again, he fumbled for the spread bag and wrapped himself in it, meeting no damp patch, then turned on his side, away from the window where morning when it came would fade the black hooked blanket to a rectangle of grey, and bent his knees, rubbing his feet together. If he lay still, if he warmed his hands between his thighs, he could slip back into it: *a little sleep, a little slumber, a little folding of the hands to sleep.* And he did; and dreamt that he wandered into a city cut by generous avenues, stitched by lanes, and studded with towers and bells and courtyards above whose fountains as they played hung blurred, passionate stars.

Maxine came to herself in the upstairs hall outside the bathroom. The gentle trickling of the cistern oriented her, and she padded away from the lavatory and down a perfectly ordinary staircase, through the living room and the kitchen, and across the blank, wet garden to her shed.

She slipped between the bedclothes and curled up, holding herself in her arms. Her bladder was empty. Its flatness rested pleasantly in the bowl of her pelvis, a comfortable absence of anxiety. There must be a nightie in the bed somewhere, but it could wait. She lay in the dark, broad waking.

In a while, when the blankets had loosened again with her warmth, she felt around on the fruitbox beside her for the matches, and carefully lit the hurricane lamp. Up out of its clean crease slid the bud of flame. She adjusted it, lowered the glass hall, and drew both arms back under the clothes.

In jerks, it seemed, then with a smoother radiance, the lamplight grew and spread. It washed in stages across the crowded domain, and watching it from her nest, she saw how it hesitated at obstacles: the tiny cradle's tremulous scaffolding, the dense protest of a cupboard door, the flourish of a chairback where a damp cloth hung: how it nosed this way and that, located a passage, and rushed on. Soon the standing furniture, like a flock grazing, was bathed in a steady, mild and shadow-making element. Maxine bunched up a pillow under her neck, and lay surveying her handiwork.

She tilted her head back and looked up for her poor bride.

The shelf was bare.

She had to dive and fumble for the thing. It had fallen head-first down the crack between the fruit-box and the pillow, and there it stuck, undignified, with its blue skirt hitched up around its cruppers and the tips of its grass-bursts gesturing inanely in the dusty gold air.

Maxine laughed. 'You look silly,' she said. 'You *are* silly.'

Sitting up, she seized the bride by its straw crossbeam and pulled it up from its hiding place.

The sudden movement brought forth a bubble of hot fluid from between Maxine's thighs. She let the bride slip to the floor, burrowed under the covers and pushed one finger into herself. She whipped it out, and seeing that it was not blood and would not stain, she wiped the colourless dew on to the folds of the sheet, and lay back down. Her whole body sank into a lagoon of wellbeing. Any minute now she would be too hot, and would have to kick off the top blanket; but her thighs and belly, humming with warmth, struck a perfect temperature and sustained it. Every muscle glowed. She was content.

The rain began again. It fell heavily, easily, with no meaning or intention but the fulfilment of its own nature, which was to fall and fall. How long this long night was! Perhaps it would go on forever. Maxine followed with her eyes, until their lids relaxed and drooped, the folding filament of smoke sent up towards the roof, but never quite reaching it, by the clean-burning, well-trimmed lamp.

At dawn, a bird began to sing in the saturated garden, a humble riff of notes, repeated in descending triplets.

Janet opened her eyes. She saw the wrong wall, the wrong picture, the wrong pattern of cracks in the plaster. It took her several moments of thick pondering to work out where she was, and to identify the room's queer smell as that of cold ashes. She sat up; she was still wearing all her clothes. The night's mortifications rushed back at her, and she threw off the rug and and stepped in her socks to the window.

The rain must have stopped hours ago: the house-sides opposite were sparkling, and the tips of their high chimneys were flushed with a secret, tentative pink. I have become, she thought with sudden clarity, a know-all, a bully and a prig. I am a really unbearable person. Ashamed and sore, fed up with sorriness and shame, she leaned her forehead against the glass.

Her breath coated it with a pearly cloud which came and went, spread and shrank, according to the rhythm of her lungs. She saw that the outline of this haze was new every time, a completely fresh and original shape, and that the vapour itself was composed of minuscule droplets, each of which prismed with colour on the flawed glass as it blossomed and died.

How fleeting everything is, she thought. How soon gone.

With this thought, so hackneyed to her, so unoriginal, came a wave of strange relief, almost a kind of comfort. She moved away from the glass. It cleared; and through it she saw a small bird land on a twig. It flipped, perched, whirred, only a few inches in front of her face. Its movements were not fluid, but were rather a series of different postures which it struck one after another, held briefly, then broke to shift, shift, shift again. Janet's mouth dropped open. She contemplated. The bird was fat, with a pale brown belly and darker wings patterned, like its head, with a row of evenly spaced white dots, as perfect as an aboriginal painting; and on its back, just above its stumpy tail feathers, she saw a flash of red.

Janet's heart was oddly light, floating high in the cavity of her chest. She turned away from the window and stooped over the couch to plump up its cushions and rearrange the woollen cover; and as she stooped, the dark column swelled behind her and slightly to the left, not touching her, and not visible unless she should frankly turn and face it. This she dared not do; but she straightened her back and bowed her head, in respect, while the column insisted behind her left shoulder, calm as a soldier, tenacious, incorporeal, and endlessly patient.

Was something burning? Maxine rolled over. Yes, but only the lamp, still faithfully simmering on the box by the bed; and already the cactus-shaped flame was superseded by a milky, rose-coloured light that leaked into the shed through the unpolished panes and round the doors which stood partly open. The rain had stopped, and a bird was calling in the garden: a dove, quietly practising its tune. Maxine wound down the wick and blew out the lamp.

The bride, poor scrap, lay in its inky skirt and hood on the ground beside the bed where last night it had slid. The air above it was dead: its energy was used up. Not a buzz, not even a crackle. I will take it apart, thought Maxine; right this minute. I gave it a chance, and it failed. I will pull it to bits and burn it.

She tunnelled into her clothes, pulled on her boots,

and picked up the bride by one leg. But halfway through the stand of furniture she noticed a piece of cloth hanging from the tip of a chairback. It was striped, domestic, out of its element. It was a teatowel. In *here*.

She stood still for a moment, thinking, then folded the teatowel into a neat square. She wedged the bride into a cleft of the chairback, and turned away to rummage among some sheets of paper on her workbench, one of which she drew out and rolled into a cylinder. Her face was vaguely smiling, but as she rolled she was already scanning the shed. Somehow she must clear a conduit through which a thousand dollars' worth of energy might flow to her. She let her gaze roam smoothly over her assorted creations. It settled, finally, on the twig cradle. The little thing stood on the very end of the workbench, trembling like a well-bred dog, ready, avid to be made use of, dying to be of service.

No sun reached Ray's window, but through the walls the bird called, and he woke on his side, utterly relaxed, as if while he slept all the knots and tangles in him had been untied. He crept out, and crouched in the greyness to flatten out his sleeping bag. The crux of his body, where hair brushed his thighs and his clump of genitals loosely hung, gave off an intimate, salty whiff. He paused. It was a scent he had forgotten, natural but at the same time disagreeable, like fish, or seaweed. Puzzled, he sat back on his heels, but where he expected only cold to be, soft cloth caressed his buttocks. He leapt up, and turned on the light.

A threadbare, cream-coloured garment lay on the floor beside his foam-rubber strip. It was patterned with small flowers, and the neck of it was trimmed with tattered and rather grubby lace.

He looked at it.

No.

He poked out one foot and stirred its folds.

No. Not possible. Absolutely not.

He seized his towel off the door-handle and covered himself, then stooped and picked up the garment with fastidious fingers. A woody, peppery perfume rose from it.

No. His heart gave one slow, colossal thump, and the shock reverberated along every vessel, right out to the tips of his nails and hair.

He closed his eyes and leaned the point of one shoulder against the cold plaster; but he hardly needed support. The disbelief that was suspended in him threatened to raise him off the floor. He felt so bamboozled, so ridiculous, that it was almost exhilarating. If he had opened his mouth, mad laughter would have come rushing out.

If this were true – if this were possible – then what would – what must – *No.* Stop now. Follow that thought where it led, and everything he'd gained and earned, all his plans, would shatter. Swallow it, brick it into a bunker. Never speak of, never think of it again.

He dropped the nightdress and kicked it into a corner. He shook his hands in the air as if to dash them free of something.

But he felt so *well*.

He opened the door and stuck his head out into the hall. The house was silent. The rain had stopped. From two streets away he heard the croon of traffic. He looked right along the upper storey of the house, past the locked room and the bathroom and Janet's bedroom near the stairs, past the two anonymous rooms where once or twice he had peered in at the sad, unsorted debris of earlier households, and as far as the ornate door of the very front room with the balcony, the one that had no lock but was always closed. The mood of the hall was different: the door of the front room was ajar.

Back behind the house, in the garden, the bird worked on its riff again. Nothing else stirred. Ray crept out and along the hallway. Janet's door was open: he braked, but the blind was down, the room was grey-shadowed, and the bed was flat and undisturbed. He tiptoed past the other two rooms and came to a stop outside the front one, between whose door and jamb stood a narrow pillar of yellow. No movement. From inside, a drip of water plopped, then another: plip. He leaned forward against the heavy timber, and pushed.

The room was enormous. Except for a couple of brimming saucepans stationed on the floorboards under leaks, it was completely empty: but its two french windows, though closed, were glossy with morning, for the room faced due east. The intensity of light grew as he entered: it grew and swelled like a vast orchestral chord, and wearing his towel like a loin-cloth he paced forward, grimacing, into the radiance of an exuberant sunrise. An observer might even have thought he was dancing. He wrenched open the right-hand window and burst out on to the balcony.

How could he not have noticed how high the house was built? Through the bald stubs of a wisteria vine he saw the winter sky roll away across the city and the plain to a horizon where great loaves of cloud lolled against a low mountain range: and up out of this bed of mist and rock rippled band after band of colour, ridges of brick-pink, smoke-grey, lavender, shuddering upwards through the chill air like undulations working their way up from the bottom of a river. Ray's heart was in his throat. Electric power poured through his limbs. He felt a violent, a pagan urge to cry out, to sing, to scramble over the rickety balustrade and beat away above the glittering streets, jostling the birds and shouting canticles of praise.

At least for breakfast there was bread.

Janet hacked it into stale slabs and toasted them while the kettle boiled. The smell brought Maxine in from the shed, picking her way across the puddled garden with the teatowel up her jumper and a roll of cartridge paper in her hand.

'I thought you didn't eat bread any more,' said Janet, straight-faced. 'I thought it made you go all mouldy inside.'

'Oh,' said Maxine, sliding the teatowel discreetly on to the corner shelf, 'I might make an exception, just for today. Look, Janet. Look what I brought you.'

She untied the sheet of paper, lifted off the tissue covering, and held it up across her chest like a scroll. Janet turned to look, with the buttery knife raised. It was a pastel drawing, very dense and worked, of a sea- or river-scape: the banks were dusk-coloured, rapidly being obscured by night, though on the water still glimmered steadily a furrow left by a passing boat; and right down the centre of the picture, dividing it exactly in two and frustrating the careless glance, a column of darkness loomed, an elegant, awesome pillar of smoke.

Janet's heart bounced. Her knees trembled. She stuck the knife into the honey jar.

'I'll buy it,' she said. 'Will you sell it?'

'No,' said Maxine. She re-rolled the drawing with deft movements, doubled the ribbon and began the bow.

'I'll pay you,' said Janet. 'How much?'

Maxine held it out, neatly rolled and tied. 'Here,' she said. 'I'm giving it to you.'

'You're poor,' said Janet. 'Let me pay you.'

Maxine laughed. 'Take it,' she said. 'If it means something to you, then I must have done it for you.'

'But your game,' said Janet. 'You need money. For your golden thing – the aeroplane.'

'Don't worry,' said Maxine with a shrug. 'The money will turn up.' She held out the scroll to Janet. 'Take it. You've been good to me. It's yours.'

Abashed, Janet took the drawing with both hands, and opened her mouth to ask the next question; but Maxine's eyes glowed, glazed, and refocused past Janet's ear, and a convulsion of amorous eagerness transformed her face.

'Hullo, hullo, Ray,' she carolled, shouldering Janet aside and rushing up to him. '*You* look beautiful this morning. I see you're wearing healing colours. You must have slept well – did the bird wake you? What did you dream of?' She pinned him from under her lowered brow with a dreadful, scorching ogle.

Janet saw him recoil, saw his bright face fade and go panicky. She was stabbed with pity: oh, poor Maxine. She was hopeless – *hopeless*. She had a bottomless pit of tactical blunders at her disposal. Someone had to help her, to advise her, or she would never get what she longed for. Janet laid her hand on the back of Maxine's neck, and Maxine, glancing up at her like an over-excited child calmed by its mother, subsided.

'Sit up, for God's sake, you two,' said Janet. 'Breakfast's ready – sit up.'

So they ate together after all, they offered each other bread, and milk, and coffee; and they were as cordial and uneasy with one another as strangers on the morning after a testing journey who, aware that they may have betrayed more of themselves in the night than they had meant to, scarcely know in daylight where to put themselves, for fear of their own openness, and of what might next be required of them.

Ray got himself quickly back on to an even keel. It had never happened. *It?* What *it?* He was firm. He would go to the wire on this. But he was always on his guard, ready for the intimacy to be presumed upon, and though Maxine's manner towards him did not change, though she said not a word about the whereabouts of the nightdress, which he had bundled up and kicked out of sight into a corner, the suspense was terrible. It was wearing him out. He slept with a chair wedged under his door handle; but in the public rooms of the house her ardour intensified and became a burden to him, a gauntlet of smiles and strokings which he had to run whenever he staggered in from work exhausted and half-frozen, craving only a hot shower and a feed and a couple of hours to read his book before he crashed into sleep.

She would run him to ground anywhere, she had no shame: pestering him while he picked gloomily at the bones of the cold rabbit, tapping on the bathroom door, yoohooing outside it while he was in there at the mirror shaving, or sitting on the dunny reading the newspaper; she even followed him along the upstairs hallway when once he tried to visit the big front room again; but it was closed, and to choke her off he had to crouch down in the hall and pretend to be inspecting the timber floor for borers. That impressed her too: now she thought he knew everything.

At the same time she started pressuring him to join some loony pyramid scam that she wanted to be part of.

Blokes at work, specially those mad gamblers the Irish labourers, were into it too, but casually, cynically, while for Maxine the scheme carried an idealistic meaning that put the wind up Ray almost as much as her adoration did. He would not touch the game with a barge-pole, and neither, to his surprise, would Janet.

Besides, he had saved, by self-denial and by camping for nothing in Janet's comfortless house, more money than he had ever possessed in his whole life before, and when Alby at last came down to get him out of here, they would be able to go out and rent a place together straight away. This month Ray's savings had broken through the four-figure barrier, and, awestruck by his own self-discipline, he segregated his opening thousand by rolling up the wad of notes in the first thing his hand fell on in the dark, and stashing it in the dirty clothes carton under the window of his room. For the first time in his life Ray had done something that would impress his brother. Alby would not credit it. Alby would demand to be shown. The thought of this triumph made Ray's head spin with joy.

Maxine, meanwhile, had selected her sacrifice, her precious thing to sell, but she had no buyer. Janet was an obvious candidate: she cherished the cradle, had witnessed its power, and could probably scrape up the asking price; but Janet would also know what Maxine planned to do with the money, and Maxine lost her nerve at the prospect of another blast of that articulate and hostile disapproval. As for Ray: since despite her best efforts he flatly refused to join the game, and because what she needed from him was far more intimate than money, she saw that it would get her nowhere to press him, and soon gave it up.

But all the while, as the weeks passed and passed, her

urgency grew. She laid aside her tools, and cleaned all day for money. They heard her on the phone under the stairs each evening, calling the merest acquaintance, the dimmest connection from the most imaginary past, pestering, persuading, pleading: they heard her deep, tearing sighs. What if the pyramid's energy-flow should flag before she could bring in two guests and afford a ticket? She took to carrying the twig cradle, quivering on her outstretched palms, out of the house and along the streets with her wherever she went; but the world, previously so rich to her with its constant swarm and flutter of meaning, its brilliant auras and suave rainbows of psychology, was daily shedding its glory. A pale whisk in the corner of her eye was only a dirty plastic bag stuck on a branch. The pavements, once alive with phosphorescence, were nothing but grit. Faces were flat maps of weakness and regret, and she read them awkwardly, like anyone else, making mistakes and having to ask questions whose answers disappointed her. Where she had veered lightly, she now marched flat-footed, with her eyes pinned to the ground in case of ordinary luck: dropped coins, stamp booklets or unscratched lottery tickets. Something had got out of hand, but in her obsession she did not even ask herself what it was.

Late one afternoon, in a milk bar far from home, the serving girl greeted her like an old customer. When Maxine hesitated, puzzled, the girl said, 'Aren't you the one who carries the little – the little – on your back?'

'Oh, my little back-pack,' said Maxine. 'Yes, I do.'

'No,' said the girl. 'I meant the baby.'

A shiver ran through the cradle.

'On my back?' said Maxine. She moved up to the counter.

Seeing her mistake, the girl tittered and flapped one hand across her mouth.

'Sorry!' she said. 'You were standing against the light. I was sure I saw a head pop up behind your shoulder.'

Maxine raced home rejoicing. She found Janet upstairs in her room, facing a blank wall and banging away on the typewriter in her lamplit snug of dictionaries and reference books, with an old crocheted blanket wrapped round her to hold a hot-water bottle against her kidneys.

'She saw it, Janet!' cried Maxine, stampeding in. 'She saw the baby!'

Janet looked up in alarm. Maxine's hair stood on end round her face, and while she jabbered out her tale in the doorway, the cradle on her palms was buffeted by a heavy surf of agitation.

'Hey. *Hey*,' said Janet. She pushed away the machine and struggled to her feet in the tangle of paraphernalia. 'Put that thing down and come in here.'

Maxine placed the cradle on top of a filing cabinet and, full of trouble and exultation in her looks, came to attention beside the table like a schoolgirl.

Janet laid her hands on Maxine's shoulders. 'Now listen to me,' she said. 'Are you quite, quite sure that this is the right thing for you to be doing? Don't you think you might have let it go far enough?'

Maxine dropped her head to one shoulder and gave a slippery smile. 'Tell me, Janet,' she said in a conversational voice. 'Why don't you move your desk so you can look out the window? Then you would be inspired by what you see outside.'

Janet shook her gently. 'Maxine. Please do not change the subject. I am only a shit-kicking journalist. I am what is commonly known as a hack. For what I write, inspiration is not required.'

Maxine's eyes focused and filled with tears. 'Oh, don't speak about yourself like that,' she said passionately. 'It's so *cruel.'*

'Maxine,' said Janet, with a hard throat, 'I'm worried about you. I'm afraid you're going to get hurt. Can't you accept that Ray just isn't interested?'

'I know – he won't join in the game,' cried Maxine. 'I can't blame him – he works so terribly hard and he's afraid to risk his money. If only I could make him understand that there *is* no risk.'

'Not that. I don't mean the game. I mean your other plan.'

'But I can't do that without the *money,*' wailed Maxine. 'He can't stick around afterwards to look after me. I've got to make everything ready *myself.'*

'But even if you do,' said Janet, 'you can't just *hijack* a bloke! For God's sake, Maxine. Be *reasonable.'*

Suddenly Maxine's cheeks bulged, her nose went red, and she exploded into great, racking sobs. She made no attempt to smother them, but stood with her hands stiffly by her sides, and howled with a square mouth, staring straight into Janet's horrified face.

It was the despondent time of day, when the failure bird dragged its gauche stepladder of notes into the garden and propped it against the nearest tree, making everything within earshot forlorn; but now Janet pulled Maxine clumsily into her arms, and found herself rocking the scrawny, sweating little figure to and fro; a few tears of her own slid into the bush of Maxine's hair; and while she murmured foolish endearments that came percolating up out of some half-remembered reservoir of comfort, her mood of dread dissolved, and she was filled instead with a calm, maternal daring.

Presently Maxine's gusty sobs spaced themselves further apart, and lost their rhythm, and stopped. Janet slid her hands down Maxine's arms to the wrists, and let go.

Maxine wiped her nose and slug-lidded eyes on the sleeve of her jumper.

They looked at each other in silence.

Then Maxine heaved a bottomless sigh, and said with a gasp and a hiccup, 'Help me, Janet. You've been around. Can't you tell me what I'm doing wrong?'

'You're asking *me* for advice?' said Janet. Her laugh cracked in two. 'About a *man*?'

'Is it my looks?' said Maxine humbly. 'Can anything be done about them or is it too late?' She closed her eyes and tilted up her face.

Silenced by a helpless sympathy, the kind for which there is no remedy, Janet swung the planet lamp away from the typewriter and aimed its beam on to Maxine's face. Maxine squinched her eyes more tightly but continued to hold up her head, presenting her face like a lake waiting for a wind; and Janet, in this moment of strange privacy, examined her from forehead to chin, from ear to ear and back again. Perhaps she would soon need glasses, perhaps it was a trick of the light, but she had to focus all her will into this act of looking; she was obliged to lug the grid of her concentration with force over the resisting planes and excrescences of Maxine's tear-puffed face; and her gaze, as she hauled it along from right to left, from bottom to top, trailed behind it a gleaming furrow of meaning, of intense significance which she could neither read nor interpret.

Maxine gave a husky giggle. 'That feels funny,' she said, squeezing her eyes shut. 'It tickles. What are you doing?'

'Looking,' said Janet, and sighed. 'Just looking.'

She bent the lamp's heavy head away, and patted

Maxine on the cheek. Maxine opened her eyes.

'Well?' she said eagerly. 'Is there a special cream or something? Or should I cut off my hair?'

Janet rested her bottom against the table and folded her arms. This undefended innocence. It was almost Martian. She spoke with difficulty.

'Don't you read the magazines? That's where you find out what men are supposed to like.'

'But Ray's not an ordinary man,' said Maxine. She stared at Janet, bewildered.

Outside, closer than the hum of home-rushing traffic, the failure bird carefully stacked its tower of notes; losing heart before it reached the top, it climbed back to the ground and prepared to start again. Maxine was beyond reason. All that was left was kindness – or bluntness, even if you had to pick up the pieces afterwards. Janet filled her lungs and jumped.

'You haven't looked after your hands,' she said.

Maxine glanced down at them, and shrugged. 'It's the work I do,' she said. 'Does it matter?'

'And your face. Is your skin that rough all over?'

'I don't know,' said Maxine. 'Probably.'

Janet got to her feet. 'Okay,' she said. 'I think we should start with a massage.'

'But it's nearly night,' cried Maxine. 'Everywhere's closed now. I was counting on doing something straight away. I can't wait, Janet. My time's running out.' Her red eyes swelled with tears, and she began to wring her hands.

'Don't start again,' said Janet, hearing in her own voice the strident note of haste. 'I can do it. I'll do it myself.'

'You?' said Maxine. 'How?' She scrubbed at her eyes with her cuffs.

'How do you think we used to pass the time when we

were hippies? I've still got the book. It's on the shelf next to the dunny. Nick in and get it for me while I warm up the room.'

She pushed away the typewriter, and began to heave the unmade bed about. Maxine, unwinding her scarf, hurried out the door and along the hallway towards the back of the house.

It was quite dark now, though judging by the frequency of passing cars it could not have been later than five-thirty, and no other lights in the house were on. Maxine slithered her hands along the wall, and reached the bathroom by feel and smell: but its light showed her that Ray's door, further down the hall, was open, just a crack. Many a time she had loitered outside it, not daring even to knock. Now, in the boldness of relief that follows tears, she simply strode up to it, pushed it open, and stepped inside.

She flicked on the dull overhead light. The window, its panes thickly clogged with creeper, was jammed shut, but one tendril had forced a way between the ill-fitting sashes, and hung out into the room. Maxine's hands clasped and butted under her chin. So this was where her angel lodged and slumbered: this was his place of dreams. How spartan his needs were. A sleeping bag, a narrow pallet, a pillow with a book beside it; and under the window, a cardboard carton of possessions. She tiptoed closer, and bent over to admire.

Clothes. Oh, his darling garments. She knelt by the box with her hands on the floor, and pushing her face right into the jumble of sweat-rank laundry, breathed her fill; then she sat back and plunged in both arms, to the elbow. Her fingers struck a firmer object at the bottom. She fished it up like a prize from a lucky dip, and drew it out towards the light. Something small was tightly rolled in layers of cloth. The wrapping was soft and flowery, and trimmed with torn, discoloured lace. She raised it to her nose.

It was her nightdress.

The floor foundered under her knees.

Ray had visited her shed. He must have pushed his hands right down to the foot of her bed.

Dumb with jubilation, Maxine laid the bundle on the floor and unrolled it with steady hands. The flannelette peeled away, and from a nest between the stained folds sprang up the core of it: money. A wad of money. A thick, rubber-banded, perfumed clump of brand-new notes.

She knelt quite still.

It was not necessary, but she licked her fingertips and daintily counted the cash. A thousand dollars. A thousand dollars *exactly*.

Out in deep space the planets swept, inexorable, along their splendid orbits. Maxine bowed her head. From now on she would take the gods' dictation.

She thrust the roll into the pocket of her tracksuit, paused for a second with her head strained up to listen, then bounced to her feet, leaving the nightdress spread-eagled under the window, and darted along the hall to Janet's room.

Janet's back was towards the door. She had turned on the radio, very softly, and was bent over the bed, singing to herself, while she stretched the sheet tightly over the mattress and spread out a towel. A plastic bottle of oil stood beside her on the night-table. While Maxine watched, with one hand round the door jamb and her fingers almost touching the nearest strut of the twig cradle, Janet stooped again and pulled out from under the bed a small brown instrument, with strings. She positioned her fingers, turned her back more fully to the door, and struck a chord so timid, so uncertain, that even the tiny cradle failed to register it.

Maxine whisked the cradle silently off the filing cabinet and sped away down the passage.

Her heart was absolutely tramping, inside her ribs. Kneeling again under Ray's window, she laid the cradle on its side, rolled it up with rapid strokes in the flannelette nightdress, and worked the new bundle, her side of the bargain, deep into the box of dirty clothes. Then she let her head swoon again among the shirts and underpants, drinking in his smell.

Downstairs, the back door crashed shut.

Maxine frisked the top layer back into a casual arrangement, snapped off the light, and shot out of the room like a rabbit.

In the bathroom she pulled the lavatory chain at once, and while the water roared and gushed, she scanned the shelf for the massage book. There it was, smelling of patchouli, its covers and page-corners splodged with oil-stains.

Janet was waiting for her, not with her customary irritable finger-tapping but sitting quietly on the tight-sheeted bed with her hands resting in her lap; she was almost smiling. The guitar – the banjo, whatever it was – was gone.

'Hop up,' she said, as Maxine came skirring round the corner with her arms flying wide and slung the greasy book on to the pillow. 'Get your clothes off and hop up here.'

'I think I just heard Ray come into the kitchen,' panted Maxine. 'Shouldn't we shut the door?'

She pulled off her soft boots and her old, rainbow-striped, woollen sweater, and while she folded the track-suit pants with meticulous care and laid them on top of the pile, Janet walked to the door and closed it.

'Back in the seventies, you know,' she said, 'we used to massage each other blatantly on the dining-room table. We had no fear. Nothing was sacred.'

She laughed, and turned from tuning the radio just in time to see Maxine, lit by the blush of the one-bar radiator, scrambling out of elephantine cotton knickers and a sagging singlet. Janet did not miss a beat. She snatched at the grey rags before they hit the floor and corrected their trajectory so that they flopped into the waste-paper basket under the desk.

'It might be an idea,' she said, squirting oil on to her palms from the plastic nozzle, 'to pay some attention to your underwear, later. Lie on your stomach.'

Gloriously, Maxine dived face down on to the towel, and closed her eyes. She was too porous to stay bed-bound: any minute now the mattress would drop away from under her, and she would rise to the ceiling and bob among its garlanded cornucopias. Thoughts of bluestone ballast weighted her. She heard Janet's feet shift round to the top of the bed, heard her draw a first, formal breath, and felt the shadow as Janet leaned forward, blocking the light. The oiled hands swooped, skimmed, and pounced. With a grunt, Maxine let go.

But the surprise of touch! Where Janet had expected a coarseness, desiccated, even flaking, her palms surged down a back whose skin was as cool and as dense as yogurt, and across whose shoulders was tossed a starry shawl of the palest, finest freckles. Maxine's ribcage sank under the rolling pressure like a little bellows, and rose again as the hands glided, one on each side of her spine, all the way to the waist, drawing behind them on the skin a quickly fading double stripe of flush.

All Ray could find to eat, down in the cold kitchen, was a rind of cheese. He attacked it, and while he chewed, his eyes roved along the bench, looking for fruit, for something with juice in it, something that had grown on a tree.

But instead, poking out of a bundle of old catalogues and supermarket specials behind the toaster, he saw a letter.

Upstairs, water groaned and beat in the pipes.

He put out his hand, but he did not need to touch the letter, or even to see the writing on it, to know that it was for him. He spat the rest of the cheese into the bin and ripped open the envelope. It was from Alby.

Alby was coming. Alby was on his way. Alby would be here, with a rented truck of household things, in a fortnight. At last, at last he could get out of here. Ray clenched both fists in the air, threw back his head like a boxer, and jogged on the spot in his socks.

But when? Which fortnight?

In vain he read and reread the short letter. There was no date on it anywhere, only the scrawled word *Thursday* at the top, and the postmark was a grey blur, completely indecipherable, as if the corner of the envelope had been lying in a pool of water. How long had it been stuck there with the junk mail? It could have been days – a week. Those bloody – it was Maxine. She had no morals. She was mad keen on him. She would stop at nothing to keep him hanging round. Pushing his feet into his boots, he leapt off the back verandah and galloped across the garden to her shed.

He thundered his fists against the double doors. The failure bird broke out of the branches and flapped away.

No answer.

He gave the bolt an irritable twist, and turned to stamp back to the house; but behind his back the latch came loose, and one of the big doors swung open and whacked him across the square of the shoulder. He seized the heavy door to heave it shut; but then he glanced up the length of the yard to the gate and the high windows of the house-back. He had a minute or two. He slid between the doors and stepped down on to the beaten earth floor.

Phew. It was like a forest in there, half dark and full of gestures. He almost expected bats, or those flights of twittering birds that explode in old cartoons, making the explorer flinch. How did she get to the bed, over there in the corner, without having to twirl and stoop? Tingling with the intruder's thrill, he advanced into the dimness, holding one arm bent to protect his face, and groping for matches or a torch. Maybe the pieces of furniture had not been carpentered at all, but had reproduced themselves: maybe they had mounted and mated clumsily in the dark while Maxine slept, like reptiles, or prehistoric monsters. The thought made him shiver; but the shed smelt of sawdust and wood, clean smells, and over there against the window's square he saw a tapering limb, the back or arm of something otherwise invisible: the grace of its curve brought him up short. He leaned towards it. Something dry and crackly fondled his cheek, and he let out a snort of fright. He jerked upright. A hat-rack crowned him, and the air round his head blossomed with stars; but snatching about his ears he got hold of the thing that had touched his face, and backed to the door with it, out into the cold evening garden.

Janet did not open the book at all. She did not need to. The strokes returned to her hands, efficiently and in perfect sequence, as if the seventies were only yesterday, or as if

Maxine's body by its very contours had called them back to life; and now Janet herself was stripped down to a singlet, flushed and sweating, all her muscles warmed by exertion and a growing sense of usefulness and power. Perhaps, if somebody *really sensible* took over this business and *did the talking*, something along the lines of Maxine's fantasy might possibly be arranged. Stranger things happened every day, and were reported in the news. She hummed along to the music, under her breath.

'What's the time?' said Maxine vaguely.

'You're not supposed to be thinking about time,' said Janet, working away on the front of Maxine's right thigh. 'You're supposed to feel "like an embryo floating in space", according to the book.'

'Will it take much longer, though?' said Maxine. 'It's lovely, what you're doing, but there's somewhere I have to be by half-past seven. I have to deliver something. To somebody.'

She raised her eyelids a sliver to check Janet's face for suspicion; but Janet, absorbed, paused in her rhythm only to shuffle sideways and begin again on Maxine's belly.

'I'll just whiz up your front,' she said. 'You're not ticklish there, are you? Bend your knees.'

Maxine obeyed, and Janet laid the palm of one hand flat on her belly. Clockwise, she thought. *The colon is coiled clockwise.* She began a full, slow circle, passing across below the ribs, swooping down to the pubic bone, and rolling round towards herself and up again to the ribs.

Maxine was scrawny and relaxed. Her abdomen was slender. It was almost flat. But it was not hollow. It contained something. A lump, a thickening. It contained a lump.

Janet's hand faltered; then round it swept again, pressing firmly, in a full, slow circle.

Something was there, all right. Something firm and

hard. In the middle, way down low.

Janet forced herself to breathe out.

'When was the last time you had a pelvic exam?' she said casually, keeping the sweeping stroke going.

'A what?' said Maxine, with her eyes closed.

'You know,' said Janet. 'A pap smear. When the doctor examines your insides, if you're a woman. For lumps. Fibroids, and so on. For, you know – cancer.'

'Oh,' said Maxine, 'I never go to doctors. I lost my faith in western medicine years ago.'

'Isn't that a bit risky?' said Janet. 'At our age?' Round and down and up again went her oiled hand, sleeking over the site of the thing.

'My breasts are *full* of lumps!' said Maxine airily, not opening her eyes. 'And I often feel rather weird before breakfast. But if I'm out of sorts I just take a dose of some special drops that my iridologist made up for me. They drive out the toxins. I won't get cancer. I don't choose to – therefore I won't.' She smiled, with her eyelashes resting on her cheeks.

Sweat popped out under Janet's eyes. Her tongue felt like metal. But she kept up her steady, churning abdominal stroke, round and round and round, remembering to flex her wrist, watching the belly button's neat little knot change from a circle to a lozenge to a circle, and feeling the crisp bush of Maxine's pubic hair graze the side of her hand with every downward pass.

Outside the shed it was too dark to see. Ray was hungry and tired, but needled by a cranky curiosity, he carried the doll back across the garden and into the kitchen.

Its garment was so faded and dusty that even in the lit room he did not recognise it. He laid the shaggy-legged thing on the bench. Was *this* art? But wouldn't a real artist have given it feet, and a proper face? Its head was blind. It had no nose or mouth. It was as clumsy and inaccurate as if it had been made by a child.

Somebody must be in the house: the pipes upstairs were still ticking. Any minute now Janet would come down in a bad temper, trailing her rug, and catch him here having a snoop. He picked up the bride, to sneak it back; but it clacked. He heard it, a clear enamel sound. He seized the doll by its legs and whacked it hard against his thigh. Dust flew off it in a cloud. He pushed apart the folds of its hood and held it up to the light. It was. It *was*. His stud. The mother-of-pearl snapstud on the sleeve of his blue shirt.

A bolt of rage shot through him. Witches! Bloody molls! Ganging up on him – ripping the sleeves off his clothes – starving him, holding back his mail – treating him like some sort of sex toy –

He was round the foot of the stairs, cannoning off the landing wall, pounding across the dark upper hall before he remembered his noble resolution: but too late. There was a strip of light under Janet's door. The radio was going softly inside. He heard voices murmuring. He wrenched at the handle and burst through, taking a breath to start his diatribe –

– but the room was warm. It was a curtained cavern, tranquil, pink-lit, full of music; and women were floating in it. One was stark naked on the bed, flat on her back, showing everything, and the other one, bare-limbed, flushed, damp with sweat, was leaning over her, tending to her, doing something, sliding one hand right down her belly to her –

He shut his mouth. He let the doll fall. He turned on his heel and spun out of the room. Someone squealed. He was halfway down the stairs before the laughter started, and the door was kicked shut behind him.

Alby, for God's sake *come*. Come down, Alby, and get me *out* of here.

Anointed, dazed with luxury, and wearing under her clothes a pretty camisole and Janet's last pair of real silk knickers, Maxine promenaded down the stairs: but Ray was nowhere to be seen. He must be resting somewhere in the house, composing himself. She would track him down tonight, as soon as she had bought their ticket, when she got home from the meeting. Out the back gate she stepped, pressing one hand flat against the wad of notes in her pocket, and hurried away along the dark street to the tram.

Ray hid in the phone cupboard until he heard the gate rasp shut behind her. Then he climbed the stairs to his room and dropped his boots on the floor and his socks into the dirty clothes carton. It was filling up faster than usual: soon he ought to contemplate running a load through the machine. He thought of digging out his money stash and counting it again, for the glory of it: he thought of warming himself with a shower and trudging over to the shop for a tin of tomato soup; but he was exhausted. He felt stunned, like a blur, as if he were leaking out of himself through puncture holes, losing outline and shape. He crawled fully dressed into his bag and lay down. Just for a minute, to get warm. These women. They were making him sick. They were crazy and bad. He lay flexing his toes, waiting for them to thaw. The terrible sight, in the pink bedroom. A gold wine-cup overflowing with the – with the lust – the something – they were haughty. They *walked with stretched forth necks and wanton eyes*. Walking and mincing as they went.

They weren't separate any more, in his imagination. They were a kind of swampy, fluctuating element that he lived in. They took all his clarity away, and left him with a bitter vagueness. His stomach was hollow, but to eat he would have had to creep out of the bag and drag himself downstairs and face Janet in the kitchen, smirking at him over an empty plate. He flattened out Alby's letter under the pillow and turned on to his belly. There were worse things in life than going to bed hungry.

Janet folded the oily sheet and sat down at the table, wiping her hands on a hanky. Poor Ray – the horror on his face. All was lost, of course, though Maxine would never be made to see it; all was lost, and it had never really been anything else. How would they face each other in the morning? Weak laughter overtook her, and she rested her forehead on the metal body of the typewriter. She tapped a few keys. Her glance dropped off the table edge and encountered, on the floor half under the bed where it had skidded, the bride.

It was the thing she had seen in Maxine's shed, the night she snooped. It was cute. She picked it up and propped it on the table against the wall. It kept toppling. Its dress and hood had faded right out, but they must have been beautiful once – a real cobalt blue. She touched the skirt with her finger. The press-stud under the chin was clever. It was put together with skill. It wasn't a patch on Maxine's real masterpiece, though, the twig cradle.

Still, it was fanciful. Rather decorative. Janet stood up and hooked the light, grassy doll on to the top corner of a picture that hung above the worktable.

This was Maxine's pastel drawing, her gift, and Janet had rushed out at once and paid an arm and a leg to have

the thing decently mounted and framed; but the framing
had not worked out satisfactorily at all, for the picture was
so dark and so densely layered that once enclosed behind
the sheet of glass, it vanished. It completely disappeared.
No wonder Maxine had trouble making ends meet. The
drawing had retreated into its own mystery, and all Janet
saw, when she looked up at it from her chair, was herself:
her thought-darkened face, her penitential haircut, and a
deep and detailed reflection of the room behind her.

She was not interested in eating. She read on until
half-past nine, and then went down to the kitchen to make
herself a cup of tea. While the kettle boiled she stood at the
door with her arms folded and looked across the garden
for a light in the shed, thinking to offer Maxine a cup; but
the shed was in darkness. Where *was* that girl? What was
she up to?

It was ten-thirty before Maxine came tripping, empty-
pocketed, rose-faced with cold, round the corner from the
avenue and down the street toward the house.

She had arrived at the meeting slightly late; but the
door was still open, and she saw from Hawkwind's wild-
eyed face that it must be his night to fly out: indeed, he
was already stuffing fistfuls of cash into his suit pockets,
and veering about the crowded room in a fluster of
congratulations and farewells. Someone approached her
with a hand out. Maxine laid the bundle of notes on its
palm. The hand closed; the shoulder turned.

Maxine looked round the room. She was by ten years
or more the oldest person present.

She was still hovering just inside the door, furtively
filling up on the cheap peanuts the hostess had laid out in
bowls on a table there, when Hawkwind passed her at a
leaning trot, making for the street; and though he ignored

her she caught on his face, as the cold air struck it, a shift of expression from gratitude to incredulous glee which kicked her pulse up a notch and made her stomach drop like a stone. She craned after him, chewing, but he was gone, elbows up and pumping, shoe soles flashing, and as he rounded the corner to the tramline the fringe of his scarf fluttered back over his shoulder like the tip of a wing.

She was light-headed. The speed and efficiency of it took away her breath. That was Ray's money. I gave it to Hawkwind. There was no receipt. He took it. He left. It's gone. She licked her lips. They were crusted with salt. She closed the door with a soft click and turned back to the room.

It was ominously still.

The eyes of the wingless ones met, and fell away.

One by one, then, they were obliged to report that they had failed again to attract any new recruits to their chapter of the game. Maxine, too, the last joiner, made this confession. Some people present, to her dismay, lost their charm and became quite nasty. They cast dark looks and launched accusations of fearfulness, of loss of faith. *Someone*, they said, must have imported the virus of negative thinking. It had spread, and was blocking the free flow of energy and love.

The hostess's boyfriend scribbled something in the margin of a magazine, tore it off, and passed it to Maxine. 'It's an affirmation,' he hissed. 'For *you*.'

He watched her while she read it. '*My attitude to money needs looking at. If I re-evaluate my attitude I can win at this game and learn what money really is.*' She looked at the man, who tossed back his glossy forelock, challenged her with a large, intense smile, and strode away. Maxine glanced down at her jumper front. It was sprinkled with peanut husks and crystals of salt.

She strove with her vestigial radar to scan the room.

It resisted. All she could perceive was a phlegmy, inert quality in the air round people's heads. She sat cross-legged on the carpet, working chewed peanuts out from between her teeth, while the meeting broke up around her into altercations and vain strategies. Silence fell. People stood scattered for a moment; then they gripped hands and formed a circle. They concentrated their energies and directed them: they visualised volcanoes, king tides, inexhaustible fountains and the like. They called on a power for which they had no name. Under her lids Maxine sneaked sideways glances at her companions in their loose, handsome clothes and identical tortoise-shell spectacles. Their faces were stiff with foreboding. Surely, *surely* they must know that the game was dead. They were its corpse. Nothing they said or did would revive it. But they would not acknowledge it, let the thing drop off them, and go home in resignation to their rooms. No – they were going to *soldier on*.

This is stupid, thought Maxine. I am too old for this.

She let go her neighbours' hands, joined them to each other like children, and stepped quietly out of the ring.

No one noticed she had gone. She crept away to the door, and looked back.

There they stood in their circle, squeezing hands and labouring at their imaginings. So strenuous! So hopeless! She could have laughed; but the sight of their bowed shoulders touched her, and she beamed a kind ray into the room in parting, to bless them. She was about to turn away, when it struck them. They raised their faces; and with a whisper and a rustle, a fuzz of colour sprang out round each person's head. Their auras blossomed for her. They flourished madly, they proliferated and radiated and swarmed like mould. Each skull sprouted its unseemly halo of avarice. Oh, it was pathetic! It was almost beautiful.

Dizzy with wisdom, Maxine slipped out the door and on to the street.

Fresh air.

Breath billowed in front of her as she jogged home. The houses squatted in their winter gardens, bathed in tides of moss-smelling night, and few lights showed. She had had no dinner, but her stomach, packed with greasy peanuts, sat roundly against the elastic of her silk knickers; Janet's camisole too was rather tight, unless it was the cold that made her breasts twinge with every step. And yet her limbs were *warm*: ripples of warmth beamed out from the core of her, a rose tightly furled in the bowl of her pelvis. She gave a smooth skip, and a twirl.

Was it wrong to feel so cheerful? Surely, after what she had done tonight, she should be heavy-hearted, weighed down with guilt and fear of the consequences? But what she felt, cantering steadily home along the avenues where she was the only one on foot and cars tore the damp air into strips, was a kind of broad, easy calm: a purity. Had she really sobbed, pleaded, rushed about? Janet must have thought she was crazy. A great tide of anxiety had turned in her, and gone out. She had grown all simple and virtuous.

Of course, it would not be an easy thing to explain. Ray loved his money. She tried to foresee his reaction, to think like a hoarder. His insides would knot with rage when he went to his clothes box and found out what she had done. It might take him quite some time to realise what a favour she had done both of them – what an ugly blockage in his nature, and in her own plans, she had cleared tonight.

How *would* she explain? There would certainly be unpleasantness. Ray might shout. Her heart gave a little trip and her skin tingled. Perhaps it would end in serious trouble. Really, for an angel he was not very highly evolved at all. This would test him *severely*. Oh, she longed for him not to disappoint her ... but if he did, if he took this badly, she might have to accept that he was the wrong angel, and let him go. She had pressed him hard, after all: the load of responsibility she had heaped on him had made him stagger.

A carefree tram went streaming by, lit and rocking like a boat. Maxine heard the chatter of its wheels and was filled with elation. It was travelling northwards on its smooth and endless rails. How lovely, to take off and speed away! For a moment she envied Ray his poverty. He was light, now: he was empty. He had nothing, while she was all dragged down and hung about with possessions: the furniture, the tools, the bench, the bed, the cradle –

The cradle. Perhaps after all it would be wiser to postpone the moment of truth, at least till she had prepared a soothing explanation. She turned the corner into the side street and approached the house, as always, from the rear. It looked bulky. It was a blank against a cobalt sky faintly smudged with stars. She raised her eyes to its high windows. They were dark. If the others had gone out, she could slip into Ray's room and dig out the cradle from its hiding place.

She stepped quietly across the verandah and tiptoed through the rooms to the stairs. Up she went, treading with care on the outer edges of the boards. All the doors were closed. Each bedroom was a private fortress of sleep. For long moments she stood outside Ray's door. Nothing stirred. The house was so silent that she might have heard him breathing, but for the bumping roar of her own blood.

At seven-ten in the morning there was a commotion in the street. Maxine woke in her thin-walled shed, with her nostrils full of the stink of exhaust. A truck out there was chugging. It did not pass, but paused, and began to manoeuvre itself backwards, as if trying to park under the trees on the other side of the fence. Out of habit and training, Maxine raised her head. She paid attention. There was meaning for her in the engine's labouring note. This was not just any old truck. Someone was coming.

She crawled out of the blankets and into her clothes. The driver was inexperienced: he was making heavy weather of it. Fumes were being pumped through the slits in the shed wall. She breathed as lightly as she could, and ran out across the yard to the gate. Dragging it back over the concrete, she emerged on to the footpath just as the motor choked and died, and the truck's red cabin burst open to eject a booted, jacketed man in flight. Head forward, arms out, he dropped to the bluestone cobbles with a grunt, jarring his knees, and recovered himself in a footballer's graceful forward stumble.

Maxine drew herself up, hands on hips, and inspected him with narrowed eyes.

He was tall, dried out, masterly. His face was thin and weathered. His eyes crackled with nerve, his fingers were long sinews, and his palms were seamed with the scars of action. Did she know him? The ghost of something flickered in his face, where his eyes embedded themselves in the skull and his mouth cut into his cheeks.

Keenly he returned her stare as she stepped towards him. But the knot in her belly gave a deep, wriggling flutter, and uncoiled. Ouf! The power of it doubled her up, and she staggered forward into the gutter, almost head-butting him.

He seized her by the wrists and steadied her.

'Whoa there,' he said. 'Are you all right?'

Confused and suddenly queasy, she waited, bent over, for the pulse to kick again; but it subsided, and she straightened up. He let go. His arms dropped to his sides, and hung there in lightly flexed curves.

'Does Janet still live here?' he said. 'I'm looking for Raymond.'

At once she saw his toughness. He was wirier than Ray, faster of mind and metabolism, longer-thighed, broader-backed. He meant business. She stared at him with respect. The street behind him glittered with sun: its brightness stung her. There was no time now to think. This one knew no fear. He was here to rectify.

'They're still asleep, I think,' she said. The tremor in her voice surprised her.

He strode past her, through the gate and up on to the verandah. Maxine thrust her hands into her cuffs, wheeled about, and fell into step behind him.

In his heavy boots he was already over the step and into the kitchen. He paused at the fridge and opened it. It was empty. He kneed it shut, and took two more steps along the bench to the breadbin. While Maxine watched, he slid up the lid and saw the carpet of stale crumbs on its floor.

'Crikey,' he muttered. 'Hasn't anyone been to the market? A bloke used to be able to get a feed here. At any hour of the day or night.'

'We've all been rather busy,' said Maxine. 'Every-one's been working so hard –'

He turned and raked her with a silent look. She strained for his aura, but there was not even static. His eyes were red with fatigue.

'Strike a light,' he said. 'People ought to *eat.*'

'Shall I put the kettle on?' she said. 'I could run to the shop.'

'Good on you,' he said. 'I'd love a great big meaty cup of something. Get coffee. Get bacon. Get milk. Get bread. Spare no expense. Here.' He pulled a handful of coins and notes from his jacket pocket and held them out to her. 'Look at that. You've cleaned me right out.'

He grinned. She saw that some of his back teeth were missing.

'Will I wake the others up first?' she said.

'Don't bother,' he said. 'They'll come slinking down once they smell bacon cooking.'

'I know who you are,' said Maxine, turning round at the door with her hands full of cash. 'I've been told about you. You're Alby. You're Ray's brother, aren't you.'

'That's right.' He picked up a sheaf of junk mail, and leaned back expansively against the bench. 'I'm his no-hoping brother. I'll be taking him off your hands today.'

Today. Something revved inside her, an excitement. She tried to take a hostly tone.

'Oh, there's absolutely no hurry! No hurry at all. Stay a while. We'd hate to lose him. We've become awfully attached. To Ray.'

'No doubt,' said Alby. He leafed through the brochures. 'Still – he's been expecting me. And I'm late, as usual. Is he crooked on me, do you know? It took me longer than I thought to organise transport – rent it, and that.'

Maxine dawdled, twiddling the door-handle. 'What's in your truck? You haven't got any washing in there, have you? That needs doing?'

'I've got furniture,' said Alby. 'Ray's supposed to have the money, and I've brought the gear. That was the arrangement, anyway.'

Maxine bit her lip and bolted, with her loose pockets jingling, out the gate and on to the street.

There stood the truck, awkwardly parked with its back to the house, on the paving stones disrupted by thick ridges of root. It was old and unstable, and under the black-trunked, leafless elms it was very, very red. Its redness leaked out into the surrounding air, tingeing and staining everything, imbuing the morning with a hectic flush: the truck seemed to be bobbing there, in the sharp early chill, like a barge tenuously moored to the bank of a current that was urging it to keep moving, to untie and swing out on to the stream and be gone. Maxine shoved her hands into her sleeves and danced on the spot. Too late to think, to soothe, to explain. Get ready. Something big was going to happen. Nothing could stop it now.

Alby made himself wait till her footsteps drowned in the river of early traffic. Then, holding his breath, he stepped through the kitchen door into the living room, the central room of *Sweetpea Mansions*.

These ten years, no matter where he travelled, he had kept a picture of the household folded in his mind, as an image of the way a life might be lived. He treasured the tomato plants heavy with fruit, the trim rows of lettuces; the washing flying high and fading on the line, straw brooms with their driving rhythm, the casual giving and lending of everything you needed, the unlocked doors and windows through which fine breezes wandered: surely he must have lived through a winter here, but all his memories were of warm air and thin clothing, and every day was Saturday. Any room you peered into had its little drama going on: two women haranguing some poor bastard about house-work; a couple of blokes in armchairs with cups of tea on the floor beside them, arguing about a strike or a distant war, or working away on acoustic guitars, learning and teaching; a girl in a floppy, flowery dress mending a bike or covering page after page of her diary, never needing to cross out, or reading the long summer afternoon away with the book propped on her chest, while round the next half-open door a lover, pale with jealousy, leaned over a table to snoop on a letter; upstairs in their wide front room the kids – whose were they? which ones actually belonged to the house? – paraded about in dress-ups making imperious gestures, or crawled naked up the bunks, or madly scribbled with the pencils, colouring in; along the hall someone waddled backwards on her haunches, painting the skirting-boards blue, or teetered on a ladder with a roller tray and the radio; if you tapped on the bathroom door you would be screamed at by someone inside who was trying to develop photos; downstairs a visitor picked out a walking bass line on the gutted pianola; on the back verandah somebody's boyfriend since last night sat grinning, head bowed, caped in a towel, submitting to the application of shit-brown gobs of henna; and three times a day the food hit the table, great crocks and tureens of it, coarse with garlic and beans, weird salads hacked to chaff, onions, brown rice, the occasional sausage, vegetable curry that burnt your mouth when you gulped it and later tortured you with farts – but filling! In this house you could fill up, you could eat and hold out your plate for more, and everyone welcomed you, at first; everyone loved you, provided you could crack a joke or stagger round the yard on stilts or grab a guitar and play.

But in the end Alby didn't match up. He wasn't ready for it. Picked up at some gig, he had drifted in from nowhere, without the necessary training, without *consciousness*, and they took him on sufferance, because he was charming; but he continued to say *chick*, to say *cunt*, to say *wog* and *abo* and make them flinch; he couldn't cook and wouldn't learn, he paid no rent and offered no kitty, he'd never handled a broom in his life and he tossed his dirty clothes at the women and expected them to wait on him hand and foot: so no matter how eloquent an advocate he had in Janet, after many a warning they turfed him out, without ceremony, just a list of his crimes left for him on the dining-room table; and on the pavement beside him landed Chips, toothless, addicted, stinking – a real hard case.

Expelled, they wandered away; and then it was the downhill run: people's couches, then floors, then, when Chips got so foul, so brain-damaged that no one would have them, it was squats, tram shelters, parks, once a disused chookpen, and the odd flophouse that Alby could sneak Chips into when the nights sank towards freezing. Alby stuck with him right to the end, trying to be a reason for him; but within nine months Chips had dropped his bundle. He folded the tent. And when he died, somehow Alby couldn't seem to get over it. In a blur that lasted years he drifted; he dragged himself up and down the eastern seaboard, scrounging and scavenging, busking, in and out of no-hoping blues bands, losing his hair and the occasional tooth, always lugging his big guitar, until one night, up north, a bunch of bible-bashers including his own brother, who were doling out food in a doorway at three a.m., collared him and gave him a solid boot right up the arse.

In his exhaustion, and to please poor old sadsack Ray, he pretended for a while to go along with it, toning himself down, twanging their hymns, and they thought they had him straightened out about booze and sex and talking dirty – not that a woman had looked at him without disgust for as long as he could remember; but the day they took him to the beach he was still secretly stubborn, still clamped around the last sour pod of resistance. Even while they were leading him out through ankle-deep water and into the shallows, all he could think of was his trousers, his only good pair, the money he had paid for them.

He saw the first wave coming and dug in his heels. He leaned back against the pinching fingers, but they gripped his biceps and pressed him forward and down. His mouth clamped shut, two sharp streams shot up his nostrils, and his knees bent and drove into the sand. The wave boiled him alive, the cream of ocean rioted in his skull, but the hands did not loosen: they doubled and trebled, they gripped tight. Back drew the wave, sucking sand from round his knees and freeing his head: he opened his mouth and gobbled for air. A man was shouting, women were singing shrilly, a banjo chunked its iron chords. The hands raised him up, stood him on his feet and let go. Staggering in the drag of the undertow, his sinuses burning with an icy fizz, he dashed the hair off his face and opened his eyes. He saw in one explosion the sparkling world, the striped sails beating, the bottomless blue of the sky. Something was dissolving his face. Scalding tears gushed out of his eyes and ran in sheets down his cheeks, softening his mouth and melting its hard muscle until unbearably it burst open and his own voice set up a hoarse babble of sound which he had never heard or made before but which must mean something, for when he turned, jabbering and dripping, to face the curved line of people up to their thighs in foam, they heard his cacophony and threw up their arms and struck their palms together to show him that at last, at last he had done something properly: at last, after all this time, he had got the whole thing right.

Even now, though, years after he had *been saved*, the house still visited him in dreams; and while its layout would metamorphose in a multitude of ways, revealing here a bright attic he had somehow never noticed, there a splendid prospect of rivers and pastures out a window which had previously given on to a brick wall, it was always the same house: he knew it every time, and entered it with joy. Every other set-up he lived in, no matter how correct and courteous, how Christian, felt timid by comparison, apprehensive, without adventure. What was the quality he longed for? Hilarity. A full-frontal spontaneity. A fearless trust that whatever cropped up might be made holy: singing wildly without words. It's the drugs you miss, he told himself, always alert to his own bullshit; it's the sex, the women and girls strolling around half-naked. It's a hippy fantasy of radiant idleness. But the house lived on in him, an oasis of deep and complex blossoming, all the while his spirit, as they called it, was being cleaned and straightened and dried out to uniform beige. The house hung on, and he boasted to his brother about it and persuaded him to go on ahead as a kind of buffer: for in his heart he believed against all odds that he *could* go back, knowing what he knew now: he took the punt and believed that the warmth and the music of it, if only it was still there, embodied what he was starved for, something to do not with religion and spirit, but with soul.

And *now* look at it. Look at the state of this room.

The white table under the window, where they used to eat, still collected the light; but the couch with the tartan rug, down at the far end of the long room, had sagged and grown shabby, and the walls were stained with red dribbles. A huge crack ran across the ceiling, right through the beautiful moulded rose, as if the foundations had shifted, and in the corner where the canary-yellow pianola used to stand there was only a mean little CD player and two lethal speakers.

He propped in the doorway, open-mouthed. All the colour had leaked away, the brightness. The truth of it was gone.

Serves you right, you stupid bastard. What did you expect. But it hurt him. His legs trembled with shock.

Steady on. He had been on the road all night: his eyes were crossing, the engine was still churning in his ears. He was probably hallucinating. Take it easy. Wash, eat, and look again.

Unbuttoning his jacket with clumsy fingers, he dragged himself across the room and headed for the stairs.

Under the doona, Janet heard slow steps come round the top of the staircase and trail away along the upper corridor. She cursed. Maxine's endless, dreaming showers were famous for emptying the tank of hot water, not to mention clogging the plughole if she shampooed her unspeakable hair. Janet allowed her five minutes. Ten. Twelve. The water was still gushing and tapping in the pipes. She tossed away her magazine and dropped her feet off the edge of the mattress.

And smelt bacon.

Saliva rushed into her mouth. She smelt coffee. She smelt toasting bread. This could not be. It *could not be*. Ray was cooking. Ray was rattling the pots and pans. He was down in the kitchen making breakfast.

She set off for the bathroom at a fast clip, whisking off her nightdress and dropping it as she went. Steam was billowing out under the door like dry ice at a bad gig. She drummed her knuckles against the panel and barged in.

The smell was wrong. The top layer was her own shampoo, her expensive skin soap, as usual – but behind the fogged-up glass screen was a larger, darker, lankier

shape than Maxine's; and the deeper reek in the room was
the smell of a man.

Janet turned to flee, but the dark form froze, with
its elbows curved high round its head like a dancer's,
and spoke.

'That you, Raymond? Who's there?'

'Alby,' said Janet. 'Alby. Is that *you.*'

He stood rigid under the thundering cascade, wigged
and shawled in perfumed foam. He should cover himself.
He should cover, or turn – but Janet had never had any
shame, and she had none now. Without a stitch on she
stepped up to the side of the bath and folded back the
screen. Drops pattered on to her up-turned face. They
stared at each other. They stared, and they saw. Alby
dropped one hand to his genitals as if to shield them, but
she stood there carelessly, her arms loose at her sides, and
with a curious gentle smile she skimmed her eyes as soft as
fingers up and down his filleted carcase; in a minute he
would have to open the cold tap on to himself, although
her body showed so sorrowfully what time can do to a
thin woman: the boxy hips, the knotted knees, the little
breasts hanging unevenly on the framework of the ribs.

'Janet,' he said. He cleared his throat. 'What happened
to the piano?'

She brought her eyes to bear on his face, and kept
them there. 'Remember Philip?' she said. 'It was his. He
took it.'

'Where *is* everyone?' he said. 'There's nothing to eat.
Where are the kids?'

There was a long pause. The water was hot, but he
was shivering.

'Alby,' she said. 'It's ten years.'

'I got a fright,' he said, placing his free hand over his
heart. 'Everything's the same – but changed.'

'Yeah, well,' she said. 'I didn't expect you to remember anything at all.'

'You'd be surprised,' said Alby. He turned his front away, and pushed his face into the stream of water. 'Pass us a towel, old girl. I don't have to do this any more.'

She laughed quietly. 'Me either. You can use the striped one. Call me when you've finished.'

The hall, as she ran along it and stooped mid-stride for the dropped nightgown, was rich with the smell of bacon frying.

Her room was stuffy. She zipped up the blind, threw open the lower sash, and, turning back to order the mess of bed and table, caught in the tail of her eye a large dense scarlet mass down there in the street: a truck parked under the bare tree, its flank blasted with cold morning sun.

She heard the taps snap off, and the air and water go chugging back along the ancient pipes.

I don't have to do this any more. Me either. Put like that, it was quite a simple proposition. It had dignity. It was a relief. Janet laughed. Waiting to be called, she glanced up at the bride where it hung, hooked by its cape to the corner of Maxine's invisible pastel. Janet raised her hand to take it down. Her reflection too reached up towards itself, out of the blurred lake of black. The glass gave back to her, tilted, her whole length, foreshortened, naked, with one arm stretched upwards in a mysterious gesture – drowning? volunteering? Her fingers touched the grass of the doll's wild legs. She paused – and behind her left shoulder, just outside the range of the reflecting glass, the column of darkness shimmered into position.

She felt it manifest, towering, svelte, featureless. If she took one step to the right it would follow: she would be able to see it in the glass: but if she looked, if she acknowledged it and turned to face it, her defences would be breached: without a word being spoken her swaddling of scepticism would burst open, and some appalling and total submission would be demanded of her, a surrender of self with no hope of back-tracking. In terror, she closed her eyes.

The column hovered nearer, almost singeing the skin of her shoulder. She dropped her arm and clung to the table edge with both hands. Tears of bliss pressed behind her eyelids and she clenched, she clenched them back; she held them in. She heard herself panting, roughly, like a wrestler, like a labouring woman: she stitched her lips shut with her front teeth and hung on. How long did she struggle? She felt the vast patience of the thing, its utter imperviousness to argument; but she fought it, with a mad pugnacious hubris she pitted herself; and at last a tremor rippled through the pillar, a slow, long shudder; and then it thinned, faded, and was gone.

A stream of cold air was pouring through the open window, but feathers of sweat burst out of her, all down her back. Something was tapping behind her, outside the door, very light and quick. A man's voice was softly calling her name.

'Janet! Janet! I've finished. All yours. I'm going to wake up Raymond.'

'All right,' she said. 'Coming.'

Her voice sounded composed, but she was as weak and trembling as if she had just run a mile. She let go of the table. A tram went racketing across the intersection. In the bare tree outside the window a sparrow curvetted, and flipped away. The room was full of sun. It was a winter morning.

The bacon was for the visitor, of course. Maxine had given up meat. She couldn't touch it, with a metabolism

like hers, this squeamishness in the mornings. Oh, perhaps a skerrick, the merest shred of curled rind, to check
that it was cooked: otherwise, no. Really. Well – to trim
off the ragged edge . . . Picking and nibbling, she heard the
two men's heavy steps on the stairs, and began with guilty
swipes to lavish butter on to the toast.

'Maxine,' said Ray from the kitchen doorway. 'I'd
like to introduce you to – my brother Alby.'

Maxine turned, and made a little bow. 'How do you
do,' she said. 'Actually, we've already met.'

'That's right,' said Alby, running a pocket-comb
through his thin hair. 'We introduced ourselves. At dawn.'

Maxine saw Ray's hastily donned clothes, his sleep-
stunned eyes and expression of sober pride, and the tread-
mill inside her whirred again.

'Yes, we did,' she said. She flashed her most brilliant
smile, and beat at her hair with the backs of her wrists.
'Alby's come to stay, he was telling me. For a while.'

Ray swung round to Alby. 'No,' he said. 'That's not
what we planned. We'll find a place today, won't we, Alb?
We'll be moving out today.'

'Take it easy,' said Alby cheerfully. He stowed the
comb inside his leather jacket and gave his chest a pat.
'We'll be off as soon as we find something decent.'

But Ray's face, turned away from Maxine, was rippling with unreadable grimaces. He shirt-fronted Alby
back through the door into the living room and grabbed
him by the arms.

'I have to get out of here,' he whispered. 'They're
crazy. They both want to fuck me. I'm not *safe* here.
They're witches. They're lezzos. They *do* things.'

Alby stared at him. 'Sit down here, Raymond,' he
said. 'The woman's going to serve us. What's the matter
with you? Don't you know when you're on to a good
thing? Be thankful.'

Maxine streamed into the room with a piled dish held high. She placed it between the brothers and stood back, clasping her hands loosely in front of her. Her lips gleamed with bacon fat.

'Ask a blessing, Alby,' said Ray. He lowered his head.

Alby flicked a glance at Maxine. 'I'm a bit out of practice,' he said. 'Is that the way things are done here?'

'It could be,' said Maxine, gliding forward. 'It could be any way you want it.'

Ray recoiled; but Alby looked up with interest. He seized a chair and pulled it out for her.

'Sit down, Maxine,' he said. 'Join us. What do you do, in life?'

Maxine blushed, and sat on her hands beside him. 'I make things out of wood,' she said. 'Furniture, mostly.'

'Ah,' said Alby. 'A carpenter, eh. That's the spirit. Good for you, love. Lord! Our thanks for these thy gifts.'

He heaped bacon on to a slice of toast and took a comprehensive bite. He was so thin that when he chewed, the ligaments of his jaw popped in and out like rivets. 'And,' he said, swallowing voluptuously, 'I guess that as an artist you'd have a hot line to the Almighty?'

Maxine's hair was as dishevelled as a bird's nest. She flattened it, racking her brains for an answer.

'Yep,' continued Alby, 'I've always thought that real artists don't need to go to church. The whole principle of creation is acted out through them, every day. That's *my* theory, anyway.' He stuffed the rest of the slice into his mouth and munched with abandon, keeping his sore-rimmed, sparkling eyes fixed on her face. 'Would there happen to be a coffee available, out there, at all?'

Maxine leapt up and dashed away to the kitchen.

'And Max?' Alby called after her. 'Heat the milk, darl, will you?' Grinning, still chewing, he looked at his brother and winked.

Ray dropped his eyes, trying not to laugh. 'You ratbag,' he said. 'How do you do it?'

'What?' said Alby.

'I haven't had a square meal since I got here. You've been here five minutes and already they're running round waiting on you.'

Alby shrugged. 'It's simple,' he said. 'I like 'em. And they like me. She's all right, don't you reckon? Whatsername? Maxine?'

'All *right*?' Ray lowered his voice. 'She's *trouble*, mate. She's not a "real artist". You should see the stuff she makes. It's unscriptural. No one'll buy it. She's been driving me crazy. She's sort of' – he glanced at the door – 'in love with me. Or something.'

Alby raised his eyebrows, and cackled.

'*You* can laugh,' said Ray. 'She's a monster. She stalked me. She wouldn't take no for an answer.' He bit his lip and examined his nails through half-closed eyes.

Alby flicked him under the chin with a hard fore-finger. 'What have *you* been up to?'

Ray bridled, unable to control his smile. 'Never mind that,' he said. 'I'm telling you I have to get out of here.'

'I can see that,' said Alby. 'I think you'd better.' He stretched both arms back behind his head so that a crack-ling ripple ran all the way down his spine, then dropped them to his sides and gazed into Ray's face with refreshed attention.

'She even tried to con me into one of those yuppy pyramid schemes,' Ray went on. 'The aeroplane game.'

Alby sat up. 'That scam!' he said. 'You didn't fall for that, did you?'

'Course I didn't. What do you take me for?'

'Phoar,' said Alby. 'You had me worried there, for a minute.'

'So don't let's hang around,' said Ray. 'I've been

having a shocking time here. You wouldn't believe what these women get up to. I saw them yesterday. In Janet's room, with their clothes off.'

Alby burst out laughing. 'Oh, come off it,' he said. 'No – really.'

'That's not all,' said Ray, warming to it. 'They ripped the sleeve off my only good shirt. They used it to make a doll's dress. They don't care *what* they do. They're loose. They're all over the place. But I don't care now. I don't have to live here any more. I'm on my way. I'm going to shake the dust from my feet.' He made brisk trucking movements with his bent arms.

Alby yawned. 'Don't rush me,' he said. 'I'm not ready yet. I'm buggered. I like it here. And I want to talk to Janet.'

Ray struck himself on the forehead with his open hand. 'Oh *no*. You're not going to socialise, are you? Come on, Alb! Let's say goodbye and get out of here.'

'Settle down, Raymond. There's coffee coming. Look – we'll have a coffee with the girls, and then we'll buy a paper and work out what to do next.'

'*I* know what's next,' said Ray irritably. 'You'll get glamorous. You'll start singing. The women'd love that. The "girls". Go on. Go out and get your great big guitar.'

For three beats Alby sat quite still. Then he leaned back, folded his hands behind his neck, and said, 'Want me to tell you what happened to my guitar?'

Maxine came into the room, carrying a coffee pot and a saucepan of milk. Cups sprouted from her fingers. Hearing his opening line, she rose on tiptoes and pantomimed a self-effacing walk to the table, where she began to arrange her offering. Her red cheeks and complicated demeanour threw Ray into a spasm of frustration.

'Can't you sit down?' he said. 'You're always *fussing*. Sit down.'

Maxine shot him a wounded look and slid on to a chair. Poor Ray. She longed to reach out for his clenched fist, to stroke the tension out of it, but the time for that had passed. She poured the coffee, surprised that her hand did not tremble, and passed the two men their cups. Ray took his without a word; Alby nodded to her, and showed his chaotic teeth in a smile of theatrical sweetness.

'Wonderful, Max,' he said. 'Perfect. And now all I fancy is an apple. One of those green ones you grow down this way, that make your hair stand on end when you bite 'em. Is it the season?'

Maxine raised her shoulders to her ears and giggled. The fruitbowl of course was empty; but if that was what he wanted; if fruit would delay the moment of reckoning – she pushed back her chair and made as if to oblige.

'Only fooling, dear,' said Alby. He pressed her on to her chair with his callused hand. 'Stick around. Raymond wants to hear about my guitar. Don't you, Raymond.'

Ray hardly knew whether to laugh or scowl. He subsided. The sooner the performance began, the sooner they could get away.

'It was a great big Ibanez.' Alby bent his arms and dropped his hands to hip level, wide apart. 'Huge. Remember, Raymond? So big I could hardly play it. But I was used to it. I'd been busking a lot, up north, making a few bucks, living on it – I was doing all right.

'Well, on the night in question, round about eleven o'clock, I got an urge to go and see the *Blues Brothers* again. I started walking down the avenue. I was hungry. Pretty soon I saw a McDonald's coming up. I was thinking, oh, I'll have a Coke, or maybe a hamburger; but before I could get into line, this bloke comes up to me. Drunk, and smelling of it. He engages me in idle chat, then after a bit he says, Look, how's about buyin' me a hamburger? I go, Sure I will. Nothin' special, he says –

just a liddle piece of meat. Don't bother with the lettuce or tomato or any of that. No, I say – mate, I'll buy you a jumbo burger. Hang on to this. And I hand him the guitar.

'I get into the queue. A lot of people there – the place is packed. Ten minutes later I fight m' way back to him, with the food up over m' head, like this – and he's gone. Taken the guitar and run off. Oh, I was thrown. I was foaming at the mouth. What was I supposed to *do*? Go back along the avenue and start asking *questions*?'

Alby picked bacon from between his front teeth, and ate it.

'I went to the movie. The shine was taken off it, for sure – but I did quite enjoy it. Then two days later, on the Sunday, I went to church. They have this system – as Raymond knows – where you write down on a bit of paper if there's someone who needs praying for. I thought, Oh, why not. So I wrote down on the paper, *Someone stole my guitar*.

'When the preacher goes through the little bits of paper, he picks out mine. He goes, Now here's an interesting one! Brother's lost his guitar. Everyone laughs. Don't laugh, says the preacher. It must mean a lot to him. And he prays.'

Footsteps drummed on the stairs. Alby paused; and Janet, with her head wrapped in a towel, came rushing into the room. Ray averted his eyes.

'Did you save some?' she cried. 'Where's mine?'

'Pipe down,' said Alby. 'Let me finish my tale. *As I was saying*, he prays.'

Janet looked at him sharply, then at Maxine; but Maxine was enthralled, Maxine had not even noticed her; so with ironic resignation Janet sat down and began to fossick among the crusts and rinds on the plate.

'He prays,' said Alby. 'And afterwards, outside, this

bloke comes up to me and says, Alby, I think God's telling
me to give you my guitar. It's been lying round the house
for years and I never play it. He took me to his place and
gave it to me. It's Australian, nice, a Maton, but still *big*.

'So I'm glad and I take it; but I'm thinking to myself,
one of these days I'm going to buy myself a ukelele, one of
those curvy little ones with the singing tone – small and
sweet and easy to carry – like a baby. I'm fed up with
lugging a huge great axe wherever I go.

'Next day I'm walking past a secondhand shop, down
along the avenue, when as if by magic I spot one, among
the junk lying in the window. Oh, it was a beauty.
Genuine Hawaiian. It had a lovely little waist on it' – with
two hands he made the wavy gesture that used to mean
stacked – 'and get this: it was only twenty dollars. The old
bloke in the shop had no idea what it was worth. I had to
struggle with myself, I can tell you. The devil was abroad
that day. Up on Sapphire Street they sell for, oh, four or
five hundred!'

Janet leaned forward. 'You mean *dollars?*' she said.

Alby nodded.

Ray's face went stern. 'You don't mean to say you –'

Alby lowered his lids, arched his brows, and held up
one flat hand for silence. 'Don't rush to judgment,' he
said. 'Hear me out.

'Right. I went into the shop, and I put a dollar down.
And then I walked home, to think about it.

'I came round the corner into our street – and what
should I spy out the front of our house but a police car.
Now what's happening, I thought. Old habits die hard:
I felt like ducking into the alley and waiting for them to
leave: but I get a grip on myself and I stroll in, cool as a
cuke, and find two cops standing in the kitchen with their
guns on. Everyone's there, and when I walk in they all

swing round and call out in a chorus, *Here he is*! Believe me, my whole life flashed before my eyes. I had to sit down.

'But it wasn't me they were after. Turns out a couple of junkies had burgled the house. And what had they knocked off? I don't need to tell you. It was the Maton.

'I went upstairs and I lay on m' bed, and I thought, Alby, this is a sign. Music is your livelihood. You are otherwise totally and tragically unemployable. This is a sign from the Lord.'

Ray clicked his tongue and rolled his eyes to the ceiling.

'And I got up,' said Alby, unperturbed, 'and walked straight back to that secondhand shop, and I bought the ukelele.'

He paused, and ran his half-closed eyes over the listeners' faces. The room was throbbing.

'Now this particular ukelele,' he continued, changing modes like a champion, 'was fashioned in the nut orchards of paradise. Through the rent in the ozone layer it dropped, straight out of the celestial meadows where the morning stars clap their hands for joy – and my out-stretched paws snaffled it before it could hit the ground. It was meant for me. It had my name on it.

'From the hole in its belly rose a fragrance like wood; like apples; like the cedars of Lebanon. It was made for the express purpose of accompanying chants of joy. I want you all to know that I was . . . *in love* with this ukelele.'

Maxine glanced at Janet with shining eyes. Janet had her elbows on the table and was gazing at Alby with astonished admiration. Alby nodded superbly, and paused to polish off a tiny morsel of flesh that clung to the dish's rim. He brought his hand away from his lips in a showy arc that galled Ray into protest.

'Alby!' he said. 'I can't *believe* you'd do a thing like that.'

'Wait,' said Alby, with another splendid gesture of restraint. 'Vengeance is mine, *I* will repay, says the Lord. Romans twelve nineteen.

'So. I took the uke home. I sat on the porch steps in the dark, and I worked out the chords of all the songs I knew. It was so easy! Compared with the guitar, its notes just placed themselves under my fingers. It had a human scale. It had a voice like an angel's. Sweet, and clear – it *rang*. It was the perfect instrument. I was made. My future was assured. I thought I'd died and gone to heaven.'

Ray could scarcely contain himself, but when Maxine laid a hand on his arm to calm him he twisted away from her. Alby took a long swallow of lukewarm coffee and set down his cup. Janet sat perfectly still.

'The very next night,' said Alby, at his leisure, 'round about a quarter to seven, I put on my good jacket, I picked up my bag, and I set out for the avenue. My repertoire was secure in my head. I was about to pull in a small fortune. I had just the spot in mind where I'd set up – in a certain corner where the acoustics would make me sound gorgeous. I had the uke under my arm, wrapped up in an old jumper and round that a newspaper, to cushion it from jolts. And away I sailed.

'Down by the station, as I went rolling along, I saw the row of phone boxes there, under the colonnade, and I suddenly thought, Why not ring up this girl I fancied, a great big bustling blonde from church, and see if she felt like hopping on the bus and rocking down to the avenue to see me put on the show of my life? I stepped into a booth and dialled her number. We got talking: I put the hard word on her, and she seemed keen to come; so I told her where to find me, I described the exact whereabouts of my spot; and we hung up with mutual expressions of goodwill.

'I stepped out of that phone box like a king. My feet weren't touching the ground. It was a beautiful evening. Cool, but clear. The sky was turning a sort of pinkish-green. The harbour down the bottom of the hill was so calm, it could have been a sheet of aluminium. A full moon was bouncing over the cathedral spire like – like the dot on an i.'

'Oh Alby,' said Janet. 'I don't think I can bear this.'

'It's like a poem,' said Maxine faintly, 'the way you tell it.'

'Keep going,' said Janet. 'Don't stop.'

'I'd got all the way down the hill,' Alby went on with a gracious smile, 'past the Town Hall and the cathedral, and I was bowling along in front of the Law Courts and the National Library, glorying to myself out loud, when a kid stepped out of a lane and put the bite on me for a dollar. I laid down my bag and went for my pocket – and that's when the penny dropped. Apart from the bag, I was empty-handed. I'd left the uke on the shelf in that flamin' phone box.'

Maxine gasped. Janet closed her eyes. Ray sat forward.

'I ran back, of course,' said Alby. 'I went like the clappers. I was knockin' pedestrians flyin' – I was leap-froggin' cars. But when I got back to the station, the cupboard was bare.'

'Did you check *all* the boxes?' whispered Maxine. '*All*?' She clasped her hands tightly under her chin.

'Course I did,' said Alby. 'No use. The bird had flown.'

Outside, the low morning sun had heaved itself far enough over the house to land its first direct beams on the surface of the white table where they sat, and lit from below by the rebounding shafts, Alby's face, to Maxine, was a mask of drama, its lips hardened by suffering, its eyes sunken almost to vanishing point. She groaned out loud. Ray flashed her a jealous look.

'I searched for it,' Alby went on, 'high and low. I resolved to check out every secondhand shop and pawn shop and op shop within a three-mile radius of the station. That's all I did, day in, day out, for a week or more. I tramped the streets. I wore out m' shoes. I made great sweeping reconnoitres. I took no rest.'

He permitted himself a very small sigh.

'Now in itself,' he said, 'a ukelele's not such a rare thing. In a day's march you might stumble on half a dozen – but fakes, right? Cheap, stringless, broken ones. Ugly workmanship. Rubbish from Taiwan, poor quality, crudely tacked together, hopeless action, with tuning pegs you can't tighten and horrible sticky yellow varnish. Trash. But you would expect to *find* 'em.

'The funny thing was, though, that search as I might, I never spotted a ukelele. In ten days I did not clap eyes on a single solitary one, of any standard or quality whatsoever. I was bluffed.

'Then, late in the afternoon of the tenth day, I staggered into a hockshop in a lane off Mandrake Street. They had nothing in the way of stringed instruments hanging in the window, but I went in anyway, according to my vow, and asked the lady behind the counter if she had any ukeleles.

'Sorry, she says. None left. With my heart in my boots I make as if to leave, but she calls after me in a friendly way and says, Are you with that girl from the Workers' Theatre, are you? I go, No – what girl? Oh, she says, I forgot their show closed last night. What show was that? I say, just to be polite. The show that girl did, she goes, with all the ukeleles. I turn around. Pretty modern show, says the lady. Different. She was in here looking for ukeleles nearly every day. I've been putting them aside for her. She needed one for each performance.'

Breathing more heavily than before, Alby raised his cup and swigged its remaining drops.

'My knees were knockin',' he said. 'But I forced myself. I go, How come she needed so many? Well apparently, goes the lady, she jumped on 'em. *Jumped* on 'em? So I'm told, goes the lady. Smashed 'em. Ground 'em to powder, right up there on stage in front of everyone. Kids and everything. She used up eight ukeleles a week. One per night, and the extra was for the Saturday matinée.'

Dumb as fish, the three faces swallowed the story. They released their pent breath in a grand, lingering sigh. Then, in unison, as if choreographed, the two women lowered their heads on to the table and drooped there, limply, while Ray, his face mantling with envy and admiration, sat gazing at his brother. Alby rested on his oars. He let the table drift and swivel on a tide of satisfaction.

'So now you know,' he said at last. 'Now you know what happened to my guitar.'

The women stirred, and raised their heavy heads. Their eyes were glazed, their features relaxed and smooth.

'How *awful*,' said Janet. 'How absolutely *terrible*.'

'Still,' said Ray, arranging the dirty plates in a square. 'You can hardly complain. You had it coming to you.'

Janet and Maxine looked sharply at him, then at the table. Somebody's tongue clicked.

'And what about the girl?' said Maxine, presently.

'What girl?' said Alby.

'Yes,' said Janet. 'The so-called "great big bustling blonde". What became of her?'

Alby laughed and turned his face away, but Ray's brow knotted and he shifted sideways on his chair, to realign himself with his brother.

'Trust you,' he said. 'Trust you women to completely miss the point.'

Alby let it pass. He laid his hand on Ray's shoulder.

'I'm broke,' he said. 'I haven't got a brass razoo. The last cash I had went on hiring that truck. I'm throwing myself on Raymond's mercy. He's my brother – he'll look out for me, even if he does secretly think I'm a ratbag and a hoon.'

He jostled Ray's shoulder back and forth, and with the rough movements Ray's pack-ice began to melt and break up. His cheeks flushed. His mouth broadened and split into a smile.

'Come upstairs now, Alby,' he said. 'Come up to my room. I've got something for you. Something to show you that you won't believe.'

The last blur of the story's spell cleared from Maxine's eyes; but her movements, as she rose to her feet, had a feminine languor she did not know she possessed: trailing her fingers along the tabletop, she glided to the window. She rolled up the sash. Cold air and traffic noise flooded in.

'What sort of furniture have you actually got, Alby?' she said over her shoulder. 'Out there in your truck?'

Her tone was almost melodic. Ray saw Alby's head come up in response: he was *programmed*, where women were concerned. Ray glanced at Janet. She pulled a comical face. He scowled and stumped away to the stairs.

'In my truck?' said Alby vaguely. The girl had run to the shop for him, she had cooked his breakfast: to humour her, he stood up and sidled along the table to the window. What was there to say, about his furniture? It was everything he owned, that was all. A table, a bed, a wardrobe. Some kitchen chairs. Maxine made room for him, and he leaned out. The pink had returned not only to her face: it extended in a long streak down the side of her neck and into her jumper collar. She slid her eyes towards Alby.

'Janet's got one of those banjo things,' she murmured. 'Like in your story. It's under her bed.' She rubbed her cheek against the cracked leather of his sleeve; the tips of her crazy hair scraped across his ear. He glanced down at her, curious, puzzled. What did she want? He breathed in a strangely pleasant, woody perfume that her clothes and hair emitted. Wedged there in the window frame, with their backs to the room and their heads and shoulders hanging out over the street, the two of them were encased in an unexpected privacy.

Alby had forgotten how pure the winter air was, down here. It sizzled in your nose like that green stuff in a Jap restaurant. Your head felt cleaner. You could breathe, and think. A tram went clanking loosely across the inter-section, dinging its chime. A pretty sound. Polite. Trams might be cumbersome, but they had manners. The sky had started to cloud over. Still, low down there was a big yellow stripe. It was a pleasant morning. A couple of crows were gargling on a lamp-post. Pity about the house. It needed major work. Only a dill would have expected it not to have changed. The wonder was that it was still here at all. All those rooms, though. The joint was empty. There was no hurry to move on. Give the girls a hand to sling some paint and Polyfilla round. Janet had had the stuffing knocked out of her; but she seemed pleased to see him. So did the woman beside him in the window, pressing her arm warmly against his. She had muscles. Handy with a roller. Might be a job to sort out Raymond. He was touchy. He still needed kid-glove treatment. Couldn't handle women. Basically he was what Janet used to call *a sensitive plant*. Alby couldn't help himself. He grinned. He chuckled. Maxine looked up at him. She smiled. Boy, was she weird. Wacko. The eyes of someone who at some stage had fried their brains with acid. Maxine would have heard the angels sing, for sure. But he liked her. He did. She was game. She was all right. He unplugged himself from his cosy spot beside her, and turned around.

Janet had pushed the breakfast dishes aside and was sitting quietly at the table with her head still wrapped in a towel, reading yesterday's paper. She raised her face as Alby sat down beside her, and though he was still part dazzled by the street, he noticed the wrinkles of her upper lip, the marks that make women look as if they have been whistling all their lives instead of speaking. But she smiled at him, and they vanished. Surprised by tenderness, he shoved his hands into his pockets and tilted his chair, feigning nonchalance.

'Stop tipping that chair,' said Janet absently. 'You'll break the legs off it.'

'Sorry.' He planked it down flat, snipping the lining of his cheek and tasting blood. He wanted to laugh, it was so silly to be here: they spoke to each other like an old married couple. In a rush of affection he curved his arm to put it round her.

But from the top of the house a cry broke out. Feet crashed along the upper hall and bungled down the stairs. Maxine drew her head in from the window and scanned the room. Her forehead cramped. Ray had got away. This was it. She braced herself.

He came hurling and flinging into the room, his eyes starting out of his head, his arms barely keeping up with the rest of him – and when he dived to a halt in the middle of the carpet and crouched there staring and speechless, Janet saw that in his hand he was brandishing the twig cradle. He had such a grip on its little frame that she started to her feet with a gasp of warning; but Ray was after Maxine, and spotting her in silhouette against the open window, he bared his teeth and advanced on her as slowly and deliberately as if no one else were in the room.

'Where's my money?' His voice was swollen. 'What have you done with it?'

He thrust the cradle at Maxine. His fingers were

forced between the struts. Maxine went white. So there would be violence. This she had not foreseen. Freckles floated to the surface of her skin. Her hair boiled round her head. She put her hands behind her and raised her chin.

'What is it?' whispered Alby. 'What's he got?'

'Shhhhh.' Janet leaned forward, breathless.

Ray bent his knees and flexed his hands. They heard the first twig snap.

'I know,' he said, very low and dangerous. 'You lost it. You put my money on that game.'

'Yes,' said Maxine, with dignity. She tried to keep her voice mellow, so as not to antagonise him. 'I took the money, Ray, and I gave it to the game.'

'Maxine,' hissed Janet. 'You *didn't*.'

'What? *What?*' said Alby.

'I'm sorry,' said Maxine. Her voice rose a little, and cracked. She cleared her throat. 'I know I did wrong, in your eyes. I should perhaps have asked you first. I lost patience. But it was in a very good cause. One day you'll understand. And I did leave you the cradle. I believe it was a fair swap.'

Fair. *Fair*.

Suffocating with rage, Ray looked down at the thing in his hands. His fingers, tangled in it, kicked like small legs. He closed his eyes and jerked his hands apart. It burst. He tore the fragile ribs out of their sockets. The curved rockers resisted: he wrenched them away. He crushed the whole thing back to a bunch of sticks, and flung them on the floor at Maxine's feet. They bounced on the ugly carpet, strewing themselves, and lay still.

He stepped back. His eyes blurred. Maxine was only a shape. The window behind her was open. He saw a silly bearded head in a bike helmet slide past. A woman shouted from a car in a language that sounded like barking: how heow *how*. He let out a slow breath.

Very quietly, Maxine got down on to her hands and knees. She began to scrape the pieces of twisted wood towards her. As she worked, she turned her face up to him, and spoke.

'Now you've done it, Ray,' she said. 'Now you've gone and spoilt *everything*.'

'*Me!*'

He rushed at her again. She reared up on her knees to save her fingers, and in a passion he trampled the scraps of twig with his steel-toed boots: he danced on them heel and toe like a sailor; his tantrum shook the floor and made the dirty cups jig in their saucers. Flinching, Maxine waited, holding her hands in the air beside her face; and when Alby grabbed Ray by the shoulders and dragged him away, she dived forward again and earnestly raked the shattered twigs into a fresh pile.

'The cradle was my best thing ever, Ray,' she went on in a dreamy voice, brushing and sweeping, plucking splinters from the carpet's coarse weave. 'It came from an inspiration. It came from a dream. I'll probably never make anything that good again. I've learnt a lot from knowing you, though. I'm not quite sure what – but I must tell you that I'm grateful.'

'You're a loony,' shouted Ray. 'You're a nutcase. They used to burn people like you.'

Down on all fours like a servant, Maxine laughed. They all heard her. It stilled them. Janet stooped for a piece of twig under the table, and brought it to her.

'Thank you, Janet,' said Maxine. She sat back on her heels, and smiled.

'Where's the money now?' said Janet.

'Hawkwind's got it,' said Maxine. 'Hawkwind flew out last night.'

'Who the hell's Hawkwind?' said Alby, grappling with Ray. 'What's going *on* round here?'

Maxine had all the willow pieces now, and stood up, holding them flat between her crossed palms. 'The game's dead, I'm sorry to say,' she said. 'Hawkwind got the last of the money. And he *deserved* it, Ray. For *trusting*.' She stepped up close to him, and scorched him with a reproachful look. He writhed in Alby's grip. 'I've lost all my illusions about you – but just the same, I do forgive you. I forgive you with all my heart.'

She stood on tiptoe and went to kiss him on the lips, but he lashed his head away, and her mouth grazed his cheek.

'I'll kill you,' he ground out between his teeth. 'I'll kill you for this. I will.'

'No you won't,' said Maxine. 'I may have had the wrong idea about you – but if you'd been *that* sort of person, I never would have liked you in the first place.'

She stuffed the broken twigs into her tracksuit pockets and backed towards the door, keeping her eyes fixed calmly on Ray's convulsing face. 'And now,' she said, 'I'm going to leave you. I feel much happier, since we worked it all out. I saw some jonquils sprouting down near the back fence. I'm going to pick them for the house; and then I'm going to start work.'

She gave a merry little wave and a smile, and swung away to the door. They heard her rubber soles tread lightly over the kitchen lino, thud twice on the verandah, and patter across the concrete. Ray uttered a strangled roar; but Janet darted to the door and slammed it. She leaned on it hard.

'How much was it, Raymond?' said Alby, shaking him and letting him go.

'A grand,' panted Ray. 'A thousand dollars, I had. In cash – notes, rolled up. She came into my room and stole it. She *took* it. She took it and she left that thing behind – her *art*.'

'Crikey,' said Alby. 'A thousand bucks. This is serious.'

Janet clapped her hands over her mouth. She started to giggle.

'You don't even care!' said Ray, stabbed. 'I worked for that money! I slaved for it – *I* didn't sit on my arse all day tapping on a typewriter – look at my blisters!'

Janet laughed out loud. She stuffed her fingers into her mouth. 'Sorry – sorry, Ray,' she said; but she could not stop. It was a kind of hysteria.

'I'm going out there,' raved Ray. 'I'm going to drag her out of that shed. She won't get away with this.'

'Face it,' said Alby. 'Face it, Raymond. She already has. Calm down, mate.' He gripped and squeezed his brother's shoulder. 'She shouldn't have done it – it's lousy – it stinks. But you've got to bloody calm down.'

'It's all right for *you*!' shouted Ray. He threw off Alby's hand and rushed about the room, butting the walls with his shoulders. Janet had never seen anyone in such a frenzy: she gnawed at her nails: it was wonderful.

'How long was it up there in your room?' said Alby. 'All that money?'

'Weeks. *Months*. I saved and saved – I hardly spent a cent.'

Alby punched him in the arm. 'Haven't you ever heard of *banks*?' he roared in sudden temper. 'You might just as well have buried the money, as leave it upstairs in a flamin' *sock*. What's the matter with you? And what was she doing up there in your room, anyway?'

Ray froze, shocked. Then he seized his head in both hands and began to pace up and down.

'Okay. Okay,' he muttered. 'Okay. I'll go after this Hawkwind. Where does he live? Does anybody know where he lives?'

'Oh, come on, Ray,' said Janet. She left her post at the kitchen door and returned to the table, unwinding the damp towel from her head. 'The money's gone. Can't you get it through your skull? You're back to square one. *The money has been spent.*'

Ray dragged a handkerchief out of his pocket and blew his nose with a sharp report. 'All right then,' he said. He took several deep breaths, and gave a resounding sniff. 'I'll go to the cops. I'll dob her in.'

'Huh,' said Alby, sitting down at the table. 'Don't waste the taxpayers' money.'

'She's got no *morals*,' said Ray. He leaned against the wall, exhausted. 'She's certifiable. She's a witch.'

'She's not like anyone else,' said Janet, 'that's for sure. She's like somebody from another planet.'

Alby tapped one forefinger against his temple. 'She's weird,' he said, 'but she's kind of brilliant, too. She doesn't care!' He started to laugh. 'She's so oblivious. You almost have to admire her.'

'Why should she care?' cried Ray. 'It wasn't *her* money!' He kicked a lump of plaster out of the wall. 'I'll fix her – I will. I'll get her for this. I'll get her – just watch me.'

But even as he gloried in it, he was running out of righteousness, and soon he stopped his stamping and stood in the middle of the room with his arms hanging, like a shag. Alby pulled out a chair and Ray cast himself on to it in an abandoned sweep, spreading his arms on the table and laying his head down on one cheek. 'Why'd you send me here, Alby,' he said dully. 'It's not my kind of place. It's a nut-house. I don't belong here.'

'Better get used to it,' said Alby. 'We've got nowhere else to go.'

'I'm not living with *her*,' said Ray. 'Maxine. *Maxine.* That maniac. No one can trust her.'

'What are we going to do about her?' said Alby.

Janet came and sat down opposite them. 'We have to look after her,' she said. 'She needs us.'

'She's not *my* responsibility,' said Ray, half raising his head. 'You can't expect *me* to . . .'

'Where'd you find her?' said Alby. 'Can't we just send her home? Where does she come from?'

'Same place *you* came from, Alby,' said Janet, 'when *you* first turned up here. From nowhere.'

Maxine picked her way, eyes down, through the damp, knee-high grass. The jonquils led her down the yard by means of their piercing perfume: metal, citrus, rotting meat: you could hardly call it scent; but her flair, sharpened by the adrenalin of confession, sucked it in. Ah – here they were, the chilly flowers of winter: clumps of cream, tightly clotted as if just that minute extruded through the pale-green, ridged stalks. Their smell sickened her. She knelt to them, holding her breath, and broke them off one by one, working her fingers down to the succulent, squeaky crowns: they came away with a hollow snap. Sap oozed on to her hands and hung in strands. Her stomach rebelled: the knot pulsed its amoebic boundaries, and subsided. She squatted, holding on; then reached forward and plucked, snapped, plucked again. Her breasts, tight and sore, pressed against her thighs, and she tried to straighten her back, to relieve them: but she was so dizzy from holding her breath against the flowers' stench that all she could do was squat and waddle forward, squat and waddle. The flowers multiplied as she gathered. There were always more. Who on earth had planted them? The wind? Herself, perhaps – they were so familiar, the zigzag stagger of the clumps. Her hands were full. She pressed her knuckles against the ground and rose to her feet. The garden spun. Oh, she would have to vomit – but the house slowed, it settled – and suddenly she saw the others, Janet, Ray and Alby, step out the back door on to the verandah, and stand there quietly in a row, gazing in her direction, peering, studying her with their six eyes. Ray was in the middle, poor furious false angel, and the others were holding him by the arms, as if to restrain or comfort him. She had enough flowers now, flowers for the house, two stout bunches of them, dripping curved trails of sap down the front of her trousers: she raised them in her fists, like trophies. The house would be full of the stinking flowers, every vase and jar and bottle stuffed tight. But first, for this sick feeling, she would take a dose of her drops. In silence she turned and walked diagonally down the garden to the shed.

The air was milky, grey and mild. The sky was clouded. Every few steps she looked back at the verandah to see if they were following. They had not moved. The wind made the sides of their hair stand up in identical crests. Don't follow, don't step down, don't come after. She plodded down the yard, left foot, right foot, making no sound in the thick grass. She looked back. They had not moved. They stood in a row, their necks craning forward and their shoulders curved. With every step she felt a huge, disappointed love for all three of them growing under her ribs: she could hardly breathe for the weight and sweetness of it: goodbye! The shed rose in front of her, with its double doors ajar and the furniture looming inside – but as she stepped between the doors, her foot flexed its tiny cathedral of bone and muscle and vaulted her lightly into the air.

What?

Into her other sole pressed the iron pattern of the shed roof.

Oh!

She paced along it in two booming strides, and skimmed away.

Angled at thirty-five degrees, pop-eyed and dangling-breasted, both hands flowering, she looked down.

The shed roof – so that's where my bow-saw got to! – was a grey rectangle below and behind her: the house a peaked, L-shaped ripple of green, the truck a scarlet box. The bouquets let loose into her hair a long drool of sap: bewildered, she muffed at it with the back of her wrist, and the turbulence stirred by her arm's bending dropped her twenty feet into a gauche somersault among the chimney-pots: sprouting elbows and knees, she tumbled like a pigeon, and dodged the antenna only by a jerky jib and tack. But when by instinct she rolled on to her side, stretched out, and thrust forth one arm as she had seen heroes and old-style swimmers do, the air smoothed into a bounding field of congratulation: its sleekness answered hers and taught her the hang of it, surging under her flank, giving purchase to her striding feet and parting to the chunked wedges of her knuckles. Chiffon vapour whizzed along her cheeks. The air was alive: it was her element: she dared a kick-turn and it sang a welcome, making the clutched flowers and every layer of cloth on her body whir.

She banked to fire one last look into the shrinking canyon of the yard. Pedalling madly and dropping her head like a chopper, she plastered both arms along her sides and unclenched her fists to let the seeping jonquils scatter down the rips of wind. *Janet!* she yelled after them. *Your knickers! I've still got them on!* – but too late, too high – for *I* was over: *I* dropped off her like a split corset: there was no more *I*.

With a churning roll and a trample she picked up speed and rocketed, whistling-eared, dead vertical from the city's paltry pencil-clump towards the meniscus of day. Her hair, streaming stiff as a helmet, was suddenly drenched in droplets: shrieking, she burst through the membrane into blinding upper sky.

Now, at a velocity as prodigious and as still as reverie, she cruised the cloud gorges: outcrops, woolly plains, escarpments, and mighty, toppling towers. She wept with awe to see the merciless delineations of their extremities, fantastical, curly-horned; and then, where the cloud-floor broke, the sea: a wrinkled skin of lead, sheeted with excruciating silver.

Inside her the little creature heaves for joy, her *Cosmo, Cosmolino*, the errand on which she is speeding: can she endure this purpose? Is this what it has all been for? And does he hear it too or is he secreting it, this wild interior music of gland and sinew, these grids of tough chords on which tremendous explosions leap and scamper, where nameless souls and sacraments outrageously disport themselves?

'Now what,' said Alby.

He stepped off the verandah on to the concrete and leaned one creaking leather shoulder against a post.

'She'll come out when she's hungry, I suppose,' said Janet.

Ray shuffled mutinously on the boards. 'I feel like barging into that shed and dragging her out,' he muttered.

'Oh, drop it, Raymond,' said Alby. He gave a huge yawn. 'I'm stuffed. I need a couple of hours' sleep.'

'You can crash in my bed,' said Janet. 'Till lunchtime.' She bent over and scrubbed at her damp hair with her fingertips.

But Alby sat down beside Ray on the woodbox. They rested their elbows on their knees and stared at their boots. How low and flat the morning seemed; and the garden disheartened Alby terribly, choked as it was with wandering weeds, nasturtiums, rampant vines and other remnants of vegetable fantasies. The work needed to get the place into shape – the labour!

'Was it true,' said Ray, 'that story about the ukelele?'

'True enough,' said Alby with a sigh. 'If you believed it. Though maybe I dreamt it. I don't know.'

He raised his head and gazed blankly at Janet. Her hair had half-dried into an unfortunate shape imparted to it by the towel, and her fringe had got squashed: it looked funny, as if it were welded to her eyebrows. He drew a breath to remark on this, but thought better of it. 'Not much of a morning after all,' he said. 'Clouded right over.'

'I've got to work,' said Janet. 'I've got to "sit on my arse and tap a typewriter". But first I think I'll clear the decks.' She pegged her towel to the wire and sauntered away into the house. They heard her start to sing, and to rattle the dishes in the sink.

'One thing about Janet,' said Alby. 'She's always cheerful in the mornings.' He laughed.

'Alb,' said Ray. 'Don't you care at all? About my money?'

With an effort Alby roused himself. He clicked his tongue and blew out air. 'You're my brother, aren't you? Do you think I'd heave all my stuff into a truck and drive a thousand K's to pick up a bloke I didn't care about?' He buffed Ray hard between the shoulder blades. 'Course I care. I know you worked for that money. You shouldn't have left it lying about, that's all. And I got cranky when you put on a song and dance about it.'

Ray blew his nose and shoved the hanky back into his trouser pocket. He stood up.

'You duffer,' said Alby. He stuck out one foot and kicked Ray lightly in the calf. 'It's only money.'

'You don't know what I've had to put up with, in this

house,' said Ray. He had his back to Alby; his neck and ears were huffy.

'Sounds to *me*,' said Alby, 'as if you had everything laid on.'

Ray glared at him over his shoulder.

'Look,' said Alby. 'Janet'll give us a bed for a while – just till we scrape up some more dough. I'll get a guitar from somewhere. Something will turn up. In a couple of months it'll be summer. We'll fix the bike. We'll go to the baths. After tea we'll sit out here and have a beer and listen to the vegies grow.' He got to his feet with a grunt. 'Come on. Give us a hand to unload the truck. I can't leave the stuff just sitting there.'

Together they stumped out the back gate on to the street. The air was cold and still. Buildings a block away looked dark but intensely visible, all their detail in sharp focus, as if distance had ceased to exist, and there was an iron quality to the light that meant rain. Ray shivered.

'Open it up. Show us what you brought.'

Alby hesitated. 'It's not much chop,' he said. 'You mightn't like it.'

'We'll sell it then,' said Ray, rolling up his sleeves. 'To reimburse me.'

'*To reimburse me*,' mimicked Alby, falsetto.

Ray turned away to hide his smile. He punched the truck's rear door.

'Stand back,' said Alby. He rammed the key into the handle, sprang on to the step, and heaved the rusty roller up to the roof.

Ray elbowed past his legs and peered in; but even before he could make out in the dull light the composition of the load, the smell of it rushed out and swamped him: the smell of pre-used, fourth-hand, of boarding house, of skulking and scrounging, of failure: everything he had come here to get away from. He rested his forehead against the red paint. He felt weak. He wanted to howl. Couldn't they do *anything* properly? Couldn't they get *anything* right?

'Well?' said Alby, towering over him on the step. 'What do you reckon?'

Ray could not meet his brother's eye. He could barely speak, for something like shame.

'It's junk, mate,' he whispered. 'It's garbage.'

'What? Oh, it's not *that* bad, is it?'

'It's not made of wood,' said Ray. 'It's not even plastic. What *is* it made of?'

Alby scratched his head. 'I see what you mean about the wardrobe,' he said. 'But it'll do us, won't it? How about that armchair?'

'It's *ugly*,' shouted Ray. He clambered on to the step. 'It's the sort of thing they have in video shops. In tattoo parlours. The stuff bloody Maxine makes is better than this. What's the matter with you, Alby? Why'd you lug it all this way? You could have saved the truck hire. We could have waited, and got ourselves something decent!'

Suddenly overwhelmed, Alby stepped down on to the kerb, sat down with his boots in the gutter, and dropped his head into his hands.

'It looked all right when I left,' he said. 'Maybe the light's different down here. Things look shabbier.'

Ray ploughed a path into the depths of the truck, and sank on to the split vinyl armchair. He laid his arms along its puffy purple rests. God, he was tired. From where he sat, the outside world with its treacheries was reduced to a simple rectangle: a frame containing a fence, a tree trunk, a gate, and his brother's bowed head down in the bottom right-hand corner. He wished he could press a button on the remote, and make the whole rotten thing fade to black.

He leaned his head against the chairback.

'I don't want to *live* like this any more,' he said. 'I can't. And I'm not going to.'

Alby sank his neck into his collar. Cold struck up through the seat of his pants and entered his bones. Rain began to fall at random, a drop here, another there. The rich smell of wet bitumen rose in the street. Janet, drawn by the shouting, came out the gate with the rubber gloves still on, and stood next to Alby at the open back of the truck.

'Look,' called Ray bitterly from his throne in the truck's deep room. 'Look at what he's brought. This is what he dragged down the highway. I give up. I just give up.'

Alby raised his face to Janet and gave a sheepish smile. He got up from the kerb and stared down the street, with his arms folded high on his chest. She saw that he was beyond argument. He was too tired to think. He should be asleep.

'It's certainly not very stylish,' she said carefully.

'He can drive the whole thing away,' shouted Ray. 'Tip it off a cliff. That's all it's worth.'

The rain fell more heavily: Ray heard the drops clang on the truck's red body and roof. He drew a hollow sigh, and got to his feet. He leaned for a moment against the inner wall; then he climbed out on to the step, seized the roller handle, and pulled the door down. It struck the step with a crash. He jumped to the ground.

Off the rim of the truck's down-slanting roof plummeted a streak of cream and green.

'Look out – birdshit!' yelled Alby.

Ray leapt back. But a flower, then two more, their stems oozing fresh liquor, landed on the spotted pavement behind the truck.

They stood in a line on the kerb, with the jonquils spread out at their feet.

'One each,' said Alby wearily.

A fourth one teetered, and fell.

They tilted their heads back and scanned the street, the trees, the steely sky.

A tram went shattering across the intersection.

Rain struck their cheeks and eyelids, and wet their lips. Glances flashed between them, of bewilderment, suspicion, respect. They blinked, hunching their shoulders, and turned up their collars. The flowers lay scattered, in no particular formation, on the blackening asphalt.

We're not finished yet, thought Alby.

Blossom as the rose, thought Ray.

Our minds are not hopeful, thought Janet; but our nerves are made of optimistic stuff.

The rain was falling hard. Janet bent down and picked up the flowers with her pink-gloved, clumsy hands.

'Come on then,' she said. 'Come in and choose a room.'

A NOTE ON THE AUTHOR

Helen Garner was born in 1942. Her first novel, *Monkey Grip*, was published in 1977 and won the National Book Council Award in 1978. It was followed by *Honour & Other People's Children*, *The Children's Bach*, and a short-story collection, *Postcards from Surfers*. She lives in Melbourne, Australia.